It's late March in Fairhope, Alabama, and artists from around the country are flocking to the bayside town's Arts & Crafts Festival. The annual tradition has something for everyone, only this year, the main attraction is murder . . .

Cleo Mack's life has been a whirlwind since she inadvertently became the executive director of Harbor Village, a retirement community bustling with energetic seniors. Juggling apartment sales, quirky residents, and a fast-moving romance is tricky business. But on-the-job stress develops a new meaning when Twinkle Thaw, a portrait artist known to ruffle a few feathers, arrives unannounced for the weekend's festival and drops dead hours later—mysteriously poisoned . . .

Twinkle's bizarre death doesn't seem like an accident. Not with a sketchy newcomer slinking around town and a gallery of suspects who may have wanted her out of the picture for good. As Cleo brushes with the truth, she soon finds that solving the crime could mean connecting the dots between a decades-old art heist and an unpredictable killer who refuses to color inside the lines . . .

Books by G.P. Gardner

MURDER IN HARBOR VILLAGE
MURDER AT ROYALE COURT
MURDER AT THE ARTS AND CRAFTS FESTIVAL

Published by Kensington Publishing Corporation

Murder at the Arts and Crafts Festival

G.P. Gardner

LYRICAL UNDERGROUND
Kensington Publishing Corp.
www.kensingtonbooks.com

LYRICAL UNDERGROUND BOOKS are published by
Kensington Publishing Corp.
119 West 40th Street
New York, NY 10018

All Kensington titles, imprints, and distributed lines are available at special quantity discounts for bulk purchases for sales promotion, premiums, fund-raising, educational, or institutional use.

Special book excerpts or customized printings can also be created to fit specific needs. For details, write or phone the office of the Kensington Sales Manager: Kensington Publishing Corp., 119 West 40th Street, New York, NY 10018. Attn. Sales Department. Phone: 1-800-221-2647.

Lyrical Underground and Lyrical Underground logo Reg. US Pat. & TM Off.

First Electronic Edition: December 2019
ISBN-13: 978-1-5161-0903-6 (ebook)
ISBN-10: 1-5161-0903-1 (ebook)

First Print Edition: December 2019
ISBN-13: 978-1-5161-0904-3
ISBN-10: 1-5161-0904-X

Printed in the United States of America

Chapter 1

"It's felt like Friday all day."

Patti Snyder, Director of Resident Services, was standing beside the ficus tree that filled most of my office window, looking out at the sunny March afternoon in Fairhope, Alabama, the most charming little village on the shores of Mobile Bay.

It was actually Thursday, not Friday, and I was clearing my desk, preparing to slip out of the office a little early. For several minutes now I'd been bombarded by Patti's silent urgings, like a drumbeat: *go, go, go.* She could scarcely wait for me to leave. Was she was planning to close shop as soon as I was gone?

She stepped away from the window. "It's because of Arts and Crafts, I guess." She sighed for the third time in as many minutes. "Don't you feel like some big holiday's right around the corner?"

Anyone who didn't know her would think she was bored, but I detected barely controlled electricity as she swished around my desk, dragging her fingertips across the polished walnut. Her nails were peachy orange today, with tiny white dots and bright blue lightning bolts. Usually the nails matched her eyeglass frames, but she must've left them on her desk. I wondered if she even needed glasses, beyond their value as a fashion accessory.

She flopped into one of the armchairs and looked at me. "I thought you were leaving early."

Now I was the one doing the sighing. "I'm going right now. It's too fidgety in here to concentrate."

I stuck a draft copy of a half-completed HHS questionnaire into the top drawer to work on tomorrow, grabbed a couple of tissues out of the box, and began wiping the desktop. "I like to find a nice clean desk when I come in every morning."

I brushed a few eraser crumbs, a sprung paperclip, and two crumpled sticky notes into my palm and then rubbed at some smeary fingerprints. No sense pretending housekeeping would attend to such details. Just as I swiveled and reached behind me for the trash can, my desk phone rang.

Patti snatched it up like she was expecting a call. "Harbor Village, Cleo Mack's office."

I dumped the litter and wiped my hand with the clean side of the tissue while Patti listened, playing with the phone cord and admiring her flashy nails.

"Oh, I'm so sorry. Should I check on her?" She listened for another moment. "She's right here."

She handed the phone to me.

"Nita. Dolly Webb's sick."

"Oh, no," I said into the phone. If I'd swiveled around again and leaned to one side, I might've seen the front door of Nita's apartment, right from my chair. "Anything serious? Should I send Nurse Ivy?"

Nita Bergen's voice was normally low-pitched, but at that moment it carried more than a trace of tension and annoyance. "Of course it's not serious. One sneeze. Now she's in bed. How many people get to celebrate fifty-one years of marriage? You'd think she could be happy for us."

"Oh, I'm sure she——"

"Forgive me, I'm just disappointed. I'll be over it by the time you get here. I promise. I'd ask somebody else in Dolly's place if I knew anyone who could get ready in an hour. That's why I'm calling you. Patti's too young to enjoy a fifty-first anniversary dinner, but what about one of your neighbors?"

"Ann, you mean? I can check. I'm about to run home and get ready."

"I just think five people is so much more festive than four, don't you? Especially with me in a sour mood. And it's not just Dolly. Everything's going wrong. I can't get my necklace fastened and Jim's taking forever in the shower."

I winced. The festive aspect of our evening clearly needed a rescue. I flailed about for humor. "Seems like you'd be used to his routines after fifty-one years, doesn't it?"

Nita laughed, and I continued to tease. "I've seen his bathroom, with all those moisturizers and sprays and lotions. All that takes time, but it's what keeps him young and handsome, you know."

Jim was about to turn eighty-four, and Nita was only a year or two behind him, but both of them were still healthy and attractive.

"I'll see you at five." Nita chuckled lightly. "And anyone else you can round up." She disconnected.

I shut down the laptop and closed it, pushed my chair back, and got up just in time to see a woman walk briskly across the drive outside my window. I paused to watch her. This was the second time I'd seen her since lunch. She'd been walking in the other direction a couple of hours earlier, toward the entrance. I'd immediately thought *sales rep* and expected her to show up in my office after the minute or two she'd need to get inside and cross the lobby. But she hadn't appeared.

I looked a little closer this time, seeing only her back. "Who is this, do you know?" I stepped aside so Patti could see out the window.

The mystery woman was thirty-five, give or take, wearing a short, slim skirt with a fitted jacket and chunky heels and carrying a red handbag. That was one way of saying she stuck out like the proverbial sore thumb in our laid-back little community of retirees and vacationers.

There was no answer from Patti. I turned around and found the office empty.

Time to go.

I patted my pocket to be sure I had my keys and phone, grabbed my shoulder bag, flipped the lights off, and locked the door behind me.

Patti was at her desk out front, wrapping up a phone call. One lonely little ceramic turtle sat on the piece of driftwood that occupied a corner of her desk. It'd taken me weeks to figure out that the number of turtles was a visible barometer for her love life. There'd been as many as eight during the holidays, but not so many lately. Maybe that was the reason she was mopey. I waved to her and did a loop through the gate and the lobby, heading for the front door.

Patti hung up and stood to follow me, reading her note and calling out as she walked. "Ms. Zadnichek says to remind you of an appointment at the front desk of the Art Center tomorrow at nine thirty. Don't be late. Someone will be waiting for you and there's a tight schedule."

She looked up to be sure I was listening. She had followed me as far as the wide metal gate that secured the offices from the lobby at night. Stilts, the orange-spotted giraffe cutout, looked over the top of the bars, making the entire gate, when it was closed, look like a cage at the zoo.

"What's that about?" Patti asked. "And where did you say y'all are going tonight?"

I stopped just before breaking the beam that opened the automatic doors and held up an index finger. "Selecting a painting for the Harbor Village Purchase Prize." Then two fingers. "And Jesse's Restaurant, in Magnolia Springs. Do you know it?"

Her expression brightened. "Is this your first visit to Jesse's? Oh, Cleo, it's *wonderful*!" She grasped the vertical bar of the gate and swung around, curls bouncing, all her mulligrubs gone. "Stewart and I went there for Valentine's. They gave each of the ladies a mini bouquet."

Stewart Granger was our multitalented, multi-tattooed director of maintenance, and Patti's heartthrob. And Valentine's was a month ago. There'd been a long line of turtles on her desk then and progressively fewer ever since. Trouble in paradise, I supposed. I'd suspected all along she was too young for him, to say nothing of her immaturity. But that didn't keep me from feeling sorry for her.

"Why don't you close up early and go home?" It wasn't that I minded her leaving early. She certainly put in enough hours every week. We all did. But I hated being in the dark about whatever she was up to.

She surprised me by shaking her head. "I'm saving my perks for tomorrow. I want to go to the arts and crafts festival in the afternoon, before the crowds get too big. Wish Jim and Nita a happy anniversary for me. And tell Riley to take you down that arbor."

I nodded without knowing exactly what she meant and waved goodbye. *Arbor? Ardor?* Whatever. If she wasn't about to sneak out, what was she up to?

Patti was the same age as Stephanie, my daughter, twenty-six years my junior. Stretching across that gap every day kept me sympathetic about the years separating me from most of our residents. I wondered how often my antics had them gnashing their teeth in frustration.

Gold lettering, newly emblazoned across the automatic doors of the administration building, caught my eye as I passed through. *Harbor Village*, I read backwards. A second line, in smaller letters, elaborated: *An Active Senior Community*. Small black lettering in a bottom corner identified me, Cleo Mack, as Executive Director, and gave emergency phone numbers.

The administration building, known to residents and staff as the big house, stood three stories tall at the western end of Harbor Boulevard, looking down the wide median with flower beds, palm trees, and a row of the five-globed street lamps that dotted the Harbor Village campus. I smelled freshly mowed grass as I crossed the drive in front of the garages. The mower was still running somewhere near the highway, judging by the sound. The first grass cutting of the spring.

My path went around the pale green, eight-car garage that served the apartment building I lived in, and down the front sidewalk. I made a point of returning to my apartment by this route occasionally, rather than zipping up the wide sidewalk at the back of the building, right to my screened porch. This route reminded me to check my mailbox in the building lobby and allowed me to speak to people sitting out on the front porch. I could check the building's public spaces as I went through the hallways, spotting little problems before they became big ones. Anything I found was turned over to Stewart.

Today there was a little commotion going on when I pulled the front door open.

On the other side of the lobby, both pairs of glass doors to the courtyard were propped open. The long harvest table that usually stood beside the kitchenette, covered with pieces of a jigsaw puzzle, had been moved to the courtyard, draped with a white tablecloth, and set with elegant china and glassware. Semitropical plants, in pots and beds around the perimeter of the patio, released a flood of color and oxygen and fresh, earthy smells. It was a pleasant welcome, like a visit to the jungle.

I turned to the bank of mailboxes and heard my name called.

Georgina Burch, the retired art teacher who lived in an apartment beside the front door, was peeking out of the courtyard. "Cleo, come give us your opinion."

I walked toward her and saw Katherine Roka, another artist and mother of Harbor Village's business manager Emily, arranging chairs at the table.

"Hi, Cleo." She plopped into a chair and wiggled, testing it for stability on the uneven tiles. "I think that'll do." She smiled as she popped to her feet again, pushed the chair in against the table, and gestured to a vase. "Georgina thinks the flowers are too tall."

"I don't want people craning their necks all night to see around them." Georgina spun a fat blue vase, filled with spring flowers, to a different orientation and stepped back, giving it a critical look.

"Let's test it." I pulled out the chair at my end of the table and sat.

Georgina took the chair at the opposite end. I leaned one way and then the other but, whatever I did, one blue sprig protruded into our line of sight.

"Ah ha!" Georgina got up. "Off with his head!"

I wiggled in the chair, found that it didn't teeter, and got up. "Who's partying tonight?"

"Some of Georgina's old students are in town for Arts and Crafts." Katherine tossed her a smile that looked a little tense. "And now her sister's arrived." She looked at me. "Everyone wants to visit Georgina."

It was true. Georgina Burch was one of the most popular people at Harbor Village. I saw her almost every day, always on her way somewhere. Off to play bridge at the senior center, to volunteer at the Art Center or the Methodist Church, or to drive a friend to lunch or a medical appointment.

Georgina looked at Katherine and sighed. "I wish you were staying. I understand, but I wish things were different."

She snapped off the base of the blue salvia stem and reinserted the long part into the vase, then gave it a pat. "There. It's too early to light the fire, but I'm going to get it ready. I hope it won't be too warm tonight. A nice little fire warms the courtyard and improves the ambience. Soothes the savage breast."

"It's cool in the shade already." I walked around the table to see what she was doing.

Georgina took a knee in front of the red clay chiminea. Its spherical base rested in a heavy metal frame, and the chimney top was about as tall as I was. Dry twigs and short branches lay stacked in a basket, on top of several short logs. Georgina tossed the salvia stem into the fire pot and began breaking the twigs in half. Then she crumpled a few pieces of newspaper and put them in first, laid twigs on top, and followed up with one of the log segments.

"Have fun tonight." I went back to the mailboxes.

I opened box number eight with my key and pulled out a stack of flyers and magazines that immediately began sliding and spilling in all directions. Response cards fell to the floor and scooted across the tile. A big, glossy card slid under a barstool. I grumbled to myself as I spread the flyers on the kitchen bar, picked up the cards, and went back for a couple of letters lying on the bottom of the mailbox.

Katherine Roka came in from the courtyard and went to the sink behind the bar.

I climbed onto a barstool and scanned an invitation to an investment seminar that came with the bribe of a free seafood dinner. "I hope you'll have a great time tonight," I told Katherine. I put the invitation on the recycling stack with the glossy ads.

Katherine turned off the water, shook her hands, and looked for a towel. "Oh, I'm not staying."

"Dammit," Georgina muttered from the courtyard, and Katherine rolled her eyes.

I smiled at her. An official-looking letter was next in the stack of mail. I tore the flap open and pulled out a sheaf of papers announcing an upcoming social work convention. I glanced over the letter and saw I was scheduled to participate in a panel discussion of reversible dementias, my favorite kind. I started a new stack for real mail.

Katherine spoke in a loud voice, including Georgina in the conversation. "I'm just helping Georgina get set up. My husband was one of her students and he'll be here, but I missed out on all the fun."

"Oh?" I looked at her closely.

Katherine was petite and pretty, with thick, dark hair worn in a pointy pixie cut. Her daughter, Emily, had the red hair that identified her as a member of the extended Slump family, but that trait came from Emily's father. Katherine's hair was almost black and her skin pearlescent, even without cosmetics. I knew she was an artist, scheduled to conduct a workshop at Harbor Village Saturday, but I didn't know much else about her. "You didn't grow up in Fairhope?"

"No. Up in the hill country." She gestured toward the north. "We didn't have art courses at my high school. Solly went to school here at about the same time and had a whole slew of art classes to choose from. All taught by Georgina, of course. Solly gives her credit for steering him into the art profession."

"Blames me, you mean," Georgina voice was muffled, coming from the courtyard.

"He's a painter?" I was trying to remember if I'd met him.

"No, a potter. When he can get away from the office."

"He has a day job, I suppose."

She laughed and shook her head. "He's dean of the Ocean Springs branch of the Magnolia Art Institute. You've never heard of it, probably, but it's developing a strong reputation in art circles, thanks to Solly. You'd be amazed at the hours he puts into making that happen. He doesn't have much time for studio work now, but he's brought a few pieces for the festival. Come see them tomorrow."

In truth, I had a very good idea how much time academic jobs took. Nine months ago, I'd still been professor and chair of a social work program in Atlanta. I had a momentary flashback to that time, before I'd been offered a nice bonus and early retirement, and before I'd discovered Fairhope. I'd never pictured myself working for a big corporation like Harbor Health Services and would never have guessed how much I'd come to like both the new job and my new home. A lot had happened in the last nine months.

I shifted my attention back to Katherine and an idea popped into my head. "Solly's having dinner here tonight, and you're not? Do you have other plans?"

Katherine shrugged narrow shoulders. "I'll find something to do. Maybe Emily and I will go out."

"I'm really not a stalker, Katherine. I'm asking because I need an extra person to go to Jesse's Restaurant in Magnolia Springs in just about..." I looked at my watch. "Forty-five minutes. We have reservations for five people and one just canceled."

She smiled and didn't say no.

"You know Nita Bergen," I pressed onward. "It's Nita and Jim's fifty-first wedding anniversary, and they're treating. Nita called a few minutes ago to say Dolly Webb canceled at the last minute, and Nita thinks four people won't be festive enough. She was hoping I could find another guest."

She was listening and smiling, and I added another inducement. "I haven't been to the restaurant, but I hear it's really special."

"It sure is!" Georgina shouted from the courtyard.

Katherine frowned. "I hope nothing's wrong with Dolly. She and Nita are signed up for my workshop Saturday."

"Just a cold, I understand. Do you know Jim, too?"

She flashed a mischievous smile. "By reputation, mostly. Emily talks about him. I guess he visits the office occasionally."

"Ha!" Georgina barked.

"More like a shadow director," I admitted. "But he's a big help to us. Now, back to tonight. Jim and Nita are celebrating, and Riley Meddors is driving us. He's a retired banker."

"And Cleo's beau." Georgina popped in at the doorway and closed the doors behind her. She was wearing white running shoes, a navy-blue Auburn University sweatshirt, and cropped cargo pants. "A real sweetheart, he is. Go, Katherine. It'll make me feel so much better."

Katherine looked down at her own dark jeans, pink button-down shirt, and pink denim jacket with fringe trim. "I don't have any dress-up clothes with me."

"You look fine," I said quickly. "I'll lend you some pearls if you like." Nothing else in my closet would fit her, but pearls would dress up her outfit. "Come to my apartment and freshen up while I get ready."

I gathered up my mail, keeping the stacks separate, and Georgina came to give Katherine a hug.

"You go. Enjoy yourself and don't worry about a thing. I'll be right here, and we'll get together this weekend."

Katherine nodded. "You're the one who should be enjoying this night. Don't worry about me. And please don't worry about Solly. He's a big boy." Katherine got her purse from the counter beside the sink and froze, staring at me. "I can't believe I'm doing this. I hope you really want me."

I assured her that was the case, and we went through the interior hallway to my apartment at the back of the building.

"Your husband's name is Solly? Is that short for something?"

"Solomon. Known in the Bible for wisdom, wealth, and writings. My Solly falls short on a few counts, unfortunately. I ought to call him, I guess, and tell him what I'm up to. He's in town, waiting for five o'clock, when they begin setting up booths."

"Were you supposed to help?"

She shook her head. "The students are there. They've got their routine all practiced."

I glanced up frequently as we walked, scanning the ceiling for leaks, checking to make sure all the light bulbs were working. "This hallway always seems dark to me."

Katherine motioned toward the wall beside us. "Just think, all this could've been windows opening to the courtyard. Maybe you could install them now? Or some white paint would help."

"I wonder if windows would require structural changes."

"I'll bet they're cheaper than you think. Maybe your staff could do it. Is that what Stewart does?"

I confirmed it as I got out my key. Tinkerbelle, the fluffy calico who'd lived in the apartment even before I came, was waiting inside the door, meowing to hurry the unlocking process along.

"What a beautiful cat!" Katherine entered ahead of me and dropped to one knee. "Are you friendly? May I pet you?

Tinkerbelle meowed some more, squinting as she presented her chin and cheeks for scratching.

"This is Tinkerbelle. Belle like a Southern belle. She's very friendly but watch out, she's shedding. Let me put this stuff away and then I'll set up the guest bath for you."

I went through the living room, dropped off the real mail at the desk, and put the junk into an almost-full recycling basket. In the hall bath I laid out a washcloth and hand towel and turned the lights on. "I don't know if you really want pearls, but I'll get them and you can decide. And then I'll get ready."

"I think I have a new friend," Katherine said.

Tinkerbelle followed her to the hall, twining around her ankles.

"Her coloration is gorgeous. I'd love to put her in a watercolor sometime. Can't you just see her, curled up on a thick cushion in a wicker chair, with long fern fronds dangling from above? Do you mind if I get a couple of photographs?"

Tinkerbelle really was a pretty cat, with semi-long hair now that she'd recovered from roughing it outdoors, after her original owner abandoned her. She had a white chest and socks, a big orange saddle, and was velvet black elsewhere.

"Of course I don't mind. Remind me now, watercolors are your specialty?" I talked louder while I dashed through my bedroom to the master bath and grabbed the short strand of pearls off the carousel. I was back in a flash and handed the pearls to Katherine.

"Transparent watercolors, usually. But I've been dabbling in photorealism for a few years now."

"That's some type of photography?"

She raised her hands and watched the pearls slide through her fingers. "These are beautiful." She stepped in front of the bathroom mirror and held the necklace to her throat. "I've never had real pearls. I should get some. Photorealism is a type of drawing that strives for a three-dimensional look. Done well, it's often mistaken for black-and-white photography. It's what I'll be teaching in Saturday's workshop. Why don't you come?"

"Wouldn't that be fun?" I grabbed at a feathery bit of cat hair floating between us. "I hope it's the time of year that's causing all this shedding."

"Losing her winter coat." Katherine addressed the cat as she closed the bathroom door: "You wait here while I wash up. And then you can pose for a photograph."

I checked the cat box, got another pair of black pants out of the closet, along with a beige silk blouse and a new red stretch blazer, then closed myself in the master bath. When I'd washed and changed and brushed and freshened my makeup, I put the jacket on and smiled at my reflection. Too bright, I knew instantly. *Way* too bright. I turned for a side view. I was overdressed, in comparison to Katherine's jeans, and the red made me look like I should be on a horse, surrounded by foxhounds. The jacket still had its tags. Was it too late to return it?

I went back to the closet and selected a camel-colored blazer.

I was putting the red jacket back on a hanger when I heard an unfamiliar ring tone, followed by Katherine's voice. The ensuing conversation was short and I caught only an occasional word, but Katherine did most of the talking. When she ended the call, I went to the living room and found her preparing to photograph Tinkerbelle.

"I love your apartment, Cleo. It's so sleek and modern."

"I did some downsizing before I moved here. And I haven't missed a thing."

I went to the kitchen, checked Tinkerbelle's water dish, and added dry cat food to her food bowl. The cat charged into the room and skidded to a halt. "Sorry, Katherine. I wasn't thinking. I should've known that sound would bring her running."

Katherine followed Tinkerbelle to the kitchen.

"How do you like the pearls?" She tilted her head to one side and then the other, giving me a good look. "They lean toward yellow instead of pink, and it's a nice contrast. They're the perfect size and length to dress me up. Don't I look smashing?" She preened and smiled. "Are you sure Nita won't mind if I crash her party?"

"She'll be delighted. So will Jim. And Riley."

"I hope so. Tell me about Riley."

I got two short bottles of water out of the fridge, handed one to her, and twisted the top off the other while I gave her a quick rundown. "He's retired from a government job he doesn't like to talk about. He's lived here two years and been divorced for…forever. But he's on good terms with his ex. Two adult sons I haven't met."

I took a quick sip of water and thought about what I'd said. "That sounds so lame, like I just met the man. He's sweet and funny and sexy. Nita's known him for years, and they adore each other, which I consider a good recommendation. And he's smart and dependable."

"He sounds ideal. Sometimes you just know."

I nodded. "He wants me to move in with him."

She sprayed water. "Oh, my!"

She jumped and patted fingers against a dribble running down her chin, while I grabbed a paper towel off the roll and handed it to her.

"Sorry, but you surprised me." She blotted her chin and the front of her shirt. "That's a big step at our age. Are you going to do it? With or without marriage?"

I took a long drink and looked around my serene, monotone apartment. Then I shook my head, a reply that was more uncertain than negative. "Maybe. I'm trying to decide. I just wish I had a little more courage."

Katherine laughed. "Ah, yes. Courage." She lifted her water bottle in a mock toast. "The expressway to disaster." She took a sip then sighed and waved toward the living room. "I love your painting, but I couldn't read the signature."

"No one you'd know. My late husband, Robert Mack." I took a few steps and turned to look at it from a distance. "He was a mathematician, not an artist. Maybe you can tell."

She walked over to stand close to the bookcase, where she could examine Robert Mack's one and only painting at close range. "It's interesting. And I don't mean that in a patronizing way. Push-pull. Comforting and challenging at once."

My gaze swept across the painting, and I smiled. "That's a good description of the man."

The numbers flipped on the digital clock atop the bookcase.

"You can look at it when we get back. We'd better walk across the street."

Chapter 2

We had attempted, in the fall, to develop a simple naming system for the six apartment buildings at Harbor Village. We collected suggestions, campaigned for our favorites, and finally voted. States and bird names had lost out, in favor of numbers.

We'd held a big launch party, with posters and handouts identifying buildings one, two, and three north and one, two, and three south, based on order, beginning near the condos at the entrance and moving toward the big house, with north or south indicating which side of the boulevard the building was on. Simple, easy to remember, and precise—right?

But it didn't work.

The buildings nearest the condos were still called the front buildings, the buildings adjacent to them were called the middle buildings, and the buildings nearest the big house were the donut buildings. Yes, *donut*. Not everybody knew the origin of the term, but *donut* actually derived from the building's appearance in aerial photos, where the interior courtyard looked like the hole in the middle of a square donut.

My apartment was on the back of one donut building. My friend Nita Bergen and her husband, Jim, had a spacious, luxurious front apartment in the donut building on the other side of Harbor Boulevard.

At a couple of minutes before five, Katherine and I walked across the boulevard, from one donut building to the other. Nita was on the porch, sitting primly in a rocking chair, her purse on her lap. From the way she stared, I assumed she was trying to figure out who was with me.

Jim and Riley were in the parking lot between the garages and the swimming pool. All four doors of Riley's black BMW station wagon stood open. I waved to the men and they began closing doors and moving toward us. I couldn't resist watching. Riley was broad-shouldered with a slight thickening at the middle, but he moved with a subconscious grace even when he was just wiping his hands and tossing the towel into the back, or closing the rear hatch.

"Katherine!" Nita exclaimed as we reached the porch. She hopped to her feet in a way that belied eighty-some years, darted over to take Katherine's hands, and gave her a pair of air kisses. "What a lovely surprise! Cleo, you've found the ideal person."

Katherine kissed back. "I'm sorry about my clothes, but this was a surprise. I didn't have an opportunity to change."

Nita was dressier than Katherine or me, wearing a bright blue, high-necked sweater that emphasized her eyes; loose, man-tailored pants; and a short, fluffy jacket. Her gold pendant, the one she'd been unable to fasten without Jim's assistance, was an antique coin she'd brought back from a trip with Fairhope's Senior Travel Club.

"You look perfect to me," she told Katherine. "What beautiful pearls."

Katherine and I laughed, and Katherine admitted the pearls were borrowed.

I gave Nita a hug. "Happy anniversary."

Nita Bergen was a tiny woman, five feet tall and barely a hundred pounds, with snow-white hair that was always perfectly in place, even when she was out on the pier, which was where I'd met her nine months ago. She'd been my first Fairhope friend and was still the best, in spite of the difference in our ages.

"Yes, a very happy anniversary," Katherine said. "Fifty-one years? You must've been a child bride."

Jim's hearing was perfect. He answered from the sidewalk. "She was a widow. Old enough to appreciate a good man when she found one."

We laughed and Nita flapped a hand, dismissing his comment.

"Katherine, do you know the boys?"

The five of us convened at the edge of the porch, and Nita did the introductions.

"Katherine Roka," Jim repeated, taking Katherine's hand in both of his and shaking it as he talked. "That's a fine daughter you've got. Good head on her shoulders. Now, Katherine, are you a Fairhope native?"

"I grew up in Fayette County." She retracted her hand and turned to face Riley.

"Oh, yes, Fayette County." Jim nodded. "Near Tuscaloosa. Know it well. Now, do you know Riley Meddors? He'll be driving us tonight. I call him the human calculator, but he's actually a forensic banker. Was, I mean."

I'd never heard that term and didn't know if there actually was such a thing. Probably Jim had just made it up.

Riley Meddors was four inches shorter than Jim and twenty-some years younger, with cinnamon-brown hair and a close-cut beard that showed a sprinkling of silver and gold in the late afternoon sunlight.

"Nice to meet you," he told Katherine, giving her a smile and a quick handshake.

I loved seeing the way his eyes crinkled when he smiled, even if it was at another woman. I could see Katherine assessing him and caught the quick glance she gave me, the little flash of a smile. Riley had passed the preliminary inspection, I assumed.

Jim was, as usual, collecting information. He asked Katherine if she was a Harbor Village resident. "I don't think you're in my directory."

Riley gave me a smile and a one-armed hug, with a quick little peck on the cheek. I hadn't seen him all day, which was unusual lately. We often had lunch together in the dining room or he looked in at the office some time during the day, and occasionally we woke up together. Katherine was telling Jim what she'd told me earlier, about Solly's job and the Magnolia Art Institute, with a few details new to me. She had a studio on campus, I learned, one that allowed her a distant view of the water while she taught and worked. It sounded even more ideal than my home and office arrangement, just half a block apart.

"Busy day?" Riley asked.

I nodded. "I tried to get eight hours of work into seven. And did a pretty good job, if I may brag on myself."

Riley never failed to brighten my day. And then just as quickly, he ruined it. "Did Michael Bonderant find you?"

I shook my head. My mouth went dry at the reference to the interior designer from Charlotte, the man who'd decorated Jim and Nita's apartment when they moved to Harbor Village and was now trying to work his magic on the house Riley had purchased. Michael had boasted he could create a home I wouldn't be able to resist, and Riley had handed him the challenge. I'd been dreading the big reveal for months, and now the day had arrived, or would this weekend, and I was apprehensive. What if I still hated the house? There was more than a good chance, but it didn't necessarily mean I was rejecting Riley and his offer, whatever it was.

Nita distracted me from my thoughts. She was looking at her watch. "I think we'd better get underway, if everyone's ready?"

Jim held the car's back door for Nita and assisted with her seat belt, then sat in front, one of the perks of having long legs. I went to the other side of the car and slid to the middle seat in back. When Dolly was with us, the middle seat was my reward for being youngest. With Katherine in the group instead, I probably lost that title, but it still seemed the polite thing to do.

The drive to Magnolia Springs took us south on Highway 98, through flat land with a heavy agricultural emphasis. Jim pointed out potato fields and pecan groves that hosted a colony of fox squirrels. "Twice the size of regular squirrels, with a black mask. Tame enough to pet, almost."

Nita rolled her eyes and shook her head but Jim, in the front seat and unable to see her, went right along. He asked Riley, "You know fox squirrels, don't you?"

Riley said he'd seen them, but Jim was off to another topic. He pointed out a citrus orchard where we'd purchased satsumas a few months earlier.

"All this will be housing developments soon," he predicted.

Nita interrupted. "Now remember, everybody. We're only going to talk about happy subjects tonight. And Jim, just for the record, I do not find development very happy."

Everyone laughed except Nita.

I'd been to Foley and Gulf Shores and Orange Beach perhaps a dozen times since I moved to Fairhope, but I knew Magnolia Springs only as a minor congestion along the way. A sign beside the road announced the community.

"Have either of you been to Jesse's?" Jim half turned to look into the back seat.

Katherine and I said we had not.

"Turn at this next street," Jim directed Riley and pointed to the right.

"It's almost five thirty," Nita cautioned him.

"Won't take any longer this way, and it'll be dark when we start home."

She relented immediately. "Oh, you're right. You're right. This is worth being a little late." She patted my hand. "Why didn't you come to Jesse's with us during the holidays?"

"I went to Stephanie's in Birmingham for Christmas."

"And we were in Savannah at Thanksgiving," Riley answered, glancing at me in the rearview mirror. I smiled back, recalling our first trip together and the cementing of our still-developing relationship.

"Of course." Nita smiled at me. She still looked for opportunities to fan the flames of romance between Riley and me. "Well, we love Jesse's. We come here for all our special occasions. I can't believe you haven't come along before now. Riley has. Lots of times." She leaned forward and looked past me. "You'll have to bring your husband next time, Katherine."

We moved at a low speed, past several new houses still under construction and finally, a mile or more off the highway and after stopping at the second intersection, Riley turned left. We crept slowly around the corner.

Ahead was an oak tunnel, with moss-covered, gnarled trees stretching massive branches from either side of the road to lace together high above. Spanish moss trailed both sides of the narrow street and a blanket of leaves padded the edges, making our progress almost silent, except for the crunch of acorns. White picket fences enclosed swaths of vivid green lawns, and azaleas larger than the car crowded right to the edge of the pavement, giving me a sense of euphoria. The big blooms blended from pink to white to fuchsia.

"Breathtaking," Katherine whispered.

I agreed. The houses were mostly old but beautiful and well kept, with an elegant, cottagey look and mature landscaping. At one small white house with bright yellow shutters, a woman worked with a broom and dustpan, cleaning the driveway.

"The Magnolia River runs right behind these houses." Riley gestured off to the right.

"The last place in the country where mail is delivered by boat." Jim motioned for Riley to turn down the next side street.

Katherine had her phone out. "Will it bother anyone if I lower this window?"

Riley buzzed it down from the driver's seat, and Katherine stuck her arms out and began snapping photographs.

"Stop for a minute, Riley," Nita ordered. "Let Katherine get out to take her pictures."

She was quick. When she finished and returned to her seat, we turned down a side street and got a brief look at the quiet little river whose water looked almost black in the fading light. I could see houses, piers, boathouses, and bulkheads from the parking area beside a little boat ramp. A squat kingfisher, with its distinctive silhouette and big head, sat on a sagging power line that ran to the nearby boathouse. I hadn't seen a kingfisher in years. Magnolia Springs was quaint and beautiful, like something out of the past.

We got to the restaurant only a few minutes after our five thirty reservation. The building was long and low, white with black trim and a series of windows across the front. There was a parking lot at one end, already full of cars and pickups and SUVs.

Riley nosed into one of a few handicap spaces beside the street and Jim snapped his laminated handicapped placard onto the rearview mirror. "This building was once an old country store." Jim swiveled out of the car, hauled himself to his feet, and opened the back door for Nita. "You'll have to see the old icebox they have inside. Moore Brothers, I think the store's name was."

"It had a good bakery, remember?" Nita got out slowly and looked back to see if I was coming her way. "We got brownies every time we came."

I was following Katherine out the other door, but I heard Jim ask, "Dutch apple pie, wasn't it? And that butcher shop. Remember it?"

"Yes. We'd stop here and buy steaks and shrimp on our way back from Pensacola, when we'd just been to the commissary. People thought we were crazy, but Moore Brothers was much better."

Riley walked around the car to offer Nita his arm, and I caught up with Jim, who teetered ahead, jabbing the sidewalk with his cane. Katherine followed us.

The restaurant entrance was at the far end of the building, past outdoor tables and planters. Inside, there was a large foyer with cubbyholes lining one side. On the other side, four people waited on a long bench, scowling at the prospect of newcomers moving ahead of them in line. We went to the stand-up desk, where a young, pretty hostess waited. Layers of carpets, in various shades of red, lapped over each other, directing people to the right, where I could see a busy bar, or straight ahead and around a corner to the left.

The hostess was a skinny young woman clad all in black. She darted in from the left and greeted us breathlessly. "Do you have a reservation?"

"Bergen." Nita motioned for Katherine to move forward. "A table for five in the sunroom."

"Hmm." The hostess twiddled her pencil. "Bergen?"

She scanned her list twice before Jim startled and spoke up.

"That's Maguire. Jimmy Maguire." He cut his eyes around at me, looked slightly embarrassed, and grinned. "Can't be too careful."

I asked, quietly, "You use an alias for reservations?" That was a new one, in his vast reservoir of quirks.

"My middle name." He grinned, seeming proud of himself. "We've got to control the flow of information, Cleo. That's job one, now days. If someone calls and asks for us, there's no record we've been here."

"Right," I said.

Nita rolled her eyes at me. "The name is Bergen," she told the hostess, firmly.

The hostess marked Maguire off her list, gave Jim a curious glance as she picked up menus, and indicated we should follow her. "We're really

full tonight. Just be glad you have a reservation, whatever the name is."
She led us around the corner.

Jim wobbled along right behind her.

"It's the festival," he told her. "We've got an extra three hundred thousand
people in Fairhope this weekend. Are you booked up every night?"

She said they were and cautioned us to watch our step going up a gentle
ramp. We passed a noisy, dimly lit dining room and, across from it, a hall
that led to the kitchen and restrooms.

"Sophia will be your server tonight." The hostess laid out menus on a
large, round table in the front corner and pulled out a chair for Nita and
another for Jim.

Jim looked around the table, then the room, and pointed to a different
chair, in the corner with a view of the entrance. "I'll sit there."

I watched him sidle around the table and thought about his aliases and
precautions and the miniature revolver always strapped above his ankle.
Security was job one for Jim, day and night. I kidded him about it, but I'd
grown accustomed to seeing his flashlight play around on buildings and
bushes every night, about the time I went to bed. I took some comfort,
knowing he was out there, walking and watching. I also liked the fact he
was on good terms with the local cops—Chief Boozer and Lieutenant Mary
Montgomery, as well as the patrol officers. Jim and Boozer had dinner
together at least once a month, before the public safety committee meeting.

His attention to details had inspired me to be more observant, too.
I noticed the sunroom's other patrons, the wood floors and interesting
paintings, the trees in big ceramic pots, and vining plants hanging in front
of the floor-to-ceiling windows on two sides of the sunroom. Windows, I
knew, were one thing Jim avoided.

The wooden ceiling was high, and fans turned lazily up above us. The
tables were especially eye catching. Big sheets of white paper were angled
over the black tablecloth and served as placemats. Five black napkins,
folded long ways, met like radii at the center of the table.

I sat with my back to the window. Riley, on the other side of the table,
held Nita and Katherine's chairs simultaneously and then gave Nita a
little shove closer to the table. Katherine scooted herself while he circled
around to sit beside me.

When everyone was seated, the hostess removed the *reserved* sign from
a small vase of flowers. Sophia hovered, opening a bottle of champagne
and filling our glasses as she recited the night's list of specials.

"Just a sip for me." Riley held his champagne glass out to the server
but turned the wineglass upside down. "I'm driving."

"Someone has to drink it." Jim tapped the edge of the table and the server left the bucket there beside him. He raised his glass. "Here's to fifty-one years. May the next one be best of all." He clinked glasses with his bride, then with everyone around the table.

When we'd ordered—baked chicken for Katherine and me, Delmonico rib eye for the others—we took turns quizzing the Bergens about how they'd met, where they'd married, and all the places they'd lived together in half a century, much of it under the authority of the U.S. Navy. The questions sparked memories and polite little squabbles between them, but everyone was engaged and entertained until the salads arrived.

"How's your house coming?" Jim asked Riley. He pulled a roll out of the basket, tore it in half, and smeared on some butter.

I closed my eyes and grimaced at the question, but Riley answered. "I've been banned for the last week, but it's supposed to be finished by five o'clock Saturday."

"Banned?"

Riley nodded.

Jim looked at me. "And you still haven't seen it?"

I shook my head. "Not since December."

Nita explained to Katherine, who was looking puzzled. "The designer who did our apartment is modernizing a house at Harbor Village." She smiled across the table. "It's Riley's house, but the designer is doing it up to suit Cleo."

"And not letting her see it?" Katherine acted as if that were a serious offense. "Are you at least making decisions? Picking colors and fabrics and art work?"

I made a hands-off gesture and shook my head.

Katherine stared indignantly. "Who *is* this designer?"

Jim waved his salad fork. "Just sign a check and stay away, that's his technique. Did us the same way when he did the apartment."

"No, he didn't," Nita said. "We were there every day."

"And he didn't listen to a word we said."

She gave him a triumphant look. "And we love the result, don't we? Better than if we'd made all the choices ourselves." She laid her hand over his and squeezed. "And we stayed married."

Jim shook his head but grinned, and Riley told Katherine, "I told him he only has to please Cleo. If she's happy, I'm happy."

"What's his name?" Katherine asked again.

"Michael Bonderant," Jim and Riley answered simultaneously.

Katherine laughed with delight. "I knew it! Michael's got a lot of confidence. But anyone would have to, to take on a job like that. What if you hate it?"

"It goes on the market." Riley's answer was quick and firm. "I don't want to live there by myself. I've got a perfect place for one person." He laughed, draped an arm across my shoulders, and gave me a squeeze. "Too bad it doesn't stretch to hold two."

Nita pursed her lips, and I wondered if Riley had strayed onto one of her banned topics. She didn't approve of public discussions of personal topics, but she'd lectured me, in private, about the advantages of marriage, a shared residence, and plenty of sex. She'd introduced me to Riley on my first visit to Fairhope and now, nine months later, she didn't understand our caution and delay.

I was relieved when she didn't pursue the subject at dinner. Instead, she turned to Katherine with a question. "Do you know Michael?"

"He's one of Georgina's old students. Went to high school with Solly, or a couple of years behind him. They're both at her party tonight."

"Maybe he'll visit us this weekend." Nita gave Jim a happy glance. "I'd forgotten he was a local boy."

"Acts like he's Ralph Lauren." Jim gestured toward Riley, a cherry tomato stuck on his fork. "Reckon he'd give us a preview of your house? I want to see what he's done."

Riley shook his head. "He was pretty emphatic when he ran me out." He looked at me. "Did he talk with you today?"

I shook my head. "Haven't seen him."

"Well, he sent you a message."

The server came just then, carrying a big tray balanced on her shoulder, and Riley was interrupted before he relayed any message. With her free hand, Sophia snapped a stand open and carefully set the tray atop it. I heard sizzling and saw little clouds of steam.

A tall young man followed with another tray and a stand he set up beside hers. Then he passed plates to Sophia, who moved around the table, putting each dish in front of the right person and announcing what the dish was, or how the steaks had been cooked.

"Looks good. Looks good." Jim leaned forward, inventorying the contents of each plate. "Riley, is that the Delmonico?"

"The petite version."

"Like mine," Nita said.

"And, Cleo, you've got baked chicken? I wouldn't mind a little taste of that. Don't think I've ever had it. Katherine, I've forgotten what you ordered."

The centerpiece blocked his view and gave him an excuse for talking about the food, an important part of the pleasure.

Riley leaned close, bumping shoulders with me to get my attention. "I keep getting interrupted. Bonderant wants you to meet him at ten tomorrow at the Art Center."

I shook my head. "I've got another appointment." Marjorie Zadnichek had said nine thirty, also at the Art Center. "Harbor Village promised to make a purchase award, and the Art Center has arranged a guide, somebody to help select a painting for the ballroom. I have to make the selection, and there's a bit of a presentation. I don't know how long it'll take."

Jim was eating but still listened attentively.

Riley frowned. "Michael's put some paintings on hold and wants you to veto anything you really hate. If you decide early, the artists can get the rejects back on display before the crowds arrive."

"Well," I shrugged, "I'll be there anyway. I'll talk with him and see when we can get together. Want to go with me?"

He shook his head and gave me a tense little smile. "I'm specifically not invited. The art is to be my surprise."

"A fine steak." Jim gestured with a big knife. "Cooked just right. What's this about a purchase prize? How's that different from an ordinary purchase?"

I cut off two samples of the baked chicken. "Katherine knows more about it than I do." I put one piece of the chicken on Jim's plate and other one on Riley's.

"Just wonderful," Katherine mumbled, rolling her eyes and signaling for a delay. She chewed and blotted her lips before answering. "These big shows draw top artists by announcing the amount pledged for purchases. Businesses get some publicity for being sponsors, and artists can compare the pledged amounts to other shows to get an idea of how their sales might run."

Nita had sliced her steak into two pieces and pushed the larger piece to the edge of her plate. "They don't know in advance whose work will be selected for the purchase prizes, do they?"

I shrugged. "I've never done this before. I thought I'd just look around until I find something that speaks to me."

Katherine agreed. "That's the best way. I've never gotten a purchase prize, not officially, but Solly snares one occasionally. Paintings are the usual choice, I'm sure. But artists are an egotistical bunch. We all think our work is best. And rain can really ruin a show, you know. In that case, purchase prizes may represent the bulk of sales. Like a little insurance policy."

The chicken was delicious, as were the vegetables—peppers and zucchini, cherry tomatoes, and purple onions.

"I should've ordered chicken," Riley said. "But the steak's good, too."

"You want another bite?"

"Aren't they a cute couple?" Nita asked Katherine.

They laughed while I cut off another bit for Riley and he held up a hand to stop me.

"I'll take it, if he doesn't want it." Jim made space on his plate and pointed.

"Jim, let Cleo enjoy her food," Nita said. "You remind me of a dog that begs at the table."

"Ebony," he said, taking her literally and naming the Boston terrier they'd had years ago.

I stabbed the bit of chicken with my knife and moved it to his plate.

The glazed chicken was good and the veggies were outstanding. Steaks were offered with a choice of sides, but the people at our table had chosen baked sweet potatoes with butter and cinnamon sugar.

As we ate, Sophia attended unobtrusively, pouring wine and water when they were in short supply and bringing a basket of hot rolls and the extra napkins Jim requested.

Nita asked Katherine about the drawing workshop on Saturday. "The flyer says we don't need to bring anything."

Katherine nodded. "I've bought paper and pencils, and we'll use the studio's drawing boards. That's all we'll need. Well, there's a particular eraser I want everyone to try, and I'm bringing a bunch of those."

"I'm excited about it," Nita said, "but I have very little artistic talent. I know you don't expect any masterpieces."

Katherine told us how simple the techniques were. "You may surprise yourself. It's not a fast technique, but it's surprising how many people produce something presentable right away."

"That's my kind of art," I said.

"Why don't you come?" Katherine and Nita asked.

"Dolly's signed up," Jim said. "You can take her place."

Katherine insisted. "All the materials are furnished. Nine o'clock in the arts and crafts room."

"Please say yes," Nita wheedled. "I need someone to sit with."

"Dolly may feel like going by Saturday," I said.

Nita and Jim snorted in unison.

"Not Dolly," he said.

"She isolates herself, you know. Three days for a cold. We won't see her before Sunday. Which reminds me, we'll need a substitute for Mexican Trains tomorrow night." Nita looked at Katherine. "Can we keep you for a second night?"

She shook her head. "I'd love it, but there's a dinner for exhibitors."

"What's this dinner going on tonight?" Jim had finished his steak and now he signaled for the extra bit Nita had put aside.

Katherine's plate was nearing the empty point, too, which seemed to surprise her. "You know, I think I must've skipped lunch today. That doesn't happen often. Shows how busy I've been." She gave the plate a little push and rested her arm on the edge of the table, leaning forward to look at Jim. "You know Georgina Burch? She lives in Cleo's building."

He nodded. "Of course. Taught at the high school for twenty-nine years. Did you know that? She's a photographer."

Katherine nodded. "She taught painting and drawing and pottery, too. Then went to Greece after she retired and worked on an archaeology dig for a couple of years. She was the official photographer, but she got her hands dirty, too. Well, several of her former students are having dinner with her tonight. A mini-reunion."

I asked, "Are they all exhibiting this weekend?"

Katherine hesitated. "I'm not sure about everyone. Is Michael exhibiting?" She looked at Riley.

He shrugged. "Haven't heard it mentioned."

"No, I wouldn't think so. What would he exhibit? A room?" Jim laughed at his own joke. "I don't think he does any art."

Katherine laughed. "Let's just say I wouldn't agree with you."

"What about Twinkle?" Jim asked.

Katherine drew a sharp little breath and her face changed somehow.

There was a brief pause, until Riley asked, "Who's Twinkle?"

Nita glanced at Katherine before answering him. "Georgina's sister, the portrait artist. She came to see us today."

Katherine blinked and inhaled as she turned to look directly at Nita. "Do you know her well?"

"She owes us a painting." Jim sounded gruff. "We gave her a deposit—a *large* deposit—at last year's festival. She's doing us a fiftieth anniversary portrait."

"That was the agreement, at least." Nita corrected, sounding as close to anger as I'd ever heard her. "It was supposed to be finished six months ago, and she hasn't even started yet."

I spoke up. "It's been a whole year? And she hasn't started?" I couldn't say what I was really thinking, that it was criminal to keep octogenarians waiting a year for anything, and especially if you were holding a big chunk of their money.

"It won't be long now, she says." Jim signaled to our server, who was already coming our way, bringing dessert menus.

"Got any bread pudding?" He didn't wait for a menu. "With bourbon sauce?"

Sophia nodded. "Excellent choice."

"Five," Jim held up five fingers, giving us no say in the matter. "And give us some extra bourbon sauce in a bowl." He cupped his hands to indicate the size bowl he had in mind. "Everybody want coffee?"

Everybody did. Four decafs. Jim ordered full strength. "Make us a fresh pot. It's our fifty-first anniversary."

"Happy anniversary." She made a little bow.

When the server left, Jim looked at me. "Ought to be free dessert for an anniversary. Maybe she got the hint."

Nita frowned at him but turned toward Katherine. "I think we should ask Twinkle for our money back. Jim doesn't agree."

"She says it'll be done in six weeks," he argued. "She came over today to get another look at us before she starts painting."

Nita gave him a stern look. "It's been twelve months, Jim."

He threw up his hands. "She's in demand, Nita. That's what happens when you get the best. Isn't that right, Katherine?"

Katherine pushed her chair back. "I don't want to take sides here. I think I'll visit the ladies' room before dessert gets here. Does anyone know where it is?"

I pushed my chair back and stood. "I saw it as we came in. May I go with you?" I walked my fingers across Riley's shoulders as I went by, to keep him from standing. "Be right back. Nita, do you want to go with us?"

"No, it's a small room. You two go on."

Katherine and I squeezed past servers in the corridor, went down the little ramp, and followed the sign directing us to the left. The restroom was small but nicely decorated, with an upholstered bench, a magnifying mirror, and good lighting. I was washing my hands when Katherine joined me at the pair of sinks.

"I guess you wondered what happened at the table a minute ago."

"Did something happen?"

She laughed without mirth and dispensed a puddle of pink soap into her palm. "That woman's name still rankles me. She was Solly's girlfriend in high school. When they encountered each other again a few years ago, he helped her with a little professional problem and she decided fate had brought him back into her life and meant for them to be together."

"Oh, Katherine. I had no idea. I'm sorry." I pulled out two thick paper towels and dried my hands. "But you're still friends with Georgina?"

She smiled. "Everybody's friends with Georgina. I can't hold her sister against her. You may've guessed I was supposed to be at the party tonight." She shook her head. "But not with that woman there. Solly and I worked things out, but I won't be having dinner with Twinkle. Not in this lifetime."

"I'm glad you got past it. And you must have, since you left Solly there with her." I watched her image in the mirror.

"Serves him right." She giggled quickly and then gave an involuntary little shiver. "She just took me by surprise today, showing up early and ruining Georgina's party. She wasn't supposed to get here until Saturday. Explain to Nita for me. There's no need to tell Jim, I suppose. He'd have questions."

"Probably." Well, definitely. "But he doesn't gossip. Just files everything away." I tapped my temple. "*For informational purposes*—that's his term."

She laughed. "Riley's a nice guy." She fluffed her hair, let it fall back into place, and blotted the corner of her mouth with a paper towel. "Have you been single long?"

"My husband died four years ago from a rare genetic disorder. But we had a happy marriage. It was my second, to be precise. The first one wasn't so happy, but we've gotten past that. He's my boss now."

She looked startled and locked gazes with my reflection. "You're kidding, right?"

I laughed. "It's true. He's the CEO of Harbor Health Services. Based in Houston, not here. Thank goodness." She still looked doubtful. "Ask Emily. She knows him. Travis McKenzie. I'm not saying it was always easy, but we have a daughter together. And a grandson now, which is still a little hard to believe."

"That makes a difference, doesn't it? Well, good for you." She leaned close to the mirror. "I should've brought some lipstick."

I used a paper towel to open the door and held it for Katherine to exit then dropped the towel into the trash can beside the door.

The bread pudding, always one of my favorite desserts, was fabulous. Jim was finishing up Nita's dessert when Sophia brought the credit card slip for his signature.

"No need for takeout boxes at Jesse's, is there?" He added a tip and signed, then swiveled his torso to reach for his cane, which had been standing in the corner behind him.

"We should be treating you on your anniversary." Riley pushed away from the table.

Jim turned back and glanced across the table. "This was Nita's idea."

He grinned at me and, with a guilty expression, reached for the bowl containing what was left of the extra bourbon sauce. He spooned the last creamy bit into his mouth. "Mmm-mmm, that's good stuff." He put the bowl down and clapped me on the back. "We're just happy to have good people to celebrate with. Katherine, we're glad to have you here, too. You're a lot nicer than Dolly."

"Jim!" Nita chided. "You don't say things like that. Even when they're true."

We laughed. Everybody liked Dolly, but there was no denying she was a little short on diplomacy.

"I've got something to show you." Nita retrieved her purse and searched inside, then brought out a card she handed to Katherine. "Open it." She looked at me. "It's from Vickie Wiltshire."

Vickie was a local Realtor. She sold Nita and Jim's original house when they moved to Harbor Village and still made a fuss over them at every opportunity. Nita had arranged for her to show me around when I first came to town, and she'd been the listing broker when Riley bought his house a few months ago. She was pretty and sweet, with killer instincts where real estate was concerned, and she seemed to have staked out Harbor Village as her private hunting preserve.

Katherine took the card from its envelope and read the front. "Happy anniversary to our favorite couple." She opened the card and Bob Hope sang out loud and clear, "Thanks for the memories!"

Diners at the adjacent tables turned to look, and whispers spread across the room. "Anniversary," I heard, and "fifty-one years." With a lot of chair scraping, people got to their feet and began applauding, and we joined in, as did Sophia and the other servers. Jim, encouraged, fumbled his way to Nita's side, and they kissed before waving to their well-wishers. It was a sweet, romantic beginning to a fifty-second year. After that, we were ready to depart.

I was walking in front of Riley, who brought up the rear as we started back through the restaurant and out to the car. But, after a couple of steps, I sensed he wasn't with me. I glanced back just in time to see him slip some cash under Jim's dessert plate.

He caught my glance and raised a warning finger to his lips. I understood immediately. Sometimes Jim took a quick little mental trip back to the day of the ten percent gratuity.

Chapter 3

When we got back to Harbor Village, Riley pulled over against the sidewalk in front of Jim and Nita's building and walked with them to their door, leaving Katherine and me waiting in the back seat.

Katherine bent forward and looked past me, across the median to the building where Georgina's party would still be in full swing.

"I can walk from here. And walk off some of those calories."

I looked across the median but didn't see anything except a few lights. No people, no decorations, not many lights. "You'd get your feet wet in the grass. Just come to the apartment with me."

I unbuckled the center seat belt and slid toward the door. "Riley lives in the building next to mine. He'll loop around the median and park out front. You don't mind going in while the party's going on?"

She hesitated and I supplied my own answer. "Then we'll go around the building and use the back door. Riley can tell Solly where you are."

She nodded then. I sensed her relaxing and saw her lean against the seat back. "Riley parks on the street? I saw a long row of garages somewhere."

"Only the apartments in the donut buildings have garages."

"Donut?"

I was explaining when Riley crossed in front of the car, opened the driver's door, and slid behind the wheel.

"Well, ladies, fifty-one years down. Jim says to tell you same time next year."

"I hope this will be a good year for them." Reflexively, I buckled my seat belt and then realized what I'd done. "Look at me. We're only going a few feet."

"Nita and Jim seem strong and healthy," Katherine said. "They may last longer than I do."

"Don't be morbid," I told her.

One result of a five thirty dinner reservation was that you got home early, too. Georgina's party had started later and I expected it to last another hour at least, maybe two. But when Riley knocked at the courtyard door to my apartment, I let him in and looked past him. The party table in the courtyard was almost abandoned. A couple of people stood near the chiminea, and Solly Roka followed right behind Riley.

Katherine came to introduce us.

Now that I saw him, I was sure we'd met before—in the office, probably. We shook hands and Katherine gave her husband a quick hug.

"Everything okay?"

He shrugged and asked about our evening, and we sang the praises of Jesse's.

"We must go sometime," Katherine told him. "You'll love it."

I went back to the courtyard door for another quick look. Fran Beck, who ran the art gallery on Fairhope Avenue, was standing with her purse on one shoulder, about to leave, judging by appearance. Patti and I stopped in at her business occasionally to pet the cat that slept in the window. And I'd bought Stephanie's Christmas gift there, too—a print of Fran's painting of Fairhope's town clock, with street trees illuminated and a few snowflakes swirling in the night air. It gave me shivers, even though a cold night in Fairhope would be a rarity. I waved at Fran and she waved back but didn't seem to recognize me.

A man was bent over in front of the chiminea. He looked familiar but I was surprised and a little embarrassed when he stood up. I was accustomed to seeing Stewart Granger in khakis and a tool belt, but tonight he wore sporty clothes and his hair had a fluffy, blow-dried look. He cleaned up good, as the saying went. I closed the door, turned the lock, and returned to my guests, to find Riley calling my name.

There was a twitch in his voice and a rush in his manner. "Michael's waiting for me. He wants to give me a preview right now."

Heart attack time. I clutched my throat. "Oh, no. Do I go, too?" I heard a similar quiver in my own voice.

He shook his head. "I'll come back when we finish." He bid Katherine good night, shook Solly's hand again, and hurried out through the screened porch.

"We'll leave if you want to go with him," Katherine offered.

"We're going anyway." Solly looked at his watch and frowned at Katherine. "Hmm. Not as late as I thought. How'd you get back so early?"

"We left at five," I told him.

Solly was tall, with receding brown hair, a muscular body, and especially bulky shoulders and upper arms. He looked like Vulcan, and I wondered if he had a hard time finding clothes that fit. His brown leather boots were covered with tiny splotches of what looked like—well, I hoped it was clay.

He caught me looking, gave me a bright smile, and held one foot out for inspection. "You like my party shoes?"

"Aren't they awful?" Katherine shivered.

He explained. "I was focused on other things—packing my pieces and helping the students with theirs. I didn't think about shoes."

"And you prefer those, anyway." Katherine swayed against him and gave him a hug around the middle.

"They're comfortable," he admitted, "when you're on your feet all day."

"Why don't you sit down and I'll get us a cup of tea. Unless you'd like something stronger?"

I spent a couple of minutes in the kitchen and then Katherine helped carry out cups and saucers, a little dish of lemon slices, a ceramic bowl of peanuts, packets of sweetener, napkins, and a plate of chocolate-filled wafers.

"Tell us about this house Riley's gone to see." She squeezed lemon into a cup of tea and offered it to Solly.

I explained that he'd purchased a house that was part of the Harbor Village campus. "The entire complex is built on property leased from the Henry George Utopian Tax Colony. The houses are on Andrews Street. That's this way, just out of sight." I pointed at an angle out through my screened porch.

"Does Harbor Village own them?"

I shook my head. "No. They're privately owned, but owners pay monthly fees. In exchange for which they sublease the lot, get yard maintenance and regular visits from a housekeeper, access to the Harbor Village gym and both pools—indoor and outdoor—local transportation, classes, and entertainment events." I caught my breath. "To say nothing of an educated and caring staff and community."

They asked about meals and I explained lunches were an optional extra for all residents, except those in the Assisted Living program. "The food's pretty good, and it's a bargain for people who can stretch an entrée, a couple of sides, soup, salad, and bread, into both lunch and dinner."

"But you said Riley lives in the next building. Does anyone actually live in this house?" Katherine asked.

"Not yet. He bought it in December and Michael started working on it right after that. The problem is, at heart, we're both minimalists. His apartment is even more Spartan than mine." I waved at the bare walls, the absence of knickknacks around us. "He bought the house as a surprise for me, thinking it was big enough for the two of us and still just a short walk from my office."

I didn't say that he'd been eager, almost desperate, to get us out of the mainstream of community life, but Riley's private nature was obvious to anyone.

"I hated the house on sight and couldn't believe he was buying it. The ceiling was low, the carpet musty, the layout—" I shivered. "Just inexplicably awkward. But Michael Bonderant is a salesman. He convinced Riley he could do things to it that would have me swooning."

"I've just heard about it from Michael. And do you like it?" Solly asked.

I shrugged. "I haven't seen it since Christmas. In a way, I hope he's right. Magical thinking, I guess. Like hoping that the prince will show up with a crystal slipper that fits only you."

"Aw, Cleo," Solly said. "Have a little faith. Life is short. Riley sounds like a real romantic. And so do you."

"And Michael's a talented decorator, I'm sure," Katherine said.

Solly grinned at her. "So he says."

"I'm sure he is, but I do love my nice, simple apartment. It has everything I need. Two bedrooms, two baths, a lovely little screened porch, a nice courtyard just outside the door, a space in the garage next door."

"And you hate to give it up," Katherine consoled me.

"A house can have all that and more," Solly said.

"But it doesn't. You haven't seen this house." I sounded childish and whiny, even to myself, but this house business was taking a toll. I'd had more than a few restless nights wondering how Riley would react if I decided to stay where I was. And I was really nervous about disappointing him. I changed the subject to keep them from asking more questions. "How was Georgina's party?"

"An unmitigated disaster." Solly laughed.

Katherine clapped her hands against her chest. "No. Don't tell me that. Poor Georgina."

"What happened?" I asked. "I see you had to call maintenance in."

"Twinkle got sick."

Katherine gave him a skeptical look.

"*Really* sick." Solly helped himself to peanuts from the little dish on the tea tray. "Probably a virus. They come on suddenly, don't they? She was in agony. Couldn't even eat." He made a fist, tilted his head back, and poured nuts into his mouth.

"So why not call a doctor? And why's the maintenance man here?"

He gave me a strange look. "The maintenance man? Do you mean Stewart? That's a good one!" He had a nice laugh.

"Stewart's one of Georgina's students." Katherine grinned at my surprise. "I thought you knew."

"Really? But that doesn't...she had lots of students. I thought the party was for former students who have a career in art."

Solly said, "Stewart *is* an artist, to the extent he wants to be. He's quite exceptional with all sorts of woodcraft."

I wasn't having it. "A carpenter, you mean, but surely that doesn't qualify."

Now they were both laughing at me.

Solly sounded offended: "Am I an artist? I work with mud."

"Stewart is a master of the wood lathe," Katherine explained. "A real master. Haven't you seen the pieces he turns from tulipwood or yew? And sweet gum, sometimes, which I love, or magnolia. They're beautiful."

Solly held thumb and forefinger almost touching. "His vessels have the thinnest walls you'll ever see. He likes to leave live edges—with the bark on, I mean. And he does some fine finishing work, too."

"Really?" So Stewart had talents I hadn't suspected. "Will he be exhibiting this weekend?"

Solly shook his head. "Apparently you keep him too busy to build up an inventory. Actually, I think his work's spoken for before it's finished."

He looked at the time again and they talked about leaving.

"We're staying with Emily." Katherine hesitated. "Our car's out front? We can go out this way and walk around the building." She indicated the screened porch.

"Shouldn't we speak to Georgina?" He raised a hand to her neck and stroked my pearls. "Pretty."

She threw her hands up. "Cleo! I was about to walk out with your pearls. Thank you so much. I think pearls dress up any outfit." Unfastening the clasp took a moment and then she handed the strand to her husband. "Solly, I want some nice pearls just like these. Notice the size and the length? Maybe for my birthday."

He examined the strand and grunted what might have been acquiescence as he passed them to me. "Thanks for rescuing Katherine tonight. At least one of us had a nice evening." He wagged his brows at his wife.

Katherine peeped out at the courtyard and relaxed visibly when the coast was clear. "I think we can go now." She gave me a hug and thanked me for a fun evening. "I wasn't expecting anything so nice. This year's festival is a success already."

I followed them into the courtyard, telling them good night, and we walked toward the lobby.

"Did you thank Georgina and say good night?" Katherine asked Solly.

"Do I need to?"

"I think so. Just knock on her door and give her a hug for both of us. I'll wait out front."

But Georgina saved him the trouble. She came out of her apartment, still dressed in party clothes—an ankle-length dress, strappy sandals, a fringed purple stole draped across her back. Her pale gray hair was curly and fluffy like the little poodles that scampered up and down Andrews Street.

Stewart was still in the lobby, too. The dirty dishes were already stacked on a kitchen cart, and his tool belt was coiled on the bottom shelf. He was stuffing used linens into a bulging plastic bag.

"How is she?" Stewart asked Georgina, without breaking rhythm.

She shook her head. "Not good. Nausea and stomach cramps still. I'll take the linens. I borrowed them from Ann."

Stewart gave her the bag. She set it beside her door and came back to hug Solly and Katherine. I sneaked glances at Stewart, considering whether I preferred his workday image with exposed tattoos or this polished, blow-dried look.

"Something she ate?" Katherine asked Georgina.

I tuned in for the answer. Food for the party had come from the Harbor Village dining room. There'd never been a problem with our food, but there was always a first time.

"Hunger pains, probably." Georgina said. "She didn't eat a bite. Just picked at her salad."

"And nobody else got sick?" I asked. That would let the kitchen off the hook.

She shook her head again and sounded unconcerned. "She's always had a crazy diet. Says she feels *funny*." She did air quotes around the word. "She's throwing up and holding her tummy. I gave her some of the pink stuff, but it came right up."

"Maybe you should call a doctor," Katherine suggested.

"I offered. She says no. Says it'll pass."

"I don't suppose there's anything we can do." Katherine didn't seem eager to get involved.

"No, honey." Georgina patted her arm. "You go along. You've got a big day tomorrow."

Katherine hugged her again. "I'm so sorry. Maybe there'll be time for another visit before we go home."

"I doubt it. She's staying all weekend." Georgina had to reach up to hug Solly's neck. "Have a good festival. Don't let her cast a pall over the weekend."

Stewart gave Solly a light punch on the shoulder. "Give me a hand, Solly, before you go. We'll get everything back to normal."

They took opposite ends of the long table and, with only a little huffing and puffing, returned it to its usual position in the lobby. Someone—Stewart, probably—had already put the chairs inside. Now we all joined setting them in place around the table.

"Poor Stewart." Georgina smiled at him. "Works all day and works all night, too."

"Shoot." He gave her a hug. "This was just fun, except for Twinkle. Tell her I'm sorry and I'll see her tomorrow. Right now, I'm going to roll this cart to the kitchen." He looked at his watch. "I'll be home by nine. Here, you take this."

He got the vase of flowers from the bar and presented it to Georgina. She took it with both hands.

"Yes, I'll enjoy these. Thank you all for coming and for being so understanding. And thank you for your help, Katherine. I'd better go check on her." She turned and went back into her apartment.

Katherine leaned toward me and spoke out of the corner of her mouth, gangster style. "Good thing I wasn't here. Everybody would assume I'd poisoned her."

"You coming?" Solly was holding the front door.

She laughed and waved and followed him.

Georgina came out of her apartment, picked up the bag of linens, and said good night again.

"Well, Stewart." I walked to the front door. "I hear you've been living a double life. You're an artist. A craftsman."

He laughed and jiggled the cart to align its wheels, then pushed it through as I held the door open. "I just follow the spirit. Wherever it leads me. And right now, it's leading me home."

I walked across the porch and watched him rumble down the slope toward the big house. The lobby lights were on, but otherwise, the night was quiet and calm. The quarter moon was almost straight above me, looking remote and lonely. I went back through the kitchen and courtyard to my apartment and locked the door.

Riley returned tense and grim from the house tour soon after I got back. "I don't know about this." He paced the living room, hands stuck in his pockets and an air of distraction hovering over him. "I just don't know."

"Want something to drink? Water, maybe?"

"Yeah, might as well." He headed for the kitchen. "You want one?"

"I've got one." I sat and waited while he bumped around in the kitchen. "Now come tell me about the house."

He came back and pulled the other chair around to face me. "I'm not sure you're going to like it." He took a drink of cold water and then rubbed his beard. "That's all I'm going to say."

"You can tell me what you think, surely. Do *you* like it? Is it finished?"

He grinned finally and shook his head. "I'll know what I think when I find out what you think. Saturday afternoon at four, how does that sound?"

"Two more days? What's he going to do in two days?"

"Magic, I hope."

"Did you tell him I can't meet him in the morning?"

"Dang. I forgot. We were talking about other things. Didn't you say you can find him in the morning and make an arrangement?"

I nodded.

"Pick a nice painting you really like, okay? The whole deal may ride on it. And speaking of art, I've been thinking…what would you think about a trip to that museum in Arkansas? Crystal Bridge. We ought to get away from this agitation for a few days."

"Something to look forward to." I realized just how pessimistic he was. There'd be no time for travel if we were moving into a new house right away. I thought about the route to northern Arkansas. "Don't they offer classes sometimes? Maybe wood carving, or watercolors…something we'd enjoy?"

"I'll check. But let's make it soon. Before it gets hot. I'd better go." He gave me a lingering good night kiss that might've led to something if it hadn't already been a stressful and long day.

When he headed for his apartment, I had a little tidying up to do. I put the bottles into a recycling bin, put away the snacks and containers, added a few bowls and glasses to the dishwasher, and cranked it up. I slid the wooden tray into its slot above the fridge and had just finished wiping the countertops when the phone rang. Stephanie was calling from Birmingham, as she did every night to verify aliens hadn't abducted me.

"How was your day?" I switched the lights off and checked all three doors—courtyard, hallway, and screened porch—and closed the blinds. Then I took the phone to the bedroom to talk.

"You know I've got a birthday coming up. You haven't asked what I want."

"Okay. What do you want?"

"A condo."

I laughed.

"Just think about it, Mom, before you say anything. Here's my idea. You buy a nice place in the mountains as an investment, and we can all use it. Family time with your grandson."

"Um-hmm." I meant to sound sarcastic but didn't quite succeed. She knew how I loved the mountains. And a condo would give Riley and me a place to vacation, just the two of us. "Where is this condo? I assume you've already selected it."

"North Carolina, I think. Maybe Boone. Or Grandfather Mountain— don't you love that name? We'd use it year-round. Cool in the summer, skiing in the winter."

"None of us ski, do we?" I wasn't sure about her husband, but I imagined myself on skis and immediately pictured casts and crutches.

"I'm about to learn. And Barry's the perfect age for lessons."

"Barry's two. He can barely walk."

"He'll be three next winter, when lessons start. Now, I'm going to email you some ideas. I just wanted to be sure you'd study them."

"What does a North Carolina condo cost?"

"Whatever you want to pay. You'll see. I don't think you'll want a real cheapie, but there are some beautiful places for under five hundred."

"Stephanie! Five hundred thousand?"

There was a shrug in her voice. "I don't know, maybe half that. You keep forgetting, Mom, you've got a big salary now and you can't take it with you. You could even rent it out if you wanted to. The management office handles everything. But I really think we'd use it too much for that. You asked about my day. Let me tell you."

With that, she launched into a series of complaints about the downside of co-owning a quilting shop. Customers, vendors, deliverymen, a partner, and especially balky sewing machines...the complaints went on and on.

"How's Barry?" I asked at an opening, hoping to distract her. "And Boyd?" Believe it or not, she had no complaints about her long-suffering husband.

"Dad was here tonight," she added as an afterthought. She was referring to Travis McKenzie, her biological father. "He's going to surprise you this weekend."

"Thanks for the warning." I managed to sound normal, although I was thinking *bummer*.

Travis McKenzie had only recently backed off a little. I'd barely seen him in twenty years, but he'd come out of nowhere to finagle my transition from the academic world to business and was still overseeing my education. "He's coming for arts and crafts, I guess."

"Mom! Is that this weekend? Why didn't you tell me?"

"I'm sure I did." Hadn't I? "It's always the third weekend in March, they tell me."

"No!" She whined the word and I heard paper rustling. "I'm supposed to work Saturday. *How* did this happen?" She fumed for another minute then said good night. "I've got to call Amy and get her to trade off days."

"I may be busy during the day Saturday. There's an art workshop I may attend."

She brushed that aside. "I'll be driving all morning and at the festival in the afternoon. And don't make any plans to feed us. I've got a special invitation. We'll stay with you and visit Sunday morning, before we start back. Why don't we have breakfast at Julwin's so we can sit and talk."

"Julwin's is inside the festival perimeter. It might be overrun."

She said we'd find some place and ended the call.

The dishwasher was winding down its work, freeing up the hot water supply, so I could finally take my shower. Then I put on PJs and slid under the covers, got my Sudoku book, and opened it to a puzzle that had already given me difficulty for a couple of nights.

* * * *

I woke up and looked at the clock when Tinkerbelle began her five-alarm calling. It was a few minutes before two. I muttered out loud when I realized I'd forgotten to fill her food dish, but I rolled out of the warm bed and padded barefoot to the kitchen. There were a few bits of food in the dish, but only around the perimeter. As I picked up the dish from its pad under the window, something in the courtyard caught my attention. Someone was moving around in the far corner. I looked long enough to decide it was Georgina, then flipped the kitchen light on and measured out a quarter cup of cat food.

Tinkerbelle rubbed around my legs and made her little chirping noise, but she was quick to push my hand aside when I put the dish down, and right away she was crunching away like she was starved. Between crunches, I heard another sound. A tiny *tap, tap, tap*, almost like water dripping, but the sound didn't come from the kitchen. I went to the living room and stood, listening. It came again and this time I pegged it to the door that opened to the courtyard.

I opened the blinds and saw Georgina, just turning away.

"I know I woke you," she apologized when I opened the door.

I swung the door open. Her party clothes were gone, changed for cargo pants and a white sweatshirt. "I was just feeding the cat. Come in. Is Twinkle better?"

She shook her head and stayed outside. "Worse, if anything. I'm going to run her over to the ER. I was checking on the fire when I saw your light. If you hear noises in an hour or two, don't worry. It'll just be us coming back."

"Why don't I jump into some clothes and go with you?"

"No, no. We can manage. She's already in the car. I just came back to lock up and check on the fire." She looked terribly worried.

I stepped through the doorway and gave her a hug. "I'm so sorry, Georgina. Call if you need me. Promise?"

"Thanks, Cleo."

I went back to bed and turned the light off. But without Sudoku to aid the transition, I had trouble dropping off to sleep. I thought about Katherine. Such a nice lady. Maybe I *would* take that drawing class Saturday. I rolled onto my stomach, stretched, and pulled the pillow under my cheek. Too bad she and Solly had gone through difficult times, but didn't all couples? What had she said about Solly getting Twinkle out of a professional bind? What kind of *professional bind* did an artist get into? I couldn't think of anything, but the mental void did the trick and I finally slept.

The building was quiet when I awoke Friday morning. The sun wasn't up yet, but I thought I smelled bacon frying. Ann Slump, who lived next door, was a fabulous cook with a big family. Her relatives stopped by at all hours and expected to be fed in high style. I loved her fried apple pies, and those fluffy pancakes with real whipped cream—but nothing like that was on my menu today, not after last night's indulgences. I dragged myself out of bed.

The cat followed me to the kitchen, where her dish was empty again. She had gained a pound or two since her return to domesticity, but she still wasn't a big cat. I put another quarter-cup of food into her dish and started the coffee, then went back to the bedroom to wash up and dress.

My closet held a dozen pairs of black or gray pants and three sets of tops I rotated according to season and event. I expected to be in the office for an hour that morning and then at the arts and crafts festival, which meant I'd be out in the sun. I selected a long-sleeved white shirt and jazzed it up with a triple strand of black ceramic beads.

I'd be seeing Michael Bonderant, I remembered as I dampened my fingers and ran them through my hair. When he toured my apartment months ago, to learn my tastes and preferences, he'd accused me of hating color. I grinned to myself as I thought about surprising him with the red blazer. No, better to return it. It was a moral victory of sorts, a demonstration that I wouldn't be bullied out of my color comfort zone. I put it on my list of chores, something I'd get to next week, after the festival.

I was dressed and brushed and presentable when I went back to the living room and began opening blinds. Someone had taped a note to the glass door that opened to the screened porch.

Goody, I thought automatically; *I'm invited to Ann's for breakfast.* I was already promising myself I wouldn't overdo the pancakes, when I opened the door and pulled the note off the glass.

Twinkle Thaw died at 4 am, I read.

Oh no! Poor Georgina.

Chapter 4

I walked out to the porch and stood, gazing across the low fence to the backyards of the Andrews Street houses. Only one had a light on, in its kitchen. If I looked sharply to the left, I would see the dining room window of Riley's apartment but, since I'd never seen him inside, I didn't bother looking. A mockingbird tweeted enthusiastically in the top of a palm tree and mourning doves cooed from the front of the building.

I crossed my arms and thought about Georgina and her sister. The age difference between them must be twenty years, and apparently they hadn't been close. Nonetheless, it would be a shock to lose a sister, especially a much younger sister.

We'd had deaths at Harbor Village since I arrived, but this one was different. Twinkle was young and a visitor, not a resident. I couldn't think of any official reaction needed from the facility, but I would tell Patti. She'd been the perfect choice for the resident services position and would know how to console Georgina.

"You just never know, do you?"

I jumped at the sound of a voice and snapped around to see Ann sitting on her porch, a few feet away.

Ann was a small woman, easily recognized by an excess of energy and short red hair. She usually wore polyester pants, size four, with the crease stitched in, and must've purchased every color they were offered in. At her family's annual business confab in February, they had voted to sell Royale Court, the retail complex in downtown Fairhope that Ann had spent her whole life developing and managing. The sales process would take some time and make the family wealthy, but the downside was it would leave Ann with even more free time to fill. She was already preparing by shifting her attentions elsewhere—still working part-time in the Royale Knit Shop that had been hers, but teaching knitting classes in the arts and crafts studio behind the big house and helping out in the kitchen and dining room, where she planned menus or baked with Carla and Lizzie.

"Georgina's sleeping," Ann told me. "Supposed to be, anyway. She was going to wait about calling the family, rather than wake them up with that kind of news. Why don't you come over? I've got breakfast ready and we can talk without disturbing everyone."

"I'll get the decaf."

It took me just a couple of minutes to get the glass carafe and my cell phone and walk next door.

Ann's apartment was similar to mine in layout but polar opposite in décor. The first thing a visitor saw on walking in was the riot of color. Then the eye sorted out stacks of reading materials and CDs with the library code taped on. There were fluffy afghans, baskets of yarn, a glass jug full of coins, a row of greeting cards standing on the coffee table, pots filled with blooming African violets, a rack displaying antique china, and a wall display of family photographs, all interspersed with cocoa-colored furniture and the usual comforts of home.

Ann was often almost invisible among the things, but her personal nest was obvious—a velvet swivel rocker between windows, a matching ottoman, a true-to-daylight adjustable lamp, an oval quilting frame pushed to one side, and, with only a slight turn of the head, a view of the sidewalk. Today, a knitting project—a scarf, from the looks of it, worked on straight walnut needles with fancy carved tops—was balanced on the arm of her chair.

"I love coming to your apartment. Just seeing it makes me smile."

She glanced around as if seeing the place through new eyes. "We need some happiness today."

She took my container of decaffeinated coffee to the kitchen and I followed as far as her big dining table, already covered with enough food to serve a dozen hungry people.

"Sit down," Ann called. "I told Georgina I'd have breakfast ready when she wakes up. And I'm going with her after lunch, to make the arrangements."

"That's good of you. I know she appreciates it." I pulled out a chair and sat facing the kitchen. "It's the sort of thing she's always doing for other people."

Ann zipped back to the table. "I don't know how close she was to Twinkle, but losing a sibling is always terrible. I know." The Slump siblings—also known as the vowel siblings because of their initials: Ann, Evie, Irene, Olivia, and Usher—had lost Irene in a tragic accident years ago.

The microwave hummed for a minute and Ann zipped off again. She returned with a cup of steaming coffee and set it on the saucer beside my plate.

"I never met Twinkle." I took a sip of coffee. "Did she have children? Or a husband?"

Ann took her cup to the kitchen for a refill and the microwave hummed again.

"I can't stand lukewarm coffee. No children. Twinkle married a couple of times, but not recently, so far as I know. An artist really needs to marry another artist." She sat down and gazed out the window that opened onto her screened porch. "She and Usher were an item once, but it didn't last. Thank goodness."

Usher was Ann's baby brother. I thought of a grown-up Charlie Brown every time I saw his big round head and pale complexion.

Ann's attention came back to the table. She snapped the folds out of a cloth napkin and smoothed it across her lap. "I don't know why I said that. They had problems, both of them, but they might've been good for each other. I tried to call him earlier, to tell him she died, but he didn't answer. You like grits, don't you?"

She picked up the blue bowl and offered it to me.

It would be more accurate to say I liked Ann's grits, which were yellow and substantial, nothing like the pasty goo I'd sampled elsewhere. But I wasn't going to pig out today.

"I'd like sausage and a biscuit. That's all. I ate way too much at Jesse's last night."

"Jesse's. It's about the best we've got now." She passed me a plate of biscuits, followed by a plate with bacon, sausage patties, and links. "You like this Conecuh sausage, don't you?"

I loved it, but I was determined to resist a few temptations today. I took a round patty instead. "Got any mustard?"

She passed me the yellow squeeze bottle. "What was wrong with Twinkle, do you know?"

"Georgina didn't say?" I told her the symptoms I'd heard and, as I talked, I split a biscuit, squirted both sides with a dab of mustard, and stuck the sausage patty in to make a little sandwich. "I didn't see her. Probably wouldn't know any more if I had. Did she visit Georgina often?" I took a bite.

"Probably not since you've been here. I knew a woman once who had a bleeding ulcer. Same sort of symptoms. Maybe that was it." She indicated my plate. "A bit of kumquat marmalade would go well with that."

Her phone, an old-fashioned, wall-mounted black one with an extra-long cord twisted into a tangle, shrilled loudly and saved me from the marmalade.

Ann pushed back her chair. "You go ahead while it's hot. Don't wait." She answered the phone and mouthed the word *Usher* to me.

I tried to ignore the conversation and looked around the table while I ate. My gaze fell on a small crystal bowl filled with fat blueberries. A slotted silver spoon lay on top, easily within reach. Blueberries were good, and good for us, too. I took a spoonful, corralled them on my empty plate, and ate a fat one using my fingers. Sweet and delicious.

Ann hung up and returned to her seat, looking puzzled. "Usher told me the oddest thing. Twinkle's got a storage locker at Royale Court. I didn't remember that. If I ever knew."

"You rent storage lockers?" It was news to me. I popped two blueberries into my mouth.

She shrugged. "Just a few, stuck around in nooks and crannies. I thought they all went to our tenants, but Usher says she's had it for a couple of years." She looked at me. "She went to it yesterday afternoon. Now don't you wonder what Twinkle stores in Fairhope? She's not here more than once or twice a year."

She looked past me suddenly and pointed toward my apartment. "Are you expecting somebody? A man in a white coat just went by."

"That sounds like a middle school joke."

I went to her door and looked out. The man was on my porch, about to knock.

I opened the door and stepped out, calling to him. "I'll be right there. Have a seat for just a minute."

Ann was right behind me, bringing the carafe for me to take home. I thanked her for breakfast.

"Want to take something to your visitor? A sausage biscuit?"

I shook my head. "Call me with an update when you talk with Georgina again."

She agreed and stepped out on the porch behind me.

Recognition dawned when I took another look at my caller. "Is that you, Hunter? I haven't seen you in ages!"

I exited Ann's porch, took a dozen steps, and turned in at mine. Hunter was holding the screened door open for me. In his other hand he held a battered aluminum case.

I hugged him. "You remember my neighbor, Ann Slump? She wonders if you'd like a sausage biscuit."

"Ms. Slump," he called to the next porch. "I wish I had time. I've been working all night and I'm starving. But I'm on business."

The apartment door was unlocked. I pushed it open, and Hunter followed me in.

I met Hunter Pratt on my first visit to Fairhope, almost a year ago, when I was still teaching. He was the same age as my students and worked as a night clerk at the motel. He'd given me a map of Fairhope and advice about places to eat and things to do, and when I took over unexpectedly as Executive Director of Harbor Village, his knowledge of technology proved helpful on more than one occasion. But I'd never seen him wearing what looked very much like a lab coat.

He told me about his assignment while I poured him a cup of coffee and zapped it for a minute in the microwave. Before it was hot, Ann brought him a sausage biscuit wrapped in a paper napkin.

"Oh boy." He took it and leaned against the counter. "I shouldn't stop for this, but you won't tell." A quarter of the biscuit disappeared in a single bite.

Ann went straight to the point. "What's with the white coat?"

"Criminal Justice," he mumbled, "with a concentration in IT." He took another bite.

"Wonderful!" She didn't know what he was talking about. She knew nothing about technology or computer crime. She had a cell phone she barely knew how to use and relied on landline phones in her apartment and the knit shop.

"I'm proud of you," I told Hunter. "But does that explain the lab coat?"

His once-lanky frame had filled out a little in the months since I last saw him, and the gold ear studs were gone, but his dark hair still flopped across his forehead. He brushed it back and took a sip of coffee.

"I'm taking crime scene analysis, and Chief Boozer took me on as an intern with FPD." The food was gone and he was sipping coffee. "I do whatever Lieutenant Montgomery says. She called in the middle of the night and asked how soon I could get here."

Ann looked out the kitchen window, into the courtyard. "Twinkle died, did you know?"

"Lieutenant told me when she brought the sample case. That's why it could wait until I got off." He looked at me. "She was one of your neighbors? I was sent to this building and thought I'd check with you."

I shook my head. "She wasn't a resident. She was visiting. Her sister lives in this building. Georgina Burch. She's sleeping now."

"She was up all night," Ann said.

I looked at Hunter. "Do you have to wake her? What are you supposed to do?"

"Collect food samples and listen to the gossip. Did anyone else get sick?"

"I talked to some of the other guests last night. They said Twinkle didn't eat. Nothing but a little salad."

"Twinkle?" he asked. "That's really her name?"

"Twinkle Thaw," Ann said. "Her sister's Georgina Burch. Maybe you know her. Taught art at the high school?"

He told Ann he was from Robertsdale and didn't attend Fairhope High School.

"The party was in the courtyard." Ann looked at me. "But there won't be any food there now."

"We can check the fridge." I put his empty cup in the sink. "Stewart cleaned up afterward, but he may not have emptied the garbage." I looked at my watch. "He took the leftovers and dirty dishes to the kitchen last night, and it's not eight yet. If he left the dishes for Lizzie to run this morning, she's just now getting there."

"I'd better see if I can stop her." Hunter moved to go.

"Let me call." Ann looked around for a wall-mount phone like hers.

I took my cell phone out of my pocket, punched in the kitchen number, and handed it to her. She moved into the living room to talk.

Hunter nodded. "I need samples of everything. Even vomit, if there was any. Do you know?"

I didn't know. "It would've been in Georgina's apartment. I suppose you'll need to talk with her."

He held up the metal case. "I'm prepared. All sorts of containers in here, gloves, masks, even Vicks—that's to overpower other smells. I'd better get busy."

Ann handed the phone back to me. I saw there was a text from Stephanie.

"They don't answer yet." Ann looked at Hunter. "Why don't I run down there and stand guard while you do your thing up here?"

"That'd be great," he said. "But don't disturb anything."

Ann went out as I scanned Stephanie's brief text. **Hold on condo**. What did that mean?

I snapped the leather phone case closed and told Hunter, "You'll need to check the fridge and the garbage containers. There's one in the lobby and the big ones are out by the garage. Why don't we walk through the courtyard, too, in case anything was left there? And we'll find Stewart and ask him about the leftovers."

The courtyard looked clean. I pointed to the chiminea.

"They had a little fire in there. I don't suppose you need ashes."

He looked but shook his head.

"Then let's check the lobby."

The big table was back in place and the kitchenette looked clean. We opened every cabinet and drawer, just in case. There were plates, cups, and mismatched glasses in the upper cabinets. The base cabinets were mostly empty, except for some platters, a couple of saucepans, a big Pyrex baking dish, and a stack of cookie sheets that had seen better days. The cabinet beneath the sink contained exactly three items: dish detergent, powdered cleanser, and a yellow sponge. The four drawers, in contrast, were all in use. One held flatware, a knife, and a whisk. Another held boxes of plastic wrap and aluminum foil. The drawer beside the sink was jammed with clean but worn kitchen towels. While Hunter examined the refrigerator, I pulled the towels out and arranged them into two neat stacks. The final drawer, beside the fridge, held a box of trash can liners and a big box of matches.

The refrigerator was forlorn, with just a few jars of condiments and several wine bottles lying on their sides, each one containing a cupful of liquid.

"Those have been there since Christmas, but someone might've tasted one. You'd better test them. What about the garbage can?"

Hunter looked in the container and shook his head. "A clean bag."

I pointed out Georgina's apartment as we were about to depart.

He nodded. "Were you at the party last night?"

"No. I never even met her. Are you sure you still need to collect these samples? They're not going to do her any good now."

He shrugged. "I'm following instructions. Maybe the hospital wants them, or the Health Department. It's a public health issue if there's something contagious, like tainted food. I'm supposed to wear gloves and a mask until I get the samples sealed up."

We walked to the front door and I pulled on the door handle just as Lieutenant Mary Montgomery pushed against it from the outside.

"Sorry." I put up a hand to avoid being trampled.

The U.S. Army had made the decision that Mary Montgomery would be a police officer. When her enlistment ended, fifteen years ago, she'd returned to the Gulf Coast and signed onto the police force, first in Biloxi, near her hometown, and then in Fairhope.

She'd been designed for the job. She was six feet tall, smart and confident, and naturally skeptical. I read an article once about law enforcement officers having difficulty going undercover. They were trained to dominate any situation and lost the ability to blend into the crowd. Mary Montgomery had been born dominant, I was sure. Now, after a few years on the job, she'd risen to the apex of Fairhope's uniformed officers. Her complexion was dark—milk chocolate but not quite dark chocolate. Her hair was short and neglected, her physique that of a pumpkin with long, skinny legs, and her disposition was stable—always crabby.

There was a blond woman with her that day, carrying a shinier, less-battered version of Hunter's sample case. She greeted Hunter by name and then looked at me and paused.

Montgomery introduced us. "This is Berly McBee. Our crime scene specialist."

The blonde nodded to me and looked back to Hunter. "Find anything?"

"Not yet. I checked the kitchen here and the courtyard where the party was. And the garbage container." He looked at Montgomery and waited.

Her brows were creased together. "You're still on the case. I just brought you some help. This may turn into something." She looked at me. "We only get one shot at collecting evidence. Berly's the A-team."

I spoke softly. "You know the woman died, don't you?"

Montgomery gave me one of her looks and nodded.

"Her sister's sleeping in this apartment." I pointed to Georgina's door.

Montgomery glanced in that direction then motioned us away.

I opened a door to the courtyard and the four of us went out. The sky was blue with a few fluffy clouds to the west, over the bay.

"This is where the party was last night." I closed the door behind us. "The big table from the lobby was right here, with its chairs, and this patio set was down at the other end of the courtyard. All the food was prepared in the main kitchen and brought here on a rolling cart."

"Where's the cart now?" McBee asked.

I told them about Stewart cleaning up after the party. "He took the cart to the kitchen, but I doubt he did much cleaning up last night."

Hunter said, "Ms. Mack sent someone to watch the cart until I get there. I was checking here first. The trash can in the kitchen is empty and there's nothing in the fridge except leftover wine and mustard and stuff."

"What do you hope to find?" I asked. "Six people ate the food and only one got sick." I realized I hadn't talked to any other dinner guests that morning, and added a qualifier. "So far as I know."

"With just one victim," McBee said, "it's likely she sampled that old wine or put mayo on her salad." She looked at Hunter. "Finish up here and go through the garbage, wherever it is. I'll take care of the main kitchen."

He nodded. And just like that, a technology whiz got assigned to dig through the garbage. McBee went out the front door, on her way to the clean kitchen.

Montgomery twitched her head toward the door and told Hunter, "I'll secure the garbage containers while you finish in here. We don't want the city picking it up right now."

I walked with her. "There are several containers in front of the garage." I pointed in the direction. "I can ask Stewart which one he used."

She nodded. "Good. Save him from crawling through the slop." She took out her notepad and we stopped in a sunny spot near the corner of the garage. "Now, who was at last night's party, besides you?"

"No, not me."

She narrowed her eyes.

"I saw them making preparations yesterday, and I got home last night just as it was breaking up. Georgina Burch was the hostess. She's in the front apartment. The victim was her sister. The other guests were her former students." I told her about Twinkle showing up two days before she was expected. "It put a kink in the dinner plans." I was thinking of Katherine, wondering if I should name her as a guest who canceled at the last minute. "All of them are artists, some here for the festival."

"Great." Montgomery said. "I don't suppose anyone knows where they're staying."

I counted to six on my fingers as I named names. "Georgina Bunch is here and Twinkle Thaw was staying with her. Solly Roka is staying with his daughter, Emily." I spelled the names. "You know Emily. She's our business manager." Stewart was number four. She knew him. "And Michael Bonderant is here from Charlotte." Did I need to mention Riley's house? I didn't think so. "I don't know where Bonderant's staying, but I'm meeting him at the Art Center at ten. He's number five. One more...oh. Fran Beck. She's local. You know the art gallery on Fairhope Avenue? Not Lindstrom's, the other side of the street."

I waited until she finished writing and then asked the question that was gnawing at me. "Now tell me why you're really here. You don't go through all this rigmarole when somebody just dies."

She scowled, looking very much like a no-nonsense cop instead of the friend who met Patti and me at Andree's occasionally for a lunch of froufrou salads.

"It's looking like it might become a criminal matter. Keep it to yourself until the word gets out."

"Criminal? That means what...poisoning? What kind of poison? Why just one person?"

"We have to wait for the medical report. Did you reach Stewart?"

We went separate ways. I punched in Stewart's number as I walked back to the apartment, got my bag and a bottle of sunscreen.

"I left everything on the cart, except the garbage," Stewart told me. "Do I need to run over there?"

"Maybe so. If you haven't heard, Twinkle died."

"What? Died? Aw, Cleo! Tell me you don't mean that." He laced in a few vulgarities.

"Georgina was up all night and she's sleeping now. The hospital sent the cops for samples of the food, plate scraps, as well as serving dishes. And we want verification that the kitchen's not tainted." I asked what he'd done with the garbage.

"I'll be there in two minutes."

I locked the apartment and went out through the lobby. In the kitchen, Hunter had a row of vials lined up along the bar, each one containing a dab of liquid or condiment. He had already written out labels and was sticking them on the vials.

I told him Stewart was coming to show him where he'd put the garbage last night.

"I'm finished here." He began placing the little containers in his case.

The garage doors were on the far side of the building, still in shade at this hour. Montgomery was looking into garbage containers when Hunter and I rounded the corner.

"Two are empty," she told us and pointed them out.

Stewart wheeled up in his golf cart and jerked to a stop, spraying gravel.

A bright blue BRATS bus—Baldwin Rural Area Transportation System—was stopped at the far end of the big house. Several people were lined up to climb aboard, as I'd be doing in an hour. Harbor Village was a designated parking area for festival guests, and shuttle buses would run every hour through the weekend.

Stewart glanced at the row of garbage cans, walked to one, and lifted the top. "This one." He flipped the top back. He tipped the can forward, stuck his head and shoulders inside, stretched, and came out with a white plastic bag, half full. "This is it. You want to open it here? It'll be a mess."

"I have to get samples." Hunter already had his case open. He pulled out a sheet of blue plastic and spread it on the pavement.

"I've got an appointment," I told them. "I hope you find what you want, Hunter. Come in and clean up when you finish."

I entered the big house through the door at the south end of the building. Wilma Gomez was in the hall, humming as she unlocked her door.

"Give me five minutes," she sang out when I greeted her. "I'll put my things away and get us some coffee. Then we'll get the show on the road." She ended with one of her jungle bird giggles, a modest one this early in the morning. They became more exaggerated as the day wore on.

Wilma was the rental agent for Harbor Village. She'd joined the staff six months ago, and we had a standing appointment at eight thirty every Friday. At first, she had asked the questions and I'd provided answers, but now it was the other way around. How many vacancies did we have? Where were they located? What types of apartments and activities did prospects ask about? What maintenance and updates were needed—carpet, appliances, paint, and so on down the list. I translated the tasks into dollar amounts. All these factors were contributors to occupancy rates, the engine that drove the Harbor Village money machine. Finance wasn't my natural way of thinking, but I was getting used to it.

I went to my office and finished the questionnaire I'd worked on yesterday. Fortunately, the final pages were mostly text, and I had the draft done in a few minutes. I left it on Patti's desk. She'd key the responses in at the HHS website.

"Good morning again," Wilma sang out when I returned to her office.

Wilma was about my age, with black hair, school bus bangs, olive skin, and a big rosy dot of blush on each cheek. She had already unlocked the metal doors of the key cabinet and was folding them out of the way as I pulled a chair around. I sat, facing the wall-mounted box, crossed my legs, and balanced a notepad on one knee.

Wilma looked to see if I was ready and plunged into her report. "We have two prospects coming by today and a couple on Sunday. All three are in town for the festival. We must be running ads somewhere."

I nodded. "An ad in the program, and we contribute to a refreshment fund at the Welcome Center." We always had maps and flyers there and they had called a week ago reminding us to replenish the supply.

"Those people may be volunteers, but they're so professional."

"They do a great job."

Wilma did a great job, too. I looked at the key box, lined in black felt. Plastic tubing in various colors outlined Harbor Boulevard and the seven apartment buildings that lined it. Each apartment was represented by a key peg with a colored tag that indicated whether the unit was leased, vacant and ready to lease, or waiting for some type of maintenance. I was glad to see that three-quarters of the units were coded green, meaning a resident was in place and contributing to the bottom line.

Wilma ran through the rental numbers, pointed out the apartments she was showing soon, and summarized the condition of those waiting for attention. "Here's the big improvement."

She stretched to reach the top rows of keys and tapped on the square representing the building where Patti had overseen our biggest project since my arrival. The second-floor apartments there had been notoriously hard to rent, but Patti and Stewart had devised a way to enclose the L-shaped walkway with screen panels. Then they decorated the resulting lanai, as we were now calling it, with sisal rugs and wicker chairs and tables and pillows and blingy chandeliers that I still had reservations about.

Single women had flocked there. They felt safer on the second floor, they said. They gathered on the lanai on all but the coldest days to read or chat or share tea or potlucks. One of the residents kept a pet mynah bird in a cage on the lanai during nice weather, and his vocabulary had doubled already. I'd heard that the bird had picked up Wilma's trademark laugh, but I hadn't heard it myself. But there was no doubt that the once unpopular apartments were now the Harbor Village hot spots.

Our online reviews and ratings had improved, too. Research showed that a rich social life and heightened sense of belonging had long-term benefits, so I thought Patti had done a real service for the residents of that building.

"How soon will the other building be finished?" Wilma tapped the matching L-shaped building across Harbor Boulevard.

I didn't know. "Patti's looking for inspiration, I think. She didn't want them to be cookie-cutter, and she feels an obligation to outdo her first project."

Wilma frowned. "Well, that's fine, but it's March already. She'd better get a move on. I'll talk with her. Residents are ready for some outdoor living. I'll bet you're already using your porch."

I laughed. "I never stopped." I checked the time.

"I may come in for a while Sunday afternoon," Wilma mused as she walked down the hall with me. "I'll put out the Open House sign and see if it draws any out-of-town visitors. If they've had fun at the festival, maybe they'll decide to stay." She gave a little bird trill, ending with a bright smile.

Emily was in the reception area with Patti, just swinging the gate to the open position and hooking the bracket that held it.

Patti's glasses were peachy orange today. She looked at me and then at the time. "You'd better go. Ms. Zadnichek said the schedule's tight. The shuttle stops beside Julwin's, and you'll have to walk from there."

"I'm leaving." I went to my office for my bag, checked my phone and put it in an inside pocket, and got out the little squeeze bottle. I stopped by Patti's desk again and squirted a dab of sunscreen on the back of my hand.

"You heard about Georgina's sister dying, right? Twinkle Thaw is her name."

I heard a gasp behind me and glanced back to see Emily staring at me. She was a pretty girl with glowing red hair, a chunky build—like her father—and alabaster skin. She was the same age as Patti and Stephanie, but quieter and more professional. Her most valuable asset, as far as I was concerned, was a clear understanding of business finance. I'd leaned on her heavily in the early days of this job.

"I'm sorry, Emily. I wasn't thinking. I should've told you, too." I had no idea how much she knew about her parents and Twinkle. I should tread cautiously.

She took quick steps to my side. "She died? Is that what you said?"

Her manner was intense but not grief-stricken.

Patti swooped around her desk to stand beside us. She kept the volume down but was visibly disturbed. "*Who* died? You didn't say Georgina?"

"Georgina's sister." I spoke clearly but quietly, holding Emily's hand while I looked at Patti. "Her name's Twinkle Thaw."

Emily gave my hand a squeeze.

"She didn't live here, did she?" Wilma asked.

"No. I'm not sure where she lived, but she was visiting Georgina."

"She was at the party last night?" Emily seemed stunned.

"Right. She got sick before it ended, and Georgina took her to the ER in the middle of the night. She died there early this morning. Hunter's outside right now, getting food samples from the dinner for analysis."

"Hunter?" Patti looked even more confused. "Hunter the computer geek? What's he doing?"

"He's interning with the police department this term. They're looking for contaminated food."

"Oh no," Emily said, flustered. She flattened one hand against her throat. "My dad was there! He ate the same food."

"Stewart, too," I said.

Patti gasped and slumped back against her desk, bumping two turtles off their perch.

"He's fine," I told her quickly.

"You're sure? He's okay?"

"I just saw him." I pointed to the garage. "He's helping Hunter collect food samples."

"Oh, my God." Patti whirled and rushed back to her chair. She grabbed up the phone. "I'll call him."

"I'd better call my mom." Emily headed for her office.

Wilma picked up the turtles and balanced them on their perch.

"Well," I shrugged. "Now that I've started everyone's day with a bang, I guess I'll catch the bus and leave you here to cope." I gave Wilma a wave and a grin.

She blinked and looked around the office as though she didn't know quite what to do. There was more than a giggle that was birdlike about her.

Chapter 5

I went out the main door of the big house, turned left toward the outdoor pool, and saw a BRATS bus—this one maroon with brass trim and fancy gold lettering—just pulling away from the pickup station.

It wasn't nine yet. Was this the eight thirty bus running late, or had I just missed the shuttle I'd planned to take? I walked the length of the porch and sat in the swing outside the hair salon. The parking lot had a few cars more than usual. I turned and saw Hunter, still working in front of the garages.

At the nearer garage building, Jim Bergen's door at the end space was open. I could see him moving around inside. He noticed me, too, of course, since Jim always noticed everything. He waved and, after a couple of minutes, walked slowly across the drive, carrying his cane, to join me on the porch. He was tall and rigidly erect, still the perfect naval officer, even though he'd been a civilian for three decades.

"Is your fifty-second year of married life off to a good start?" I asked.

He grunted and wedged his way through the shrubs, pushing branches aside with his cane until he could grab one of the white columns. He hauled himself up the short step and onto the brick floor. "Morning, Cleo. You heard about Twinkle, I guess."

"Yes. I hate it for Georgina."

I held the swing steady while he rotated, grasped the chains, and lowered himself slowly. The swing gave a shudder at the additional weight. He leaned back and pushed, setting us into motion again.

"Don't see you out here often. Nita says you work too hard. She worries about burnout."

"And I'm not really relaxing now." I told him about my nine thirty appointment in town and that I'd just missed the shuttle bus.

"They're always late. Want me to run you into town?"

I knew he'd planned to stay home during the festival, avoiding the traffic that descended on Fairhope for these events. "I'll drive if another bus doesn't show up soon."

He chuckled. "You can drive. The problem is you can't park when you get there. The Art Center, you said?"

"Right."

"Well, it's early. You might still find a space on one of those little side streets. Wouldn't be a long walk from there. Uphill, though." He looked at me. "Maybe you're not old enough to pay attention to hills."

"I'll give it ten minutes and drive if a bus doesn't show up."

"Want to get coffee while you wait? I was coming to talk with you this morning."

I shook my head. "I'd better stay here. I don't want to miss another one."

He nodded and said nothing for a minute. "How much do you know about Twinkle Thaw?"

I told him the bare facts I'd picked up. "I never even saw her. What was she like as a person? Her sister's a darling."

I'd asked the right person.

"Five-six." He squinted and rubbed his chin. "A hundred and twenty pounds. Skinny thing, flat as a board. Dark hair. One odd thing—her eyes moved around. There's something to that old saying, you know—an honest man makes eye contact." He laughed. "And a good con artist knows it."

She had rung the doorbell yesterday, just as Nita was about to nap. I knew that meant about two o'clock.

"Stayed forty minutes, for chitchat." He shook his head. "I reminded her it was supposed to be a fiftieth anniversary portrait and we didn't want it looking like we do today. But she said these wrinkles have been here a lot longer than a year."

"Did she tell you when she'd do the painting?"

He shook his head. "Said she's working on cruise ships, traveling all the time. Down to Aruba, or through the Canal around to San Diego. Went to Japan twice, and up to Alaska, looking at glaciers and whales. I told her I'd been in that line of work, too. Munitions instead of art, you know. She did portraits of the passengers, or painted the scenery if nobody signed up. Said she worked out in the open and, when a crowd gathered to watch, she'd put a person in the painting, some pretty woman walking along the deck. Of course, her husband had to buy it then. Sold everything soon as it was finished. Got a gold mine there."

He rubbed thumb and two fingers together, his way of indicating money was the topic. Then he corrected himself.

"*Had* a gold mine, I should say. Full-time travel, all expenses paid. Something I might do if I were single. But the cruise line took a cut of all her sales. The ones they knew about." He chuckled, and I assumed Twinkle had done some of her work under the table.

I told him about Hunter coming to collect food samples from the dinner party.

He turned to look. "This young man here at the garage? I wondered what he was up to."

Of course he'd noticed. He noticed everything. He stopped the swing and got up stiffly, shuffling around and shading his eyes to look in Hunter's direction.

"Now what do we make of that? Collecting food samples after she's dead." He looked at me and raised his eyebrows.

I knew what I made of it—a suspicious death. "Mary Montgomery's here, too. She went to the kitchen with another evidence technician."

He leaned against a post and nodded a few times. "Um-huh. Um-huh. Somebody must've poisoned her."

So much for confidentiality. "I guess they have to ensure there's no threat to the community. Like botulism, or salmonella. Maybe there's produce they need to pull off grocery shelves."

"If this were Washington, we'd have to rule out terrorism. Have they shut the dining room down? You'll have to get box lunches brought in if they do. We can't go out to the restaurants with this crowd in town."

I pulled out my phone and called the kitchen. Carla answered.

"Have the cops said anything about closing the kitchen?" I asked her.

"No! Did they say that?"

"Don't mention it to anyone—we don't want to give them ideas. Just be aware it might happen, and call me if it does. I've got an appointment in town, but I'll have the phone with me."

"Right," she said.

Jim leaned back against the post and nodded his head a few more times. "You know, Twinkle had a fit over that print. I never thought much of it, but she's a professional and it got her attention. I'm thinking maybe we ought to keep it. Nita likes it well enough."

I stood and went to stand beside him. Hunter was still at the garages, crouched over the blue plastic. He must have been finishing up, since he was putting things back into the sample case.

"I guess you won't be getting your portrait now," I said to Jim.

"That's what I'm thinking. If we're not getting a portrait, we ought to get our deposit back and keep the loaner, too. For all the trouble."

"Is it Twinkle's work?"

"No. It's old and dark. Mostly black, and not what you'd call pretty. Not that I'm an authority." He switched his cane to the other hand. "I looked this morning and didn't see a signature on the canvas. Maybe they didn't sign their work back then."

He seemed awfully interested in a painting he didn't like.

"I can't think what it looks like." Dark, he'd said, and I could picture that, but I was drawing a blank about the subject matter. "Is it a portrait? Or a still life?"

He scowled and shrugged his shoulders. "Just an old, dark house, with people standing around. Something Fran had lying around, I guess. Michael approved the frame and the portrait light. Good-looking frame. Hardwood, twenty-three karat gold leaf. He designed everything to fit—the niche, the buffet, lamps, frame."

"Maybe the artist signature is under the frame."

"Could be. Look at it tonight." He pointed toward his apartment. "Mexican Trains at five thirty, remember. You want a ride to town?" He stood up straight.

I looked at the time. "No sense in your getting in that traffic. I'll drive. If I'm late, I'm late."

We said goodbyes.

I walked in the edge of the cross street, through the intersection, and down to where Hunter was finishing his work, near my garage. Harbor Village was quiet except for traffic noise on the highway out front. Stewart's golf cart was parked in front of Riley's building, I noticed, before the garage blocked my view.

Hunter was folding the plastic sheet, not neatly but with big, loose turns, creating a noise like the roar of surf. He gathered the corners and crammed the whole thing into a garbage container. Blue plastic bulged out the top. He pulled off his mask and gloves and stuffed them in, too, before he dropped the lid into place.

I reached into my bag for the remote and pushed the button. The door of my space, one of the middle ones, jerked and started upward.

"All done?" I asked Hunter. "It took a while."

He wiped his hair off his sweaty brow. "I got sent back, for more samples. But it's done now."

"And what happens next?"

He looked past me to the intersection and suddenly shouted a greeting, throwing one arm up and waving.

"Hey there!" he said. "G'morning!"

I turned, expecting to see Jim following me, but he wasn't there. Instead, a woman was in the crosswalk, moving rapidly toward the opposite side of Harbor Boulevard, her back toward us.

I noticed her short, quick steps, the way people walk on crowded city sidewalks, and recognized her from the red leather handbag. It was the mystery lady I'd seen twice on Thursday.

"Hunter, who is that woman? She waved at you. Do you know her?"

He squirted hand sanitizer on his hands and shrugged. "She's staying at the motel. I don't remember her name. Debbie something."

"Odd that I didn't see her a minute ago, when I was walking over here. She must've come out of my building. And she was here yesterday. What's she doing, do you know?"

He shook his head. "I can find out, if you're curious."

"You know me. I'm always curious."

He stuck the sanitizer bottle in his shirt pocket, shook his hands to dry them, and looked at me as if gauging the degree of, or the reason for, my interest. Then he looked after the woman.

She was already skirting the end of the big house, heading toward the Assisted Living building, or maybe the PT office, or the gym. Or maybe her car was parked around there, just out of sight. I was making a big deal out of nothing.

"You're thinking she might be a murderer?" Hunter made his own big deal of the situation. "If that were true, wouldn't she be long gone by now?"

"Don't jump to conclusions," I reminded him.

"Hmm," he said.

"Maybe she's somebody's girlfriend and doesn't want to be noticed." It was possible, but I did a quick inventory and realized there was no unattached male living in my building. Just Stewart's golf cart, right up the street. I hoped that wasn't the answer and felt a tiny twinge of dread, just imagining the drama that would ensue if Patti were dumped.

"She was real chatty last night." Hunter still looked toward the corner of the big house. He cut his eyes around and looked at me. "And she was just about to come over and say hello now. Then she saw you and went the other way. Are you sure you don't know her?"

I laughed. "I have that effect on people. I've got to go. I've got a meeting at the Art Center."

He gave a short bark of laughter. "You're going to drive to town? Today? Bad idea. Why don't you ride with me? I'm going to the police station. But you'll have to take the shuttle back."

I tapped the remote again and the garage door grumbled as it went back down.

"Ready when you are."

Chapter 6

We wound through back streets and passed by the old Colony Cemetery as Hunter maneuvered to avoid festival traffic. He had a card that admitted him from a back street to the private parking lot behind the police station. A yellow-and-black striped bar rose up, we entered the lot, and the bar automatically lowered behind us.

"You know where the shuttle stop is? At the corner beside Julwin's?" Hunter got his sample case from the trunk of his black Altima. "I would offer to drive you back, but I'm hoping McBee will let me help with the lab work today."

I thanked him for the lift into town. "Will you be able to tell me what they find in the food samples?"

He shrugged. "I don't even know if they'll tell me. They make a big distinction between interns and sworn officers."

He stopped abruptly in the middle of the parking lot and gave me a grin. "You suspect something, don't you? Was she murdered?"

I shrugged. "I hope not. She's been abroad, I learned this morning. Working as the resident artist on a cruise ship. I suppose she might've picked up some weird stomach bug on the ship. Be sure Montgomery knows that." I motioned with my head toward the police station. "And be careful, in case it's something contagious."

"I'll call you later with that woman's name. And if I see her again, I'll find out what she's doing."

"Oh, yes." I pictured the mystery woman prowling around Harbor Village. "I like to check on repeat visitors who aren't vouched for. I'm responsible for the safety of our residents, you know."

Hunter grinned and nodded. "And you're nosy."

"Yes. Especially when somebody dies suddenly."

He waved and headed for the back door of the police station, swinging the specimen case.

I walked around the building, out to Section Street, and merged into the festival crowd.

Streets had been blocked off a day earlier, beginning at the central intersection downtown and extending a few blocks in each direction, including some of the side streets, like de la Mare and Bancroft, where the food court was located. This morning, Section Street, the main north-south artery, had a double row of white tents down its middle, leaving both sides of the street, plus sidewalks, for the flow of pedestrians.

Crowds were thin at this early hour, but music filtered down from the center of town. The smells of popcorn and hot grease crept over from the food court but blew away when the air currents shifted. I didn't take time to browse but walked rapidly toward the Art Center, a block away. The festival wouldn't officially open until ten, but a jewelry booth caught my eye.

The artist was arranging displays of attractive pieces. I told myself I'd come back for a closer look, after my business was completed.

I did stop long enough to pet a wonderfully soft, sweet-tempered golden retriever.

"He's Barney, and this is his favorite show," his owner told me. "He hasn't missed one in six years."

Barney gave me a big smile.

A mariachi band began playing outside the Mexican restaurant up the street. I walked on, matching my steps to the beat.

Normally, the Art Center, with its terra-cotta paint and outdoor sculptures, dominated the North Section Street intersection and nestled into the woodlands that grew close behind it. Today the location was the same but white tents—officially called canopy market stalls, I'd been told—had sprouted all around it overnight, like mushrooms after a rain. Some of the tents had pyramidal tops and others were arched, and the side curtains were arranged in various positions.

The Art Center faded into the clutter. I zigzagged between the tents on the narrow strip of lawn in front, dodged groups of people on the wide sidewalk that led to the door, and entered the glass-fronted lobby.

The front desk, a sweep of curved blond wood, was a work of art in itself, positioned at one side of the lobby. Today there were four or five women behind it and a larger cluster in front, most of them female, all of them talking. They wore name tags and carried clipboards or folders.

I gave my name at the desk. "Is Marjorie Zadnichek here?"

The woman with the paperwork shook her head. "You know she still works at the Grand Hotel. She had something to do there this morning, but she'll be here after lunch. Is she a friend of yours?"

I nodded. "She talked me into this purchase prize, from Harbor Village."

"Oh, yes." She put a checkmark on a printed list then looked around and signaled to someone.

Before I could ask about Michael Bonderant, or leave a message for him, a man's voice boomed out over the twittering.

"You're early!"

Volunteers fluttered.

I looked in the direction of the voice and saw the top of Bonderant's head, six inches taller than the women in the lobby. He pushed his way through the stampede he'd caused and even grasped one woman by both shoulders to move her out of his way. She didn't protest but giggled and blushed when he gave her a big smile. That was when I realized he was aimed for me.

"Ten o'clock, I said."

People looked at me and whispered. The oh-my-god chorus that resides in my head, a holdover from my timid youth, made its presence known. I felt my cheeks burn and my pulse rate spike.

"Michael." I did my best imitation of Barbara Bush, offering my hand and suppressing the impulse to hold it palm out, like a stop sign. "How nice to see you again." My heart was racing, and not with infatuation.

Michael Bonderant was a lithe, attractive man who made a big impression. His light brown hair brushed his collar, and a shadow of stubble lay across his cheeks, something new since I last saw him in December. He was wearing jeans and a blue chambray shirt, open at the neck, with a brown leather vest. He needed only a split-rail fence to lean against and he'd look like an ad for men's cologne.

"I thought you said a purchase prize." The woman at the desk laughed as though apologizing for having misunderstood me.

"That's right." Barbara Bush was using my voice again. "The Harbor Village Purchase Prize." I looked back at Bonderant. "I'm sorry to stand you up, Michael, but I doubt I'll be finished by ten. I was just about to leave you a message."

He looked down his nose as usual—not that he had much choice, given his height. "You're doing a purchase prize?"

I nodded. "Harbor Village is. Any suggestions about what I should look at?"

He stalled for a second, smiling, and then took a few steps that put him behind the desk. "Let me see."

He peered over the woman's shoulder. Checking the amount of the Harbor Village pledge, I realized.

"She's on here." She sounded peeved, as if he were questioning her ability to read, and refused to be pushed aside.

Bonderant shifted his gaze back to me, paused just long enough to build dramatic effect, and announced, "*I'll* take her."

"Do you have a folder?" She was frowning. "Do you know what to do?"

He gave her a condescending smile and took a red folder from the top of the short stack on the desk.

"We'll figure it out." He pulled a clipboard from beneath the desk, stuck his folder under the clasp, and clamped the whole thing under his arm. "Now, Cleo, I know precisely where this work should be displayed."

"In the ballroom," I said.

He ignored me and gestured with a big, upward sweep of the arm as he headed for the door. "Right above the couches, with the bottom just about eye level, I think. High enough to draw the eye upward, toward that chandelier and the beams. You'll see it from the entrance, from the reception desk, maybe even from outside once it's lighted properly."

Oh my god, I thought. *He's going to break the budget.*

Michael sailed through the open door of the Art Center and was almost to the street before he remembered me. He paused and looked back.

"Sorry," I caught up. "I'm out of training."

And I was not about to run along behind any man whose legs were that long.

Bonderant matched his pace to mine after that and was actually quite chatty while he explained his plans.

"It isn't far, and we'll kill two birds with this one stone. I've got something on hold there already, for Riley's house, but there's a perfect piece for your lobby, too. I've been wracking my brain, trying to think where I could use it. Now, before you see her work, I want you to think of the advantages. You'll get to enjoy the painting in the house for now, but when you tire of it, Riley will donate it to Harbor Village, which will already have one work by the same artist. She'll be famous by that time. Riley gets a big tax write-off, and Harbor Village increases its collection of a nationally known artist."

"You'll thank me one day."

Nobody saw me roll my eyes.

We turned in at the third or fourth tent past the barricade. A blond woman with a Dutch Boy haircut, my age at least, sat in a tall deck chair in front of an easel.

"Cleo Mack, meet Jeanine Lawrence." Michael charged through the booth and vanished.

I barely glanced at the artist. The entire back wall of the tent was taken up by a square painting depicting a scene like you might encounter crossing the bay to Mobile, late on a winter afternoon. It seemed to glow. The sky was blue with a few small clouds and eye-popping rays of gold from the setting sun. They almost hurt my eyes. The water was misty blue and lavender and, in the foreground, walls of green sea oats divided, allowing ripples of shallow, transparent water to lap up onto sand. I thought for a moment I actually heard the ripples. It reminded me of my first visit to Fairhope, when I'd met Nita on the pier and she'd introduced me to cathedral sky sunsets. The foreground glimpse of water added a new element, something like grounding.

I drew a deep breath and relaxed as I exhaled. "How beautiful."

Jeanine gave me an appraising look and pointed. "Thank you. But Michael's selection is out back."

She was indicating a spot in the corner, where Michael had disappeared through an opening in the tent.

When I was a step away, he stuck his head back through the opening and startled both of us. "There you are! So? What did you think?"

I stepped out into the sunlight, looking around. "Where is it?"

"The big one, you ninny!" he hissed. "On the back wall." He gestured toward the interior of the tent. "Don't tell me you didn't see it! That's impossible. Didn't you love it?" He got a little louder, a little rhapsodic, and gestured with raised hands. "The way it goes from realism toward Impressionism but doesn't quite get there? The clarity of the water? The sensation of inherent movement?"

"Well, yes, I loved it. But it's big. Wouldn't it dominate the whole house?"

"It's for the lobby, Cleo! Focus, now. *This* is the one for Riley's house. Of course you love it."

He waved a hand toward a smaller but equally exquisite painting hanging on the outside wall of the tent.

I stepped back as far as possible, until my back was against the adjacent tent, and looked. It was a close-up view of sand and smooth pebbles and water, looking perfectly natural at first glance and then intensifying with depth and vivid detail, like I'd gone through to the essence of the subject matter. Water glistened in a thin layer of moss growing on some of the pebbles, so real I expected my hand would come away damp if I touched them. When I looked closely, there were dark and light grains in the sand, and they seemed to stir and resettle as the water rocked, distorting the view.

"Very nice," I muttered. "Interesting, but easy to live with."

"Exactly." Michael sounded pleased. "We'll take it. Now the question is, do we want a third one by the same artist, or something entirely different to go with this one, in the salon?" He pinched his lip between thumb and finger.

"Salon? Is that the living room?"

"It was. It's a salon now. You'll see." He shook off concern. "I think we'll look at another possibility."

He lifted the tent flap and waited for me to go through, then approached the artist.

"What's your best price on the big painting?" He waved casually toward the back wall.

I saw a little card posted to one side and maneuvered to get a look without being too obvious. Um-huh, the figure was a pretty close match to the Harbor Village purchase prize. Michael was locked in quiet discussion with the artist, his back toward me in what felt like a message. I looked at the paintings on display.

"We'll be back," he told her pretty soon, loudly. I looked and saw him motion for me.

"Thank you so much," Jeanine said to me. She looked happy. "Michael, don't I get a ribbon or something, to display on the tent?"

"I've only got the one." Michael opened the folder and fingered a rosette and ribbon labeled *Purchase Prize*, "and it's promised." He felt in the pocket of the folder and pulled out a folded strip of heavy, white plastic. "Here. Let me give you this banner for now and I'll bring your rosette in an hour."

He shook the folds out of the plastic strip, which expanded to a length of about six feet, and showed her the front. *Purchase Prize* was printed in big red letters. "We'll just hang this above the entry." Michael proceeded to do just that, handling the folder to me and reaching up with both hands to tie the flaps of the banner to the tent's frame. I couldn't have reached that high, but it was easy for him.

"Now, you two stand here together and let me get a photo." He pulled out his phone and clicked off several shots, telling us how to pose for each one. "Hold this," he told Jeanine at one point, handing her the blue rosette but taking it back after he'd made some photographs. "I know! I'll call the desk and have them bring one you can keep. How's that?"

She seemed happy and chatted with me while he made a quick phone call. "I hope you'll like living with the paintings. Are they both for Harbor Village?"

I assured her I would love them and already did, in fact. "One will be in the lobby of the administration building.Michael says. The smaller one is for a private home. A private home with a salon."

I assumed she'd share my dismay, but she didn't react at all.

"Okay, what did we buy?" I asked Michael as we walked away. He was taking long strides up the street toward the center of town but slowed down when he realized I was lagging.

"The big painting for Harbor Village, with your purchase prize funds. And the smaller one, out back, goes to Riley's house. She was delighted to get the double sale and the award, especially early in the festival. She gave us a nice discount on the two, and now we keep looking. I had another painting for you to consider for the house, but I know now exactly which one, since you have such an evolved taste. I'd rather you didn't see it yet." He grinned at me and laughed in a happy, flirty way. "More surprises. And there's some money left in the purchase price. I'm thinking a nice big ceramic piece." He narrowed his eyes like he was seeing it. "Let's go look."

The smells of funnel cakes and hot grease mingled in the air. I stopped at the jewelry booth I'd admired earlier and Michael examined several pieces quickly before hustling me away.

"There's a better option on Fairhope Avenue."

I was relaxed finally. We'd selected a painting for Harbor Village, and I'd kept my appointment with Michael Bonderant and even won his approval. Now I could enjoy the festival. The enthusiasm of the artists, the walk up the hill to town, music and dogs, hustle and bustle, and a growing crowd—it all began to feel like fun.

As promised, we stopped at a jewelry tent in the middle of Fairhope Avenue. Michael vetoed the first piece I picked up, saying I was too short for it.

"It chops you off right at the neck." He made a slashing gesture. "Look for this shape instead." He traced a deep vee on his chest and handed me a smooth stone pendant suspended from a chain of metal links. "It elongates the body. What's the stone?" he asked the artist.

"Agate. From Fayette County, if you know your Alabama geography." The artist looked at me. "Forty miles north of T-town—everybody knows where that is."

Fayette was Katherine Roka's home, I remembered.

Michael knew something else. "Jimmy Suddeth's home."

The artist confirmed it.

Michael explained for my benefit. "Georgina took us to see him when I was a senior. He was already an old man then. A folk artist who painted with mud. I didn't know mud came in so many colors. He had all these secret locations where he dug it up."

"I've got a few of his pieces," the jewelry artist said. "They're extremely fragile."

"I should think so. What's the price on this?" Michael held the pendant up. I had looked at the tag already. "I think I'll take it."

The stone was a rusty red with faint yellow streaks, smooth, and the size of a small egg. The shape of an egg, too, but a lopsided one. I handed the man my charge card and he slid it though a cube on his iPad.

"You want a bag? Or will you wear it?"

I took the bag.

Our next destination was a block toward the bay, Michael said. We walked on, passing Fran Beck's gallery.

I slowed my steps and looked for the cat, but its basket was empty.

"You heard Twinkle died, I guess."

He came to an abrupt halt and stared at me. "Died? Twinkle?"

"I'm sorry. I assumed you knew. You knew she was sick?"

He nodded. His had face turned an unhealthy shade.

I touched his arm. "Do you need to sit down?"

He blinked several times, shook his head, and moved over to lean against a pillar beside the jewelry store window. "What happened?"

I was suddenly concerned about Riley. Had he sampled any food when he was in the courtyard? Had he heard about Twinkle?

"Tell me," Bonderant urged, bringing me back to the moment.

I shook my head. "I don't know much. Georgina took her to the hospital and she died there early this morning. I can see it distresses you. I'm sorry."

"But what happened? What was wrong with her?"

"They don't know exactly. They're collecting food samples."

Grief, or maybe it was worry, did odd little things to his face. His brows pulled together. Vertical creases appeared beside the outer edges of his mouth. When he frowned, his upper lip lifted on one side, like a sneer. "I can't believe it."

"You didn't go back to the party after you showed the house to Riley?"

He shook his head. "I was glad to get out. But I hope she didn't suffer. Poor Georgina. I'll go see her." He paused then straightened up. "Let's finish up here."

We walked a long block and stopped at a double space, one side open to the sky and the other with a tent that had two flaps raised. There was a wooden sign for the Magnolia Art Institute.

Solly and Katherine stood in the shade, surrounded by people. Paintings and pottery were displayed on weathered shelves and partitions that flowed out to the adjoining space. There was a rustic bench, like an old pew, where people could sit and take a break. I was tempted to try it out, but there was a line.

"Did you hear about Twinkle?" Bonderant asked them immediately.

"So sad," Solly said.

The festival crowd was larger now, almost filling the street margins. The Magnolia Art Institute booth had several shoppers, and Katherine was busy assisting people. I circulated through the display, looking at ceramic pieces especially, and anything else that appealed to me.

Michael and Solly continued their discussion. I heard Michael say quietly, "You did her a favor, keeping that under wraps."

Solly's voice was soft and raspy. "And she nearly ruined my life."

I stopped for a close look at a tabletop ceramic fountain, and its bubbling drowned out their discussion. I found myself wondering, once again, what kind of trouble an artist got into.

Another object caught my eye, a three-foot-tall construction of clay slabs that flexed and leaned together into the general shape of an upright piano. Would anyone else see a honky-tonk piano in the way it stood, collapsed into itself, its heart played out?

"Do you like that?" Katherine asked as she passed by. "I'll give you a good price just so we don't have to pack it up again."

"Is that salt glaze?" Michael sauntered over for a closer look.

Solly said it was. "I had my fingers crossed while it was in the kiln. I always worry about air pockets in a piece like that."

"You ever blow up a kiln?" Michael asked.

"Sure. But not recently. Knock on wood." He rapped knuckles against the pew.

The glaze was a buttery brown, but when I looked closely, I saw tiny green puddles lying atop the smooth, buff-colored surface. There were some dark green streaks, three at a time, looking like finger tracks, and lots of dark flecks and shallow gashes. I liked the variation as well as the humor I imagined in it.

"How much?" I asked Katherine the next time she went by.

She looked at the tag and told me a price.

"Well, it's a bargain," Michael said, "but your purchase prize won't quite cover it. And I don't know if we can call it a purchase prize, since it exceeds the original commitment."

I didn't see why that should matter, but this was Michael's world.

He looked at Solly. "She's already picked one of Jeanine's paintings, but she saved enough to get a Roka piece, too."

"I'm flattered." Solly puffed up visibly. "Emily will be pleased. Did she put you up to it?"

"No," I said, quite honestly.

Emily knew even less about what was happening than I did, although Michael made it all sound quite deliberate.

"He accepts your offer," Katherine told me.

We laughed because I hadn't actually made an offer, but, just like that, the deal was done. The purchase prize label certainly carried clout in the art world.

While she stretched a sheet of bubble wrap around a matte black teapot that looked like it belonged at MOMA, Katherine asked me, "Do they know yet what Twinkle's problem was? Surely they would've found an ulcer, or appendicitis, or diverticular disease. Found it in time to do something about it, I mean."

"They're examining the food served at dinner."

She nodded. "Yes, I talked with Georgina a few minutes ago. Someone was there, going through her trash. They asked her about nut allergies. Do you know anything about them? I don't. I don't think we had those when we were growing up."

"Nuts?" Michael asked. "Where'd she get nuts?"

Katherine shrugged.

Michael looked at Solly. "Did you see any nuts last night?"

"Just Stewart."

They laughed.

Solly looked at me. "I'm kidding, of course. He's an inspiration. And no, I didn't see any nuts last night, not until I got to your apartment, and Twinkle wasn't there. If she ate nuts, it must've been earlier."

"Do they still serve nuts on planes?" Katherine asked. "I haven't flown recently, but maybe she had some there. What was she doing all afternoon? Does anyone know? Georgina said she was here by noon, but I didn't see her."

"Neither did I." But I knew she'd been at Jim and Nita's for some time. Would they have given her any food?

"Was she really a good artist?" I asked.

Solly nodded. "Yeah."

Katherine was more positive. "I hate to admit it, because I disliked her personally, but she was good. Quite good,"

"With portraits," Michael qualified, with a sniff of superiority.

"I'm sorry I never met her," I said. "Does the Art Center have any of her work? There's a members' show in the main gallery right now." I'd seen a sign about it in the Art Center lobby. "I'd like to see what she did."

"There's probably some of her work right up the street," Solly said. "Fran Beck's her representative."

"I've been in there. Maybe I'll stop now, on my way to the shuttle." I looked at my watch. "Are we finished, Michael? How do we get the pieces back to Harbor Village?"

"Don't worry about it. I've got a van. I'll take care of everything this afternoon. But before you go, I need photos of you presenting the ribbon to Solly. And some photos with the sculpture, too, for your PR person. Now use them, Cleo. Put them in your promotional materials. Lots of people know Solly's work and will come to see it. Jeanine's painting, too."

He interrupted himself to tell the Rokas about the pieces we'd selected earlier. They seemed impressed.

"Just wait and see how many people wind up renting one of your apartments after they visit the Harbor Village art collection." He made a broad gesture when he said *art collection*, as if he were envisioning some magnificent accumulation. "This is a good start, and it builds your connections to the art community. Maybe Solly will come sometime and do a ceramic workshop."

Katherine and I laughed.

"Katherine's doing a workshop for us tomorrow," I told him.

He was back in bully mode, almost belligerent. "I hope you've signed up for it. Maybe I'll stop by. Who knows, I may bring Nall." He was referring to the world-famous artist who lived in Fairhope now. "Do you know him? He'll certainly want to see the painting when it goes up. And Riley's house, too. I'll go by his studio right now and tell him about it. See how well everything is fitting together?"

He punched my arm gently. "Art doesn't get nearly the credit it deserves for making this a better world."

Chapter 7

Making the photographs of me presenting Solly Roka with a purchase prize ribbon, with both of us standing beside the salt-glazed ceramic piece I was already thinking of as "the piano," took a lot of time. Finally, it was done to Michael Bonderant's satisfaction, but then he decided to phone the Art Center and have them send a runner with another plastic banner. We didn't have to wait for it to arrive, he said, but Michael took a few minutes sending the photos to all interested parties, including me. Then we took more time to wish the Rokas a successful festival.

"I don't know when I'll see Georgina," Katherine told me. "We'll be here until the crowd leaves, and the exhibitors' banquet is tonight."

"I'll tell her you're thinking about her," I promised.

At last we were underway, walking back toward Fran's gallery. My phone rang just as we got there. I waved Michael ahead and paused on the sidewalk to answer.

"Where are you?" Riley asked.

"About to catch the shuttle. I've seen Michael." I looked toward the gallery, saw he'd already gone inside, and talked freely. "He was a sweetheart, if you can believe it. I've got one more stop to make, then I'll walk to Julwin's and wait for a shuttle. Of course, I don't know how long the line is. I'm not far away, but I can't see it yet."

"I can be there in fifteen minutes, and we can go somewhere in Daphne for lunch." When I didn't answer immediately, he added another option. "Or we can come back here. There's a big crowd in the dining room already, but there may be something left by the time we get there."

Harbor Village residents were notoriously early for meals under ordinary circumstances. Today, with the festival in town, many people would prefer to avoid the crowds and have their meal in the dining room. I hoped Carla and Lizzie had prepared extra food.

I made a snap decision. "Give me twenty minutes and meet me at the post office. If I'm not there, just wait a couple of minutes. I won't be long."

Michael and Fran were talking about Twinkle when I joined them in the gallery. I thought I could stay ten minutes before I left to meet Riley.

"I'm sure it wasn't food poisoning," Michael said clearly, over the tinkle of the bell mounted on the door. "She didn't eat enough to get any bugs."

Fran must've disagreed, but I didn't hear her.

He continued, "It came on quickly, and so intense. I think something ruptured. You sat right beside her. You know she didn't eat."

This time I heard Fran. "How could you tell how bad it was? She's such a diva."

She threw her pen onto the glass counter, noticed me, and changed expressions immediately. "Come in. Look around. I'll be glad to answer any questions you have."

Michael waved a hand. "Cool it. She's with me. And we've already spent all her money."

"Why didn't you come here earlier?" She held out her hand to me. "I'm Fran Beck."

"Little Franny Beck." Michael could be terribly condescending. "All grown up with her own main street art gallery."

I'd met her a couple of times, but she didn't seem to know that. She had a bushel of poufy, golden brown hair and a wide-eyed look.

I shook her hand. "Where's your cat?"

She angled her head toward the back of the shop. "He's locked up today."

"Poor kitty," Michael said.

"Are you kidding? He lives like a prince. Except that people can't resist knocking on the window and waking him. Bunch of barbarians."

He smirked. "Do I detect a lack of appreciation for the arts and crafts festival?"

Fran glared. "Look at it this way, Michael. How would you like it if your chamber brought a hundred decorators to town for a weekend and encouraged all the residents to patronize them? There's only so much money out there for art, you know."

Michael shrugged and raised his arms in an expansive gesture. "It's a sacrifice for the greater good. The restaurants and motels appreciate it, even if the galleries don't."

She gave him a hateful look.

"I was hoping to see some of Twinkle Thaw's work," I said.

Michael looked at Fran. "I forgot why we came in. You've got some of her work, I know."

Fran Beck pointed to one of the little vignettes arranged on the walls.

The center of the shop was furnished with velvet couches and shabby chic chairs, interspersed with tables and lamps and antique books and big tassels and, off to one side, a glass case filled with beetles, stuck through with long pins. Everything was arranged in a fashionable jumble, seating areas back-to-back, facing the walls. It seemed designed to appeal to a young and wealthy clientele and looked like a long, skinny living room the morning after a drunken party. Customers could sit facing either direction while they admired or studied the paintings and drawings and photographs that covered the walls. Obviously, they moved the furniture around depending on the particular view they wanted.

I went to the area Fran had indicated and found two portraits by Twinkle Thaw. Both had the designation NFS on the card where the price would've been, and both were in ornate gold frames with the artist's signature running vertically along the right edges of the canvases. Each signature sported an asterisk in place of the dot above the *i*.

There were dates after the signatures, too. The portrait depicting a family of four had been completed twelve years ago. The children would be college age now, I realized as I examined their faces.

The larger painting, probably borrowed from some boardroom, showed an older man in a dark suit, his head mostly bald and shiny, his hands crossed on a desktop. There was a large championship ring on his left hand, where a wedding ring might go. The date was fourteen years previously. I wondered who the subject was and whether he was still occupying a prominent position in life. I didn't know the people and couldn't make any judgment about the accuracy or artistry of the portraits, but they looked like work I'd expect to see in colleges or museums or old Irish castles.

Fran joined me after a couple of minutes. "These were on loan for the weekend, so people could see her work and commission a portrait. May as well take them down now. There won't be any more Twinkle Thaw portraits."

"Don't you have some of her botanical pieces?" Michael had followed her and leaned against an oak bureau. "She told me last year she had a barn full of them. Her retirement plan, she said."

There was a distinct edge to Fran's voice. "She quit doing those. Years ago."

Michael snorted. "Who do you think you're talking to? Let's see what you've got."

She shot him a warning look. "Just shut up, Michael. Anything I get, I earned, believe me." She looked at me. "Ignore him."

But he didn't shut up. "I know you're stalling because you haven't raised your prices yet. Better get it done, girl. Double at least, maybe higher. As you said, there won't be any more. I hope she really did leave a warehouse somewhere." He laughed.

Fran sent him another frosty look.

This was no fun. I looked at my watch. My ten minutes was up. "I'm going to run, Michael. Thanks for your help today. I enjoyed our shopping spree."

I stuck out my hand and he took it then pulled me to him, wrapped me in a big hug, and squeezed.

"I'll bring the painting this afternoon and get it hung before the weekend's over. That frame will be okay for now, but eventually you might want to replace it. Talk to Franny about it when you dig up the money, but let me approve it. And Solly's going to help me with the ceramic piece. Now don't forget our appointment tomorrow. Four o'clock, at the house. And don't be early this time. I won't let you in."

"Right." I wanted to leave.

"Come back next week," Fran told me. "I'm much nicer when all this crap's over." She waved toward the street outside.

I waved to them and left.

I expected Michael to stay on and visit with Fran awhile. I even imagined she would soon bring out whatever paintings she had by Twinkle, the ones she'd declined to reveal in my presence. But he caught up with me before I got to the next corner.

"Did you get one of her cards?" He shoved a business card into my hand. "'Portraits by Twinkle Thaw,'" he read from his copy then waggled the card in my face. "Maybe I should be an agent. What do you think?"

"Aren't you? Don't you get a percentage on the works I just bought?" I took the card.

He gave me a look of surprise. "Not on the purchase prize. I was volunteering at the Art Center then. My clients pay me, of course. It's a percentage of the total cost, but the artists negotiate their own prices."

"That means when you got a discount on the painting for Riley's house, you were actually reducing your own income."

He shrugged his shoulders and turned palms up. "That's why artists should never go into business. We go into an automatic physiological rejection when money's involved."

I dropped the card he'd given me into my bag. "What happens to a deposit already paid for a portrait by Twinkle? Will it be refunded?"

"If Twinkle signed a receipt, I suppose it'll be repaid when her estate gets settled. Am I right?"

"I don't know. That's why I asked you."

"I guess Georgina's her heir." He raised an eyebrow and looked at me.

Someone bumped into him from behind. "Sorry," they said at the same time, and Michael stepped aside.

His expression had changed. He grabbed my arm. "Don't tell me you paid her."

"Not me. The Bergens."

He sighed and let me go, and we started walking slowly. "Yes, I'll bet they did. I designed that niche and selected a frame for their portrait. But Cleo, that was long ago. Two years, maybe. She's done it by now, surely."

I shook my head. "No."

"Don't tell me the frame's hanging there empty."

"There's something in it. I can't remember what, but Fran loaned them a placeholder."

He shook his head with annoyance. "Did they pay a big deposit?"

"I was thinking you'd know. They didn't pay it to you, did they?"

He narrowed his eyes. "Not me. Maybe Fran. Twinkle's fee was fifteen or twenty thousand, I'd guess, and the deposit would be half of that."

"Whew. That's a lot of money to lose."

He agreed. "See if you can get the details out of them—how much was it, and do they have a receipt. It's none of my business, but I do wonder. Will Georgina settle the estate, do you think?

I didn't know, but I knew Jim would have any important receipt he'd been given. I told Michael I'd explore the issue.

I was thinking, too, about Ann saying Twinkle had a storage locker at Royale Court. I didn't mention it to Michael. We'd been friends for only a couple of hours at that point, and I wasn't eager to look foolish when the storage locker turned out to be full of dried up paints or old shoes, rather than lovely finished paintings. We were passing Julwin's, the oldest restaurant in Baldwin County, according to the sign on the window.

"I like Riley," Michael announced suddenly, giving me mental whiplash. "But I'm not sure I'd take this job again." He was watching me from the corner of his eye.

"I hope you enjoyed it." I wasn't sure Riley could say that.

"I did, very much. And the place looks fantastic. Wait until you see it. But this thing you're doing to him, it's just unfair. Cruel, even."

I was shocked. "Cruel? What are you talking about?"

"He's such a special man, our spy guy. And crazy about you."

"Well, I'm fond of him, too." What did he mean, *spy guy*?

He made a derisive sound. "Pshhh! *Fond* of him." And rolled his eyes. "Honey..."

"You're not being fair." I sensed a previously unknown emotional dam was in grave danger of bursting. I stepped off the sidewalk, into the shade of the mini-park's holly trees, and faced him. Then I said all the things I should've been saying to Riley for the last three months.

"Moving in with somebody is complicated, Michael. What if I give up my apartment and we find out we aren't compatible on a day-to-day basis? What if I lose my job, or go back to teaching? What if his sons resent me? Things like that can kill a relationship. And that house...I *hated* it the first time I saw it. What if I still hate it? Will I lose Riley over your stupid ego, bragging about how I'm going to love it..." I stopped before the tears surfaced and braced myself for his retort.

But Michael was startled into silence. He just gaped.

"Well!" he said after a minute's pause. "Well, well, well."

And all at once he grinned at me.

"Just remember to apologize..." He jabbed my shoulder. "And express your gratitude..." Another jab. "After you see what I've done. Tomorrow at four. Don't be early, and don't...be...late." Three jabs.

He gave me a little smirk like I hadn't just gone ballistic on him and turned back the way we'd come. In a few seconds, he'd blended into the crowd.

Oh-my-god, the chorus hummed. I turned toward the post office, mentally defending myself, thinking I hadn't said anything that wasn't true. But it was still embarrassing. I'd have to apologize. Thank goodness I hadn't said it in front of Riley, who hated drama and thought I did, too. What was the matter with me?

I took a deep breath and walked on, pulse pounding, past a long line of festival guests cued up for a shuttle bus. Lucky me, not to be standing there waiting. I passed the library and then a garage surrounded by old cars and was feeling almost normal again when I saw the post office parking lot. Riley's black BMW was double-parked.

I walked faster.

When I slid in beside him, I leaned across the console and gave him a kiss. "Thank you for coming."

He looked at me, frowned, then took my chin and tilted my head. "Your face is kind of pink. Did you use sunscreen?" He waited while I buckled up.

"Exertion. You should've seen me a few minutes ago." I felt like an idiot.

Chapter 8

We went to Panera Bread at Malbis, just past the I-10 exit. Riley ordered coffee, but I got iced tea and went back to the cold drink bar for a refill before our food even arrived.

"I've been on my feet for hours," I complained to Riley as I settled back into the booth and stretched my legs.

"Did you find a nice painting?"

I told him the basics about the big painting for Harbor Village. "You'll see it today or tomorrow. I'll let you form your own opinion. Michael took charge, thank goodness. Otherwise, I'd still be wandering from tent to tent, I guess. He wants to put it in the lobby instead of the ballroom. I guess that'll work. It'll be much more visible there."

"I was asking about the artwork for the house."

"Sorry." I hesitated and then grinned. "I'm not sure I'm allowed to tell you about that. Isn't the art going to be your surprise? You've seen everything else."

"Not everything. You said Michael was nice?"

I nodded and grinned. "Eventually, yes. But we got off to a bad start." I told him about the crowd scene in the Art Center when I arrived. "He wanted to make a big deal because I was early, but he changed his tune when he decided there was an opportunity for him to curate a major art collection for Harbor Village."

"Wait—an art collection? Whose idea was that? As if I don't know."

Our buzzer sounded and flashed, indicating lunch was ready for pickup at the kitchen counter.

"Stay put," Riley told me and brought back two plates.

I had a Modern Greek salad with sliced almonds and quinoa and a tangy dressing, along with a big chunk of crusty baguette. Riley had half a turkey sandwich on asiago bread and a cup of black bean soup. While we ate, I told him about the festival and took out my new necklace.

"The stone's from Fayette County. Near Tuscaloosa." I scraped the price tag off with a fingernail and dropped the chain over my head.

"Nice. Is the chain bronze? I like the color."

I looked at it. "It has a rosy tint."

The greens in my salad were cool and crisp, and the bits of grain and nuts gave it a crunchy, substantial texture I liked. "I'll bet Ann and Carla could figure out how to make this. Maybe I should take them one. Are you going to the festival?"

He shrugged. "Maybe. I've got a lot going on this weekend."

"The house," I sympathized.

He smiled vaguely. "That and a call from Washington I need to tell you about. They're inviting me to consult on a banking review."

"Really? Are you going to do it?"

He shrugged. "Their invitations are usually command performances. I may not have a choice."

I laughed and then remembered something. "Does that invitation explain why Michael Bonderant refers to you a *spy guy*? And Jim Bergen called you a *forensic banker*. Just what is that? Something he made up?"

He shrugged casually, but I saw an odd expression creep over his face. "Over the years, a few people might've learned I'm not as naïve as I look. Or as nice. What else did Bonderant say?"

"Just that. Is there something more?"

He shook his head. "He probably heard me on the phone and made up the other side of the conversation. Want to share a dessert?"

We shared a lemon teacake, with a third glass of tea for me and more coffee for Riley, and after that, I was almost desperate for a nap. But I had a meeting to attend.

"Call me when you're ready to go home." Riley dropped me off at the older retirement community in town, not far from Harbor Village.

"It's only a few blocks. I can walk," I assured him before I noticed how limp my legs still felt. "Or I'll get a ride with somebody."

"Call me," he frowned. "You've already had too much sun."

The sweet man didn't realize I hadn't been sunburned when he picked me up; I'd been in an emotional dither after my outburst with Michael Bonderant. But I wasn't about to admit anything.

Three apartment complexes that catered to seniors, several area nursing homes, two assisted living complexes, and two retirement communities all seemed to have realized recently that we lived in hurricane country, where torrential rains, wind damage, power outages, staff problems, and other uncontrollable conditions, including normal wear and tear, might one day result in sudden, unexpected demands on our services. We'd begun meeting occasionally to explore cooperative arrangements that might help us cope with such emergencies. We'd met in the Harbor Village conference room in February and discussed routine overloads, like the ones we encountered recently, when we took in respite cases at our Assisted Living program and suddenly needed an extra bed for one of our own residents. Colds and flu and tumbles happened and could cause normally healthy residents to need assistance for a day or two.

Today we were meeting in Homestead's Magnolia Room and our topic was bigger problems, like hurricanes and roof damage, for which we were developing a list of emergency repair contractors. The meeting lasted an hour and when it ended, I got a ride back to Harbor Village with the administrator from Church Street.

"We stayed open when Hurricane Frederick drove all the water out of Mobile Bay," she boasted as we drove past the pelican sculpture at the entrance to Harbor Boulevard.

"Do you realize how long ago that was? Almost forty years. You didn't work there then, did you?"

She grimaced. "I was a student nurse. And didn't know squat. Our staff today is a different generation. You think there's anything to this millennial business?"

I laughed. "We've got some good people, and I'm sure you do, too. But it can't hurt to have a contingency plan, can it? All of us are in the same boat."

She let me out at the front door of the big house. As I walked through the lobby, I was on the phone with Riley, telling him I was back at the office. I didn't want to leave him on standby all afternoon.

He reminded me we were expected at Nita and Jim's apartment in just two hours.

"Boy, this day has flown." I walked past Stilts the giraffe. "Patti's not here. Gone to the festival, I guess. Her desk is cleared off. That reminds me, I still haven't seen Georgina."

He had. "Ann was there. They're going to a family dinner tonight at Ann's old house on the bay. I didn't realize she still had it."

"She gave it to her niece. Along with the knit shop." I chuckled. "But I don't think she turned loose of either." I groped around in my bag for the office key. "Their whole family gets together and Ann cooks. I've gone a couple of times. There's a big glass porch across the back, where they eat and watch the sun set. Nice of her to take Georgina along."

He said he'd come to my apartment at five twenty and we could walk across the street together.

"See you then." I checked the phone for messages.

Patti had called twice, once at noon to remind me of the multi-facility planning session, and again to tell me, in a rush of frenzied words, that she was on her way to the festival, that Emily and Stewart were with her and Wilma would cover the phone in their absence, and that she'd decided how to decorate a first-floor lanai if I could just work out the budget. "A little bit more than the first one, probably, but worth every penny. Just wait until you see my ideas. Even Michael Bonderant was impressed."

Travis had left a message, too, saying he was detained in Tuscaloosa tonight and was wondering why he hadn't heard from me all week.

The final message was so soft I couldn't hear it. I sat down at my desk, clicked the phone volume to maximum, and started the message again. It was Hunter, according to caller ID, and he was whispering.

"Her name's Debra Hollen." He spelled both names. "Now why is that name familiar?" There was a pause and I heard his keyboard clicking. "From Washington. Just a street address and a phone number." Another pause. "Let me know what you learn."

And he clicked off with no mention of what they'd found in the food samples he'd collected. "End of messages," the phone informed me.

Debra Hollen. The name rang a bell with me too, but I couldn't place it.

I called Wilma and told her I was back in the office. "Do we have any residents named Hollen? Or any next of kin with that name?" I spelled it for her.

"Let me call up my lists."

After a delay, she said she didn't find the name Hollen, not as a resident, and not among our emergency contacts.

"How about a prospective resident?"

After another short delay, she said no again.

"Anyone here?" someone called down the hall.

"Gotta go. Someone's here."

I ended the call with Wilma just as Lieutenant Mary Montgomery, in full FPD gear, swung through the office doorway. "You busy?"

"Just imagining the stupidity of any criminal who risks an encounter with you. What's up? And why are you in uniform?" She'd been wearing street clothes for a few months.

I waved her to a chair and took the second one in front of my desk.

She pulled the chair around to face me and dropped into it with a big sigh. "Lots of visitors in town this week. Don't want anybody mistaking me for a civilian. Have you been out solving murders?"

I shook my head. "That's your job, Lieutenant. I hope you're not suggesting that Twinkle Thaw was murdered. She had a digestive problem, I understand. An allergy."

"Ah, now." She shook her head. "Maybe you haven't heard. She took in a load of toxins, right here in your *active senior community.*" She did sarcastic air quotes around the phrase and laughed at the irony.

"I can't tell if you're serious."

"Serious as a heart attack."

Something like a lead ball hit the pit of my stomach. "A toxin, you said? Is that true? What kind of toxin?"

"Alkaloid, they think."

"I don't know what that is. They've done an autopsy already?"

She relaxed in the chair and flexed her ankles. "They found this before she died. Gastric lavage—you know what that is?"

I did. "But I don't know about alkaloids. Where do you get it? I heard she didn't eat anything last night."

She had finished toying with me. Her demeanor shifted back to normal and her focus went to Twinkle Thaw. "She was one of those frail women; you know the type." She slid down in the chair, stuck out her long legs, and crossed them at the ankles. "Not old yet, but no reserves. Running on caffeine and a leaf of kale. A few alkaloids might not kill you or me, but somebody like her?" She shook her head. "What kind of nuts does the kitchen put in salads?"

I shook my head. "I couldn't say. Do nuts contain alkaloids? I talked with two people who were at the dinner last night. Both of them said there were no nuts served."

"I knew it!" She banged a palm down on the chair arm. "You've been snooping. Where have you been all day? Who else did you interview?"

"I was at the arts and crafts festival all morning and saw some people who attended Georgina's party. And at a planning meeting after lunch. A few people there offered their sympathy, but they were friends of Georgina, not Twinkle."

She was unhappy. "People just naturally tell you things. The same things they hide from me."

"I did see Michael Bonderant and Solly Roka this morning. And Katherine Roka, too, although she wasn't at the dinner. She helped Georgina set up, if you didn't know, but she went to dinner with the Bergens and Riley and me." I told her about our anniversary dinner at Jesse's.

"Yeah, I heard all about it. That bread pudding—I'd like some of that right now."

"You talked with Jim."

"Call Stewart Granger to come in, will you? So I don't have to go chasing after him. You got some private place we can talk?"

"The conference room." I got my phone from the desk and rang Stewart. "Where are you?" I heard conversation and background noise.

"On a shuttle bus, almost to Harbor Boulevard. What's up?"

I told him Lieutenant Montgomery was here, waiting to talk with him, and hung up.

"A few minutes, he says. He went to the festival with Patti and Emily. Now what can you tell me about Twinkle?"

"She ate some nuts and berries. Ingested very shortly before she got sick. Pretty straightforward, as such things go."

"Was she allergic?"

Montgomery shook her head. "Only like everybody's allergic to poisons. They don't know what kind of nuts yet."

"I had slivered almonds in a salad at lunch today."

"The kitchen does put nuts in salads?"

"I didn't say they don't. I said people who were at the dinner told me there weren't any nuts last night. I ate at Panera today. The dining room here was slammed."

"Yeah, I know. I was here. The Bergens invited the chief and me to join them." She grinned. "Jim's on the case."

Jim had been picking them for details, I assumed, but he would've called me by now if he'd learned anything really interesting. I walked with Montgomery to the conference room and turned the lights on.

Stewart Granger had a phobia about cops. I'd known about it almost as long as I'd known Stewart, but Lieutenant Montgomery elicited less reaction than Chief Boozer did. Still, Stewart looked like a trapped animal as he followed her into the conference room.

He gave me a drowning pup look as he closed the door.

I smiled at him and walked out to join Patti and Emily at the reception desk, where they were scowling and sulking and flouncing around like naughty children.

"What now? Why does she want Stewart?" Patti asked in a quiet but angry tone. "She didn't even die here. She died at the hospital."

I thought Montgomery's interest was all very natural and nonthreatening. "Twinkle's distress began here, at a dinner Stewart attended."

And he was alone when he cleaned away the remains. I was immediately ashamed of myself. I didn't want to be suspicious of Stewart. And I wasn't actually. I was just being aware of facts.

"They're right there," Emily whispered, pointing to the wall with her thumb and raising her eyebrows suggestively.

"Stay away from the door," I warned them. "You start eavesdropping and she might decide to interview all of us."

Patti fidgeted. "Cops make him so nervous."

"They make me nervous, too," I said, truthfully, and changed the subject. "How was the festival?"

They'd bought earrings, multiple pairs, which they pulled out of bags and arranged on the desktop. Patti had a tall bundle of dried plants, too. "These are perfect for the new lanai, but I'm going to do an arrangement for Stewart's living room first. To practice."

I checked the time again. "We should be going home."

"I'm not leaving with Stewart still in there," Patti said.

I decided to wait, too, at least for a few minutes.

After a ten-minute conversation, Montgomery and Stewart emerged from the conference room with Stewart looking more or less normal. Montgomery greeted Patti and Emily and asked about the festival and thanked me for the use of the space. All very polite.

"I'm trying to catch all Twinkle's dinner companions before they disappear for the evening." She looked at me. "But I know where to find you. I'll talk with you later."

I shook my head. "I wasn't there. And I never met the woman."

She gave me one of her famous stares. "You were there in the afternoon and back before dinner ended. And you had a free run of the building all night. And you were there when the evidence was collected this morning. Even told the techs where to look." She gave me an opportunity to refute her remarks, which wasn't possible, and grinned. "Catch you later."

She gave us a wave and left a distracted, silent quartet in her wake. Stewart, on second glance, seemed more dazed than distracted.

He saw me looking at him. "I told her Twinkle didn't eat last night. She might've eaten her salad, but not the lasagna. I know. I cleaned the plates when I loaded the cart. Hers hadn't been touched."

"Mary's just interviewing everyone who was there," Patti soothed him. "And you don't know, maybe you told her something important without realizing it."

"Nothing that's going to help Twinkle," he said.

She took his arm and he seemed to swim out of his daze.

"Does she know my dad's staying with me?" Emily asked. "She'll want to talk with him, too, I guess."

"I guess. Here's her number, if you want to tell her." I called it up and handed my phone to her. "He's going to the exhibitor's banquet tonight, right?"

"Unless he can weasel out of it." She got her phone and keyed in Montgomery's number then returned mine.

It was almost five. Time to go home. I walked back toward my office to close up and, on the way, detoured into the conference room to turn the lights off. Two chairs were pulled out at the end of the table. I was pushing them back into position when I noticed a diagram on the whiteboard.

There was a rectangle—the dining table in the courtyard, I decided—with a *G* written at one end. That, I assumed, was Georgina, with *SR*—Solly Roka—on her left and *MB* for Michael Bonderant on her right. Twinkle was at the other end of the table, with Fran Beck on her right, between Twinkle and Solly. The other place, between Twinkle and Bonderant, was marked with an *X*. That would be Stewart. I took out my phone and snapped a photograph before I erased the board.

Patti and Stewart followed me down the hall to my office.

"I forgot to ask," Patti looked in at the doorway. "How was your dinner last night? Did you like Jesse's?"

"Very nice. Pretty little community, too. But I overate. Seems like it was a week ago." I was looking at a note from Wilma as I walked around the desk. She'd just rented the last two units on the new lanai to sisters from Michigan.

"We're thinking about going tonight," Patti said. "Everything in town will be crowded and nobody wants to cook. What are you and Riley doing?"

"Playing dominoes at Jim and Nita's. Subway's delivering. Did you see this?" I handed her Wilma's note.

She read silently at first. "Wow! Stewart, we've got to celebrate!" She read the note aloud.

"Good girl!" He slapped her back. "That's worth a celebration."

"What do you think about Subway?" she asked him. "Not fancy, but they deliver."

He shook his head. "Jim's got some special deal. Subway doesn't deliver. Not to the turtle farm, anyway. Why don't we have leftovers from last night?"

I looked at him. "Leftovers from last night?"

"Yeah. Lasagna reheats just like new."

I must've reacted visibly.

"What is it?" Patti stared at me.

"Did you tell Montgomery you had the leftovers?"

Stewart shook his head. "She didn't ask. And there's nothing wrong with that food. I ate some of everything last night. A lot of the lasagna."

I reached for my phone. "Hang on a minute. She might want to talk with you again."

Patti grimaced and hugged herself. "Why? Why, Cleo?"

"Look, you two. I'm not saying Twinkle's death was anything other than an accident, maybe an allergy. But we don't know. The cops need all the help we can give them."

Stewart looked chastised.

Patti was squinting, looking from Stewart to me.

"We should tell them whatever we know." I got Montgomery on the phone and told her Stewart had taken leftovers home last night. I was sure she could hear Patti muttering in the background, but she just sighed and told us to wait where we were. "I'll be back in a couple of minutes."

I hung up and stood, aimed toward the window behind my desk. And there was the mystery woman, walking away from us along Harbor Boulevard.

"Look, Patti." I pointed. "Do you know this woman? She's been around for a couple of days."

She bent forward and leaned to the side, trying to see between branches of the ficus tree. "I've seen her. One of the food suppliers?"

Stewart looked, too. "I've seen her around. Maybe here with the festival."

"Debra Hollen," I said. "Ever hear of her?"

They shook their heads.

"I thought you didn't know her," Patti said.

"I don't. But I'm pretty sure that's her name."

They shrugged, and I looked out again. The woman was a fast walker. She was already past Riley's building. Once again, I wondered if she'd been visiting someone in one of the apartment buildings.

Patti was scowling. "A strange woman hanging around with no business when somebody gets poisoned. Now why aren't the police questioning *her*, instead of harassing Stewart?"

"Aw, Patti," he said.

I sat down again and reached for the keyboard. "I'm still hoping she had an allergic reaction. I've got something to look up before I leave."

They went up the hall, chattering. I clicked on the browser and typed in the name Debra Hollen.

The answer came instantly, in the form of a dozen thumbnail photos. I hadn't gotten a good look at her face yet, but it looked like the right person. Hair in various lengths, with a slight graying across time. Half-moon eyes, flat on the bottom from the perpetual grin. Chubby cheeks, also from the grin. There was more, too. A Twitter link, a Wikipedia page, links to a multitude of articles and videos. Plus a little summary box in the corner. *An American journalist*, the first line said. Health reporter for the *Washington Post*. Health analyst for NBC.

Another lead ball hit my belly.

I picked up the phone and punched in Travis's number. He answered immediately.

"Do you know any reason for a *Washington Post* reporter to be hanging out here?"

He muttered a couple of four-letter words. "What does he want?"

"No idea yet. It's a she. Debra Hollen. I think she's avoiding me. This is the second day I've seen her, but I just found out who she is."

"Find out what she's up to. Maybe she's looking for a new home for grandma. If not, well, I'll be there tomorrow. Maybe late but in time for the party."

"Okay." I clicked off.

Party? He was already anticipating fireworks? Not something I'd look forward to, but he might be right. It couldn't be good news to have *WaPo* on our case.

Montgomery's voice carried from the reception area. I shut down the computer, grabbed my purse, and got to the hallway just as the conference room door closed.

Patti was leaning against the wall, her arms crossed. I locked my office and she walked back to her desk with me.

"I don't know why you had to call her," she said. "I can't stand the way she's picking on Stewart."

"Maybe you should wait out here," I suggested. "She's just doing her job and Stewart can handle an interview. Maybe he can supply some essential information. You'll stay here until he's finished?"

"Of course."

A few minutes later I was rushing up the sidewalk to my apartment.

Riley was already waiting on the screened porch with his phone to his ear. When I got closer, I heard what he was saying. "We won't be very late, after all."

He put the phone away, and I gave him a full body hug and nuzzled his bearded cheek. He'd just showered and still smelled of sandalwood soap.

"Rough day?"

I nodded as I got the key out. "Rough, but some high points, too. And tomorrow...but let me get ready now and save the stories until I can tell everyone at the same time. Who's coming in Dolly's place?"

He didn't know. As soon as I unlocked the door, Tinkerbelle was there at our feet, meowing and twisting.

"Jim's eager for an update, I'm sure. We all are." He leaned over and stroked the cat. Hey, Tinkie. You need some food? How about water?"

Riley and Tinkerbelle went to the kitchen and I went to freshen up.

Chapter 9

I didn't change out of my work clothes but set a record for rinsing off the day's grime and refreshing my hair and lipstick. Meanwhile, Tinkerbelle instructed Riley in the fine art of cat feeding. Five minutes later we were crossing Harbor Boulevard.

Jim Bergen was waiting at his apartment door and flung it open before we could ring the bell.

"Got a surprise for you." He waved us inside. "Look who's here."

Dolly sat on the leather couch. She wore navy blue pants, a plaid shirt, a fleece vest, and a matching blue mask covering the lower half of her face.

"I'm almost well. This is just a precaution. But no hugs. I don't want to be accused of giving anybody anything." She looked and sounded perfectly normal. Her snow-white hair was nicely arranged in its usual angular style, and her cheeks—as much of them as I could see—were rosy.

I'd already taken a few steps toward her with my arms outstretched. "No hugs?"

Riley said, "I thought you'd be in isolation for another day or two."

She nodded. "Normally, yes. I'm still not going out of the building, but I thought it couldn't hurt to play dominoes. Nita's not worried about catching anything."

"And the real reason is that she doesn't want to miss anything." Jim chuckled.

"Certainly not a murder," Dolly admitted. "What's the latest, Cleo?"

"A murder?" Riley gave me a quick, surprised look.

I touched his arm. "I was about to tell you. Mary Montgomery stopped by before I left. That's why I was late. She didn't call it a murder, not exactly. She said Twinkle died from ingested toxins. Something related to nuts, I hear. I'm hoping it was an accident."

"Bah!" Jim grinned and shook his head. "Hope for the best, but plan for the worst. It's murder. Wait and see."

Dolly looked pleased, but Nita sided with me. "They have to weigh all possibilities."

Jim cast a sneaky glance at her. "I thought," he said slowly, "under the circumstances, we might break the rule and talk about this before dominoes."

Nita began shaking her head before he finished. "No, Jim. No."

She was on her feet, hands up and waving in what looked a lot like a push, an aggressive little hen herding him out of the room and toward his office. "If we start breaking the rules just because there's something interesting to talk about, soon there won't be any rules. That's what happened to the book club. Come back at six thirty. I've ordered the sandwiches already."

He gave the rest of us a helpless grin and a good-natured shrug and vanished into the other side of the apartment.

Riley and I sneaked a smile. Jim was helpless in the face of Nita's devotion to rules. As for Nita, she acted embarrassed as she motioned us toward the dining room.

"He wants to pick your brain, Cleo. I hope you have some information for him."

I doubted it. "He probably knows more than I do. I haven't had a minute to think all day."

She frowned and shook her head. "You're working too hard. Do you agree with Jim? Maybe you'd like to do some brainstorming tonight."

"While we eat," I said.

Nita's ficus tree was twice as tall as the adolescent version in my office and was covered with tiny white lights. It stood in a corner of the dining area and stretched upward, toward the skylight, except for one branch that drooped across the pass-through to the kitchen.

Dolly led us to the table, already set up for our game, the dominoes spread out in a big circle. The score pad and a sharpened pencil lay at the place where Riley sat. Dolly might have a bug, but she still looked strong, like someone who swam laps five mornings a week.

"Did you swim today?" I asked.

She shook her head. "I missed two days in a row. I'll make it up Sunday."

"Tomorrow's Saturday." Riley said it like he was correcting her.

"I know. But I'm going to pamper myself one more day."

I hid my smile by detouring back toward the front door and dropping my shoulder bag on the needlepoint chair. I gave a passing glance to the tall mahogany secretary with sparkly glass doors and an eagle finial and moved on through the seating area. Michael Bonderant had done a brilliant job of decorating their apartment and, with my new regard for him, I felt a quiver of anticipation. Maybe he was creating something equally wonderful out of that sow's ear of a house Riley had bought. Was it possible? We'd know by this time tomorrow.

Oh-my-god, the choir whispered. Whatever the result, it meant big changes in my life.

I crossed the living room's angled, thick carpet, noticing the interplay of dark red squares with the yellowy greens. The dense pile contrasted the wood floor and the slick leather couch. It was all so pretty.

Nita was watching and smiling. "How are you, honey?" She reached out an arm to scoop me toward the dining room.

"I've been waiting to tell you about Michael Bonderant. He helped me pick the painting for the lobby this morning and he was so nice. A tremendous help."

Nita was surprised and pleased. "The lobby? Not the ballroom?"

I nodded. "He convinced me the lobby was a better choice. The painting will get more attention there. I'm eager for you to see it. You'll tell me what you think, won't you?"

"Michael wouldn't steer you wrong." Nita looked toward Jim's office. "Was I too bossy with Jim? I think so."

"I wasn't saying that."

"I know. But I was." She smiled ruefully, and I gave her a hug and a pat.

Nita and I had liked each other on first sight, and knowing her had made it easier for me to accept early retirement and the golden parachute that came with it. I'd had only a few weeks to make the decision and I'd come to Fairhope to think. It was at the pier, on my first night in town, that Nita offered me a seat on her bench. We'd watched a magnificent sunset, the first of many we'd seen together since. The Harbor Village job had been a surprise, masterminded by Travis McKenzie. After seeing Nita's apartment, I'd negotiated one for myself as part of the compensation. And another surprise, which still amazed me, was that I hadn't regretted the life changes. Not that I'd had much time for regrets.

Even my off hours were structured. For nine months now, on Friday nights, if I was in town with no concert or birthday party or lecture to attend, the four of us played Mexican Trains. Sometimes there was a fifth player, but never Jim.

Stephanie had asked, a few months ago and during one of our nightly phone calls, why I did it. "It's a pleasant, low-key end to the week," I'd told her.

She had twittered. "But what's the real reason?"

"Nita and Dolly enjoy it."

She'd rejected that, too. "I'm talking about you."

Finally, I had admitted to my daughter, and to myself, that Riley Meddors was the main attraction. I'd first met him at the Bergens' apartment and our relationship had developed slowly over dominoes, with Nita's not-too-subtle encouragement. I'd been surprised, a few months later, to receive a semi-official invitation into his life, and now here we were on the verge of commitment. Maybe.

I realized I'd been staring at Riley and looked away. We didn't say a word about Twinkle and our game progressed with more speed than usual. We began with the double twelve and were about to finish the double nine round when the doorbell rang. Jim came charging out of his office to handle the delivery. Dolly rapped a domino on the table to signal she was about to go out and, on her next play, she did. Nita and I hurriedly added up our pips, gave Riley the totals, and went to the kitchen to serve the meal.

"Forty dollars," Jim announced in a loud voice, dropping two big bags on the kitchen counter. "Eight dollars apiece."

We always divided the Subway bill, which included a tip for the driver, and handed Jim the cash as we left.

"That's the same charge as last week." Nita frowned. "And I got fewer sandwiches, since Dolly wasn't feeling well."

"Nita," he frowned. "You didn't tell me that. Now I've tipped too much and there won't be any leftovers."

Chairs were being moved around, and dominoes clattered and clicked as Riley and Dolly pushed them to the center of the table, freeing the perimeter for dining. Their other jobs included distributing placemats, napkins, forks, and the plates stacked on the shelf of the pass-through. I prepared drinks. Nita cut the sandwiches into thirds or quarters and arranged them on platters already furnished with little dishes of olives and pickles.

There was a bag of chips on the counter. I tore it open and emptied the contents into a bowl and carried it to the table. Nita brought the two platters and Jim assumed his usual position at the end of the table. I took the empty chair that had been inserted between him and Riley.

We passed the platters and served ourselves, and soon Jim was looking at me over an Italian sub. "Now, about this poisoning business. What's the latest?" He took a big bite and settled back to chew and listen.

I told them what I knew—that Montgomery was interviewing everyone who'd attended Georgina's dinner party. "Apparently, I'm on her list, too, even though I wasn't there. She said she'll talk with me later." I looked at Riley. "That probably goes for you, too. And Katherine."

"I don't know anything about it," he said.

"She told you about the poison?" Jim asked. "What do we know about alkaloid?"

I pulled out my phone and keyed in *alkaloid poisoning*, then clicked on several sites in quick succession, all of which looked technical. "Strychnine, nicotine, belladonna. A lot of chemical diagrams. Here's a picture of an opium poppy." I put the phone away. "The cops are asking about nuts. Did Twinkle eat anything while she was here with you?"

"She had a cup of tea," Nita said. "I set out a plate of cookies but I think Jim ate them. That would've been about three, right?"

"There was no poison in the cookies. I've made a little list." He pulled an index card out of his shirt pocket, placed it on the table, and read off the names of the six people who'd attended the courtyard dinner.

"Where'd you get that?" Dolly asked.

He grinned. "I have my sources."

Her gaze shifted to me. "You need to do something, Cleo." Her mask wiggled up and down when she talked. She grabbed it and yanked it off. "Georgina would appreciate it, I'm sure. And the residents certainly would. We don't want our home getting a bad name."

"What if one of us did it?" Jim asked.

She gave him a sassy look. "If one of us ever murders anybody, Jim, it'll be you. And you didn't do it. Did you?"

Nita seemed distressed. "I know I'm always telling you that you work too hard and ought to get more rest, but this was an attack on our home and our values. It'll be talked about for years, everywhere her work is displayed. We can't have Harbor Village getting a reputation."

Jim always took a practical approach. "Somebody needs to take a close look at Georgina."

"Georgina?" I was surprised. "She wouldn't harm a flea."

Jim rubbed his thumb and forefinger together. "I know that. But isn't she the heir? A famous artist might leave a big estate, and some people will jump to conclusions."

Nita frowned at him. "I don't know anything about Twinkle's estate, but one thing puzzles me. If they're sisters, why do they have different names?"

Dolly laughed. "So people can tell them apart."

Nita scowled. "I mean Thaw and Burch. Neither of them ever married, did they?"

Jim said, "Probably they did, over the course of their lives. Most people do."

"Ann says Twinkle married twice," I remembered.

"Start with the dinner party." Jim automatically took charge. "One person out of six at the party gets poisoned. First job is be sure she was the actual target, not collateral damage. We don't want another incident while we're scratching our heads."

The talk lasted as long as the sandwiches did. As far as helping me think, it was useless. More of an impediment than an assist.

Jim was moving his index card in and out, trying to read the small print. "Now about these suspects. Who knows Solomon Roka?"

"Emily's father," Nita said.

"Katherine's husband?" Jim looked at her then back at his list. "Hmm. Well, don't mark him off entirely. Just move him down the list."

"Fran Beck, then." She'd been rude today, and secretive.

"Who is she?" Riley hadn't said much to that point, but he never missed anything.

"A local artist." I looked at Jim. "Was she the one who arranged for Twinkle to do your portrait?"

"She sold us the frame. And she got us that loaner." He looked up from the index card. "Remember to look at it while you're here."

I glanced toward the buffet behind him. The painting was there in the shadows, but I could tell little about it.

Nita looked at her watch and cleared her throat. Usually that was a signal to return to our game. Tonight, it was prelude to a speech. "I have a proposal. We're all interested in this. Why don't we put the dominoes away and I'll make coffee and heat some pie. And we'll get back to normal next week."

"Now you're thinking!" Jim sounded gleeful. He pushed back his chair. "Let's move to more comfortable seats."

I stacked the dominoes in their case and put it, along with the score pad and pencil, into a lower drawer of the buffet. Riley and Dolly cleared the dishes while Nita supervised from the kitchen.

When we were seated again, five minutes later, Jim asked about the food served at Georgina's party. "Did Ann help prepare it?"

I'd already checked on that. "No. She worked in the knit shop Thursday." I had passed on the pie but had a cup of decaf and was sitting on the couch beside Dolly. "Carla and Lizzie prepared the salad Thursday morning. The lasagna was one of the frozen dishes they keep on hand, and they left it cooking when they went home for the day. Stewart went in at five, took it out of the oven, loaded the cart, and rolled everything up to Georgina. She kept it warm in the community kitchen there." I told them about Stewart taking the leftovers home. "You don't suspect any of the staff, do you?"

"No," Nita answered firmly. "Not Carla. And not Lizzie, but for a different reason." She tapped the side of her head and rolled her eyes. "Just rule them out now."

"Not Bonderant," Riley said.

I wasn't totally certain of that and may have looked a little skeptical, but I trusted his judgment.

Jim was eating pie, but he continued to talk between bites. "Fran Beck's a smart lady, I know that. Good business sense but mousy."

"If you're ruling out everyone else," I reminded him, "that's going to leave Stewart."

"No!" Nita and Dolly protested at the same time.

Jim's head swiveled. "Nobody else was there?"

Nita and Dolly were consulting.

"Not Carla, not Lizzie, not Stewart," Nita relayed. "Just rule them out now and save time."

"Not Bonderant," Riley said again. "What did we say about Stewart?"

"We know everyone except Katherine's husband." Nita looked worried. "Are there no other options?"

"Nobody's mentioning Georgina," Dolly said.

Nita smiled and patted Dolly's hand. "Can you imagine Georgina harming anyone?"

"Maybe this talk is premature," I suggested. "Montgomery said poisoning, not murder."

Jim laughed. "Are you thinking there's some laboratory test to say whether or not it was murder?"

I shrugged and gave up. "I guess you're right. She ate something toxic mixed in with wholesome food. Nobody else got sick, and nothing showed up in the leftovers. That means somebody put a toxin in one serving and saw it went to Twinkle. Assuming she was the real target."

"Riley," Jim said, "you're working with Bonderant. You're not suspicious of him, are you?"

"Cleo is," Dolly volunteered.

"No, we're friends now," I said.

"Well, poison didn't put itself there," she said.

"I assume what we say here is confidential, and I do know a couple of things." I told them about Twinkle's fling with Solly Roka. "It was years ago and they've put it behind them."

"Yes." Jim nodded and smiled. He'd probably known already. "You've got to admit, it puts things in a different light."

"What's the second thing?" Riley asked.

I got my purse and fished out the card Bonderant had given to me. "This is Fran Beck's business card. It identifies her as Twinkle's agent."

I handed it to Riley, who looked and passed it on.

"I was in her gallery today with Michael, who seems to think Fran has a stockpile of Twinkle's work. He told her to double the prices, since there won't be any more."

"Very good, Cleo. Very good." Jim scribbled notes on his card. "Affair with Roka. Financial entanglement with Fran Beck. Now we're getting somewhere."

"Do you have Katherine on your list?" Nita asked him. "The woman scorned."

He hesitated, and I smiled. Jim liked Katherine.

"What about Georgina?" Dolly asked. "It's usually a family member. I've heard you say that."

"The more the merrier." He scribbled some more. Then he looked at his list again. "Did we rule out Bonderant?"

"Let's don't," Dolly said. "You just said it. The more the merrier. Now, how about her plate? Was it different somehow? She looked to me like she might be a vegetarian."

Riley gave a short laugh. "How does a vegetarian look?"

"Cleo's one half the time," she claimed.

"Nuts are going to be the critical item," I said again.

Jim's card was running out of space, but he turned it and wrote along the margin.

"Katherine said the cops asked Georgina if Twinkle had a nut allergy. And Montgomery asked me what kind of nuts the kitchen puts in salads. Solly and Michael said there were no nuts at dinner, but Twinkle's stomach contents included nuts. Any ideas how you'd add poison to nuts?"

"You've been working on this already," Dolly said.

"Just collecting information. Now we need to fit it into a theory."

"Means, motive, and opportunity," Jim said.

Riley looked at his watch and got out his wallet, actions that usually signaled the end of the evening.

"Let's look at this print before you go." Jim put down his card and pen, pushed the dessert dishes aside, and pushed up out of the recliner. "Where's that remote, Nita?"

We followed him back to the dining room, with Nita slipping ahead to switch on the lamps and direct him to a specific drawer in the buffet.

He dug around. "What does it look like? Do you remember?"

The first thing I saw, when I looked up, was a wide, ornate frame, gold colored, with a portrait light attached to the top. Jim found the remote and clicked the light on.

I'd seen the print lots of times without paying particular attention to the content. The image itself was approximately square, roughly two feet on each side, and depicted an interior scene with three people—a woman seated at a musical instrument, another woman standing, and a man with his back to the viewer. I assumed they were engaged in a musical performance or practice.

"Twinkle was impressed with it," Nita said. "She called it a Vermeer."

I recognized the name from art appreciation, thirty years ago, and the image was vaguely familiar. One of the Dutch painters, but I didn't remember much. Riley was standing beside me, totally absorbed. What was he seeing, I wondered.

"What's special about it?" Dolly asked.

"Do you like it?" Jim asked her.

"It's okay. I've seen it before. Haven't you had it a while?"

"A year," Nita said.

"No," Jim said. "We'd better get this straight. It might be relevant. We got the seascape first. She brought this one later. We've had it—what, Nita? Eight or nine months?"

"You said *she*—who was that?" I asked.

"Georgina," Nita said.

"Fran Beck," Jim answered at the same instant.

They looked at each other and frowned.

"Wasn't Vermeer known as the master of light?" Riley had a way of sounding authoritative.

Everyone must've had the same reaction. We waited, looking at him expectantly.

"What do you know about him?" Jim prompted, after a moment of silence.

Riley took two steps to the buffet and gestured as he talked. "He did several paintings of this same room. I remember the black and white floor and the light flooding in from a window we don't see. That carpet…" He pointed to the left side of the picture. "I saw a documentary about Vermeer's work a few years ago, and there was something about that very carpet. Wish I could remember the details. Seems like he invented a special lens or something."

"A camera," I remembered, out of the cobwebs.

"Vermeer," Jim repeated, like he'd just learned the name. "Look at those floor tiles. The checkerboard's messed up. You think the floor was really like that? Or did the artist make a mistake? Not much of an artist if he didn't observe better than that."

"You mean it's a real room somewhere?" Dolly asked. "Not just made up?"

Nita said, "Georgina called it a painting, but Fran's receipt said a print. How do we know what it is, for sure?"

Riley leaned across the buffet. "Can we take it down?" He grasped a corner of the frame and gave it a wiggle. The corner bumped against the wall without moving much.

"Be careful. That lamp's heavy and plugged in," Jim said. "We've got a little step ladder…"

He spun on his heel, heading for the kitchen.

"No, Jim! No ladders!" Nita said. "We could break something."

He turned back reluctantly.

"Better get Stewart to do it," Riley agreed.

"He put it up there," Nita said. "He'll know how to get it down."

"Or did he?" Jim asked. "Maybe that electrician…"

"Yes," Nita agreed, frowning. "You may be right. Or was that—"

I tuned out the argument and imagined Jim Bergen climbing a ladder and reaching across that wide buffet to unplug an electrical cord we couldn't even see. Recipe for disaster.

Riley picked up one of the buffet lamps and tipped it, adding a little more illumination to the top of painting, which was still shadowy. He put the lamp back in place.

"I saw an expert once look through a canvas from the back. He showed the audience how light came through where the paint was thin. I think the question of painting or print will be easy to answer when you get it down and examine it."

"Riley, you're a treasure." Nita gave me a look that said *snap him up.*

"You're saying it's an original?" Dolly asked. "Isn't it old?"

"What's an original worth?" Jim asked.

Riley was shaking his head. "I've told you everything I know. Ask an artist. We've got a few hundred in town this weekend."

"Do you paint?" Dolly asked.

"Not since grade school. But Diane and I lived in Boston, once upon a time, for a couple of years. We didn't know anybody but there was a museum nearby that sponsored lectures. We joined a friends' group, or something."

"We should get some art lectures here," Dolly said. "I'll tell Charlie Levine. He likes projects to work on. He should've done it like the car show, had a lecture series this week, before the festival. Jim, what did you learn about getting your deposit back?"

"Nothing, so far."

"Michael thinks you'll be able to file a claim against Twinkle's estate," I told him. "He says you're a creditor and should get repaid when the estate is settled. If there's not enough money to cover all the claims, they're prorated."

"I've got a receipt," Jim recalled. "Right, Nita? Didn't Fran Beck give us a receipt?"

"But did we pay the deposit to Fran? Or to Twinkle?"

They sparred for a minute, with Jim promising to find the receipt and Nita deciding there had been two. "One for the portrait and another for the frame and lamp. That one went to Fran, I'm sure. Her gallery, I mean. What's its name?"

"But you got what you paid for with the frame," Dolly pointed out reasonably. "Why should she give you a refund?"

"Well, Dolly, it's like this…." Jim started slowly, like he was going to explain something, but he must've seen her point. He looked sheepish. "There's the principal of the thing."

We pitched in, shifting dessert dishes from the living room to the kitchen counter, rinsing them, and adding them to the dishwasher.

"I'll look for the receipt tomorrow." Jim had stopped in front of the painting. "I never liked this one much. But now, after Twinkle took such an interest, it's growing on me. Who knows, it might have some value."

"You'll have to give it back if you get your deposit refunded," Nita reminded him.

He scowled. "Or maybe get that seascape back."

Nita shook her head and rolled her eyes.

Riley looked at Jim. "What seascape?"

"A ship in a storm," Nita answered. "Jim liked it, but I didn't. It was threatening. I didn't mind when Fran wanted it back. Did you see the seascape, Cleo?"

"I don't remember it." But I hadn't remembered the Vermeer, either.

At the next pause in the conversation, I changed the subject. "I wanted to ask if any of you noticed a young woman walking around here in the last day or two. Thirty-five or forty, wearing heels and office clothes. When I saw her, she was carrying a red handbag."

"Nope," Dolly said. "But I haven't been out. What about you, Jim?"

"Are you talking about Debra Hollen?" Nita asked.

I don't know why I was surprised. "Well, yes, I am. I guess you know her."

Jim answered. "We do now. When was she here, Nita? Yesterday?"

"She came to see you?" I should've known to ask Jim at the outset. I could've saved myself some time.

"She sat on the porch with us for a few minutes. She lives in Washington and told us what it's like now, after all these years."

"Sees the National Cathedral out her windows. You know what that says." Jim made his money sign again. "I'd take it if she gave it to me, but I wouldn't live there."

"Too crowded," Nita agreed.

"Traffic, sirens, police swooping in everywhere you go. And those motorcades speeding through, with all their windows blacked out. The worst part's the threat. Anthrax, IEDs, mail bombs. Even airplanes flying into buildings." He looked at me. "Listening to Debra made me happy to be here."

"But she's a lovely girl," Nita said. "Now tell us. Why did you ask?"

"I don't suppose she said why she's here? Like maybe her mother lives here, or an aunt or something?"

They glanced at each other. "Did she say?" Nita asked.

He shook his head. "But I know one thing. That's an expensive address she's got."

"She's a reporter." I waited for their reactions. "For the *Washington Post.*"

"*WaPo*," Jim said. "Looking into Twinkle's death, I guess. She was famous, you know." He looked at Nita. "Maybe she was painting a portrait of the president. Maybe that's why she kept us waiting."

"Debra Hollen was here before Twinkle died." I felt guilty for crushing his theory.

Nita looked at Jim and raised her eyebrows.

Jim looked at her, then nodded and grinned. "There's your answer then. A real suspect, finally. I'll call the chief. Tell him to interview Miss Hollen tomorrow."

Dolly asked, "Where she's staying? How's he going to find her?"

"She's staying at the motel where Hunter works," I volunteered.

Jim nodded. "I'll make a note of that."

"The plot thickens." Riley grinned at me.

"Dolly," Nita said, "did you talk with Cleo about the drawing workshop?"

Dolly had already picked up her purse and the blue mask. It was time for us to go.

"I've paid the fee and it just goes to waste if you won't go," Dolly said. "And Nita needs somebody to keep her company."

"Katherine says we're going for a little walk," Nita said. "Have you been to Big Mouth Gully?"

"What's that?"

"A ravine, right behind the big house. Katherine says I can do it, but I prefer to have somebody to lean on."

Riley was her usual escort. I looked at him, but he shook his head. "I'm helping Michael all morning. Wish I could go."

How could I refuse such a request? "How about I go for the morning? Stephanie's coming for the festival, and Riley and I are seeing the house at four. My afternoon's pretty full."

"I'm looking forward to that—" Dolly began.

Nita flapped a hand and interrupted her. "Wear sturdy shoes, Katherine says. I'll have my cane."

"Watch for snakes," Jim said. "Could be some big ones in that gully."

"A gully?" I just realized that was where we'd be going. "Why are we going to a gully?"

"To see that shrine, I imagine." Jim looked at Dolly, who was poking his arm.

"Eight dollars for my food." She thrust some bills into his hand. "I'll go out the back, if Nita will let me."

"Certainly." Nita led Dolly to the apartment's back door, which led to the interior hallway.

Riley and I paid up, too, and then Jim let us out at the front door. We walked into the night air, which held a bit of a chill, even though the day had been pleasantly warm.

Chapter 10

"It's Friday," I reminded Riley as we walked across the grassy median, already wet with dew. "Are you staying over?" It was semi-customary now, spending a night or two together each week, but not something we took for granted.

He gave my arm a squeeze. "Can I get a rain check? We're both going to be busy in the morning, and I'm thinking I may stay up awhile."

"Everything okay?"

He stopped suddenly and pointed toward the streetlight. "A bat! Did you see him?"

I missed it, and the bat didn't return in the minute we watched. I crossed my arms, wishing for a jacket. Or a scarf, at least, to keep my neck warm.

We walked on and Riley asked, "Did you ever hear of the Gardner Museum?"

"No. Where is it?"

"Boston. It might be a good trip for us sometime. The building is a story in itself. But I'm remembering a theft that happened while we lived there—an art heist, the headlines called it. Must've been eighty-nine or ninety. We weren't there long."

We were between his building and mine, the darkest part of the walk home, but the sand-colored sidewalk showed up clearly.

Riley was involved in his story. "Some paintings were cut out of their frames. The canvases were taken, but the museum left the empty frames hanging on the walls, to remind the public of the lost treasures."

"Must've worked, if you remember it after all these years."

"It was a really big deal at the time, several pieces taken, some of them famous. Paintings worth millions of dollars."

"Millions?"

"Literally. Some people thought it was an inside job. The guards were under suspicion at first. I'm thinking a Vermeer might've been one of the stolen pieces."

"You're not thinking this is it, are you? The one Jim and Nita have?"

"Oh, no. They were probably recovered long ago. I didn't keep up with it. Or don't remember, if I did. Either the museum got them back or they're in some oligarch's hideaway by now. Look it up when you have time. It's an interesting story. And tonight's conversation has roused my curiosity."

We turned the corner beside my porch.

"What was wrong with Dolly tonight?" he asked. "She was easily confused."

"Isolation, I hope. I wish she'd go to that class tomorrow."

"But she won't. Thank you for going with Nita." He gave me another squeeze, and we stopped on the sidewalk. I'd forgotten to leave the light on, but Ann's porch light illuminated the entire area. She and Georgina must still be out.

He gripped the screen door but was slow to open it. "Four o'clock tomorrow. And the curtain rises…."

"Are you excited about it? Glad to have the house finished?"

He shook his head. "To tell the truth, I wonder what was I thinking. I'll leave it at that."

"I think I have to investigate Twinkle's death. At least a little."

He nodded. He didn't really approve of civilians interfering in police investigations, but he usually tolerated my overblown sense of obligation.

"I know it's your job to stay on top of things that happen here. I'd feel the same way in your position, but be careful. And don't step on any cop toes, okay? I haven't seen much of them around here today. Are they waiting for an autopsy?"

"I think they have it now. She was poisoned about the time of the party."

He sighed and gave a little shrug. "Well, Harbor Village is your responsibility. It happened here and some of your staff members were present."

"I've got another problem, too. Debra Hollen."

"Yeah, I meant to ask. What's that about?"

"She's a reporter for the *Washington Post*."

"And?"

"A health reporter." I waited while he thought about it.

"You think she's here looking for dirt? Some sort of exposé."

"What else?"

He frowned. "Is something going on?"

I shook my head. "Nothing I know about. Probably a coincidence that Twinkle was poisoned, if you believe in them. I doubt she's here to write a puff piece."

He shook his head, gave me a quick kiss, then shooed me inside. I locked the door and we waved through the window, then I watched him walk toward his apartment, head down, hands jammed in his pockets. We ought to spend more time together, to make up for our late start. Maybe the house...I gave a little shudder and closed the blinds.

Tinkerbelle was sitting a few feet away, watching me with her superior expression.

I got her brush and sat on the floor with her, giving her long hair a thorough brushing. She flopped onto one side, then the other, latched her claws into the carpet, and pulled just out of my reach. I quit brushing until she wormed her way back to the starting point.

"You're a pretty girl, but you have an exaggerated sense of your importance," I told her.

"Meow." She closed one eye and rubbed her chin against my knee.

I pulled a big wad of hair out of the brush and took it to the kitchen garbage can.

I took my shower and, without really planning to, got an early start on the weekend chores. I took the hamper to the laundry room and sorted out a load of dark pants and tops.

Stephanie phoned just as I lowered the lid and pushed the washer's start button.

"Let's make this brief tonight," she said, in greeting.

"Okay. All's well here. Bye."

"Not that brief. What's new?"

"You didn't send the condo information. Or did you? I don't believe I've looked at email all day."

"Didn't you get my text? I'm rethinking all that. Which do you prefer, mountains or beach?"

One of the most beautiful beaches in the world was less than an hour's drive from my apartment, yet I seldom went there. I assumed she was up to something, but she wasn't admitting anything.

I changed the subject. "I hate to tell you this, but there was a suspicious death here last night. Or this morning, to be accurate."

There was a pause. "In Fairhope, you mean."

"Well, yes. An artist named Twinkle Thaw. Did you ever hear of her?"

Stephanie didn't think so.

"She was Georgina Burch's sister. Georgina lives beside the front door. I'm sure you've met her."

"The front door of...?"

"Of my building."

"And her sister *died*? What do you mean by *suspicious*?"

"Poisoned, they think."

"Mom! Are you doing this on purpose? I told you I'm short of time and you bring up a suspicious death right under your nose? At least she didn't live there. Where was she when it happened?"

"Here, unfortunately. Visiting her sister. They had a party in the courtyard last night and Twinkle got sick. She died at the hospital early this morning."

"Mom, that's horrible. I can't believe you're chatting about condos when someone's just been poisoned right there in your building. How did it happen?"

"No one knows."

"What kind of poison?"

"Alkaloid, I heard."

"Oh god. I hate those things."

"I'm not talking about the mints, you know. I'm talking about a plant poison."

"Yeah, I know. Like you get from too many kale smoothies. Remember when my fingertips got numb?"

What? "No, I don't remember any such thing. What are you talking about? When did it happen?"

"In college. Maybe I never mentioned it." She changed the subject abruptly, leading me to suspect she might've neglected to mention other things. "Barry's asleep already. Boyd wants to get an early start tomorrow, but I haven't slept late in weeks and tomorrow's my only chance." She asked about Riley.

"Michael Bonderant's in town. He's going to show us the house tomorrow."

"I'd forgotten about that. That means you'll be tied up, too."

"I expect I'll be back here pretty quickly."

"Don't count on seeing us before...let's say eight," she said. "We've got dinner plans, so don't cook anything."

"Riley got a preview of the house last night." I was thinking to myself, still sulking a little at being left out and at his refusal to give me any hint of what to expect.

"And...? What did he think?"

"He's not allowed to tell me anything."

"Well, what does your intuition say? I think it's going to be awesome." She clicked into her therapist voice.

After we hung up, I scooped out the cat box and got the garbage ready to drop off on my way to Katherine's class. Then I checked the doors, turned the lights off, and worked half of a diabolically difficult Sudoku puzzle before turning off the bedside lamp.

I lay awake for a few minutes, regretting I hadn't made time to visit with Georgina. I'd see her tomorrow, I promised myself. And I'd look up alkaloids. Were they really in kale?

I rolled onto my stomach and thought about the drawing Stewart had left in the conference room, showing the seating at the party table. The task stuck with me after I went to sleep. I snapped awake abruptly, dreaming about squeezing all Georgina's guests into extra seats around our table at Jesse's Restaurant.

It seemed sad, in a way, to take death so casually, but it was a natural event. Twinkle hadn't lived here, and few of our residents had known her. In fact, I didn't know where she lived. Surely not just on a cruise ship? Weren't there friends somewhere, mourning her? A newspaper, fluffing her image in an obituary? A home filled with possessions to be claimed? Paintings and plants, or even pets, to be cared for? I hoped Georgina was taking care of everything, whatever there was.

Ann and Patti would be assisting her, I reminded myself, and went back to sleep with only a slight feeling of guilt.

* * * *

I woke up at the usual time Saturday and felt perfectly fine for a minute or two, until my memory reloaded. Twinkle had been murdered, perhaps, and in this very building. I didn't see how it could've happened by accident. A big-shot reporter was sniffing around Harbor Village. Riley was hoping I'd swoon over a house I remembered as smelly and oppressive. Bad as it was, I could just about cope with all that until I remembered my one-time husband and current boss, Travis McKenzie, would be here within a few hours. He always annoyed me. And if that weren't enough, I had agreed to attend a drawing workshop this morning.

I groaned out loud and rolled out of bed. No sense in delaying. I went to the kitchen to feed Tinkerbelle and, five minutes later, I was dressed in jeans and a sweatshirt and leather moccasins. I stripped the bed and put the linens in to wash while the clothes I'd washed last night were drying.

Then I lingered over two cups of decaf, along with buttered toast and some of Ann's jelly. Finally, the dryer buzzer sounded.

As I headed for the laundry room, I saw Ann entering my porch. She waved and I detoured to open the door.

"Come in. I've got to get some clothes out of the dryer."

It buzzed again, a really obnoxious sound, and she followed me to the laundry room. I opened the dryer, removed three pairs of black pants, and draped them over the dryer door.

Ann gathered a few hangers off the rack and held one out to me. "I saw Usher last night. We had dinner at the bay house. Remember he called while you and I were eating breakfast yesterday? He said Twinkle had a storage locker at Royale Court."

I shook a black knit top and took the hanger. "Yes, I remember." I stuck the hanger through the neck. I would check it in stronger light, but it looked like it could get by without ironing.

"Last night, he said he *saw* her Thursday afternoon. Claimed he'd already told me about it, that she came to visit her locker."

"Really? That's interesting. But not what I understood."

"Well, good. He didn't tell me any such thing, I know. I was afraid I was losing my mental acuity." She exaggerated the words and grinned.

I hung a brown blouse on another hanger and buttoned the top button. Linen. I'd have to iron it. Maybe I should find it a new home.

Memory loss was a big worry for seniors, but Ann certainly displayed no signs of it. "You know, Usher didn't answer when you called him. He called you back later, about the time Hunter showed up. Maybe that distracted you and made you forget what he'd said."

I stooped, pulled a black cardigan from the dryer, and felt around for damp spots, but I didn't find any.

Ann was leaning against the washer. She made a face. "I think I'd remember that, but who knows. I was surprised to find out she even *had* a locker."

"Did he go to the locker with her? I'm curious about what kind of things she'd keep in storage, since she's here so seldom. Just once in the last year, I heard." I gave the cardigan a couple of shakes, laid it out flat on top of the dryer, and smoothed the sleeves.

"He said she called about three, wanting him to pick her up in Daphne. They went back to Royale Court. Her locker's in the anteroom, beneath his stairs, and he keeps the entry door locked."

I folded the sweater into a neat square to fit on the closet shelf. "She couldn't access it unless he was there?"

She nodded. "He said she was in there five minutes at the most, while he sat on a bench in the courtyard."

"He didn't see what was inside?"

"He said whatever was there still is, unless it was small enough to go in her purse. She came out empty-handed and sat with him for a few minutes, talking about Fairhope and how much it's changed. Then she kissed him in public. That made his day." She snorted. "And took off again."

"Wonder where she went."

"And how she got back here."

I took another hanger and inserted it in the shoulders of a black plaid shirt. Mentally, I was sandwiching the storage locker into a schedule I was composing, covering Twinkle's last few hours.

"Just being friendly, he said." She grunted and straightened up, like she was about to leave.

"She didn't put something new into the locker?" I picked up a pair of pants and snapped them.

Ann shrugged. "Didn't say so. But he might not notice. Well, I better get going. I won't be able to park if I don't get there soon. The knit shop's going to be a madhouse again today."

I matched the side seams, smoothed out a few wrinkles, and folded the first pair of pants over a hanger.

"You wouldn't believe how many people come in just once a year, during arts and crafts."

"And expect you to remember them, I guess."

"And I do, mostly." She grinned. "Not their names, maybe, but where they're from and what they buy."

We laughed and I walked to the door with her.

"Do you know if Twinkle ate anything while she was with Usher? Maybe candy from the candy shop? Or nuts?"

Of course she understood what I was asking. News traveled fast around Harbor Village, especially when there was a body involved.

"I don't know." Her eyes narrowed. "But I'll find out. I'm glad you're looking into things."

"Just unofficially. As the local representative of Harbor Health Care."

"Of course." She gave me a couple of pats on the shoulder and pulled the door closed.

I went back to the laundry room. One more pair of pants and then the dryer was empty. I verified that Tinkerbelle wasn't inside and slammed the door.

The linen shirt would stay on the rack until I had time to get the iron out, but the other hangers were ready for the closet. And when I got there,

I remembered Nita's admonition to wear sturdy shoes. My rainy-day shoes would have to do. Any other shoe option I might once have had disappeared in the downsizing before my move to Alabama. I put the black shoes on with some black cotton socks.

It was still early, so I looked through the fridge and the kitchen cabinets, making up the weekly shopping list. I planned to go to Publix after lunch. I might not be preparing a meal while Stephanie and Boyd and Barry were here, but snacks were another matter. Boyd was a world-class snacker, and Barry always expected grapes when he came. I added them to the shopping list.

Finally, with the time for the drawing workshop approaching, I gathered up the recycling, sorted it quickly, and was looking for my phone when it began ringing. It was still on the night table. I raced to the bedroom and grabbed it up without looking at caller ID. When I said hello, a familiar voice came back.

"Cleo? This is Ken. You got a minute?"

Ken Ingram was my former dean. I hadn't heard from him in months.

"Oh, Ken! How nice to hear your voice. Tell me you're in town for the festival!"

"I wish. No, I'm parked at a convenience store, waiting for the middle school soccer team to tank up on sugar. I have to talk fast, but I wanted to tell you about an interesting phone call I got yesterday. Remember Izzy Wooten?"

I did. Izzy was one of our graduates, four or five years ago. He taught at Alabama now, or did the last I knew.

"He's looking for you," Ken said.

"He needs a recommendation? Why would he change jobs?" That was the primary reason I heard from former students, but it would be about time for Izzy to apply for a promotion. Maybe he needed a letter of support. But that wouldn't cause Ken to call me on a Saturday morning.

"Their dean is retiring," Ken said. "Izzy nominated you for the job."

It was a good thing I was standing near the bed. I dropped onto it and gulped like a fish out of water. "Dean of Social Work? At Alabama?"

"Thirty-six thousand students. Half again as big as we are. If you haven't heard about it, I'm glad I called. It's not the sort of thing anybody wants to be surprised by. You got any first reactions?"

"No. Nothing except shock. I'm still getting settled in here, learning my job. I can't even imagine another change."

I heard kids' voices and the slamming of car doors.

"Cut it out, Matthew. Close the door." There was another slam. "Let me say, Cleo, that he sounded pretty serious, like the idea's already been vetted. They may send recruiters after you."

Oh-my-god, the choir was humming when we hung up. My stomach felt queasy and my hands were shaking. *Another job change?* No matter how attractive it might be, it was more than I could think about at the moment. I was going to be late for drawing class.

I grabbed my shoulder bag, dropped the phone in, ignored the garbage but grabbed the recycling, and scurried out the door.

The shuttle bus was waiting at the far end of the porch when I rounded the garage. I crossed the intersection and gave the shuttle a wide berth. Festivalgoers were lined up to get aboard, most of them Harbor Village residents.

"Good morning!" somebody shouted. "Hey, Cleo! Let's go to the festival. Let's have a funnel cake!"

I shouted back, both hands full of recycling. "Have fun! Enjoy the festival!"

The bus whined and puffed out a thin veil of vapor as the engine revved.

I walked around the gym and someone pecked on the window. It was too dark inside for me to see who was there, but I smiled and nodded my head and felt guilty. I'd been to the gym only once all week, I realized with an inner cringe. And I'd eaten that big dinner at Jesse's! I needed to do better.

The recycling shed's metal roof kept the contents reasonably dry, and partial walls concealed the contents from the view of people passing by, but primarily it was what you might call an open-air structure, with five containers lined up against the back wall. I dropped my brown sack, filled with a week's supply of junk mail and last Sunday's *Times,* into the big blue box labeled *paper only.* Plastic water bottles and juice containers and vitamin bottles went into a large green garbage bin with its top flipped up, leaning against the wall. There was a tall shiny container with a swinging door, the sort of trash can you might see in a mall, for plastic bags, but with cloth bags for groceries, I never had many of those now. Glass items went into their own smaller container. I laid an olive jar on top of the pile carefully, to prevent anything from breaking. Finally, I dumped a few aluminum cans out of another paper bag, into another green garbage container. They disappeared with a clatter, and I tossed the brown bags into the blue box.

The Harbor Village arts and crafts studio was a wing off the back of the big house, facing the koi pond. The ballroom made a third side for the pond and an ornamental garden, which spilled out into a vegetable garden maintained by residents and staff, and then the raised community garden spaces, available to anyone who lived in Fairhope. At this time of year, cherry tomato plants were already making their way up a bamboo trellis, soon to become a tomato tunnel, and azaleas were past their peak.

The door squeaked when I entered the studio. Katherine Roka stood in front of a network of long tables. She looked up from the papers she was holding, saw me, and pointed to Nita, who sat at a front table by herself.

The front wall of the studio had built-in bookshelves beneath windows that looked out on the fountain spraying up from the little pond. The back wall was solid white but mostly covered with taped-on paintings. Above them, a row of clerestory windows faced north and gave a view of clouds.

Nita gave me a big smile and patted the table as I slid into the folding chair beside her.

"Jacques." Katherine looked around the room.

I did, too. A small man seated behind Nita answered.

"Right here." He waved one finger. He was the right age to be a Harbor Village resident and had smooth, hairless skin and a nice tan, but I didn't recognize him.

I looked around at the other students. It was fun and kind of exciting to be in a classroom again. Would it be fun to return to teaching? I pushed the idea aside and shook off the emotional reaction it inspired. Harbor Village had classrooms, too.

I recognized about half the class, which consisted of eight females and four males. Eloise Levine, Charlie's statuesque wife, was there, all made up with her hair done just so, even if it was nine in the morning. She waved to me and I waved back. I couldn't see what kind of shoes she was wearing, but I knew they wouldn't be sturdy.

There were three or four teenagers in the room, probably sent by the high school art teacher.

"Dolly's not here, but Cleo Mack is taking her place." Katherine pointed to me and made a note on her list.

I waved to the class.

We were seated two to a table, with a little stack of materials in front of each of us.

Katherine leaned against the front table. Framed drawings were stacked and propped on the tabletop behind her. "How many of you have taken an art class before?"

Most people had. She pointed around the room, asking everybody to talk a bit about their art training.

Nita had taken a series of art classes, mostly watercolors, but pottery, too, and collage. "Oh, yes! A framing class, too. And let me say that cutting mats is a lot more complicated than it looks."

Katherine pointed to me.

"One art appreciation class in college," I replied. "But no skills."

"Now don't do that," she chided. "You can operate a pencil, I assume."

Jacques was an architect. "I'm competent with two-dimensional drawing and with various perspectives. But your class description says photorealism has a 3-D look, and I want to see what that's about." He chuckled as if he'd caught her in an exaggeration.

Katherine took some of her smaller framed drawings from the front table and handed them out to be passed around. The first one to reach me was about eighteen inches square and depicted a single leaf on a white background. The leaf was heart-shaped, almost a foot across, and cast a shadow on the paper beneath it. It looked real enough to pick up. Every little vein and dimple, every curled edge, a pinprick of a hole, even the slick texture of the stem was perfectly depicted.

Katherine was answering a question but stopped and walked over to me. "May I?" She took the leaf drawing from me.

"See this leaf?" She held it high and rotated slowly, giving the class a good look. "I kept track of the time that went into this one. Over forty hours. Do you understand why I cringe when someone refers to it as a sketch?"

"Amen!" Jacques the architect said.

She had examples of work by other artists, too, including a magazine cover that showed beads of perspiration that looked exactly like water drops. Other sample drawings could pass for black-and-white photographs, especially one large drawing she didn't pass around. She held it for us to look at the rocky embankment, the sky, a few puffy clouds. I had stared at it for a minute or more, thinking it rather plain, but suddenly I felt a tingle and noticed the big cat—a mountain lion, I guess it was—lounging on a ledge, staring at me.

"This is the drawing that got me hooked." Katherine told us the artist's name.

We looked at all the works she'd brought to exhibit, and then she talked us through the materials laid out for us on the tables. There were two sheets of white paper that differed in *tooth*, she said.

"Feel a corner, not the center. The oils on your hand will alter the paper. I like to work with a little piece of tracing paper under my hand. It slides easily, keeps my hand clean, doesn't smear the work, and I can see through it, so I know where I'm going."

That explained the piece of tracing paper in the supply stack. There was a little handheld pencil sharpener, too, like one I'd used in elementary school, and a couple of graphite pencils, well sharpened, with no erasers.

"Drawing pencils come in a range of hard and soft. Does everyone have an HB and a 2H? That's enough to get you started today, and you'll add more if you continue to draw. There are several brands, and everybody has their own favorites. Did everyone see Jacques's pencil set?"

I turned to look at the man seated behind Nita. Jacques had laid out a long, hinged strip of wood, nicely finished and grooved to hold pencils in numerical order. There were two dozen pencils, plus slots for a soft brush, an X-Acto knife, and a small indention for the doughy type of eraser. Some of his pencils had an inch of crudely shaped graphite exposed.

"I'm a fanatic about sharpening," he said. "Sometimes I think that's my real hobby."

Katherine began the actual instruction by demonstrating several grips for holding a pencil. Then she affixed a large drawing pad to an easel and, using a hand rest and the lightest imaginable touch, shaded a one-inch square. "Let's begin with the 2H pencil. Hold the pencil flat, like this, and use the side of the graphite, not the tip."

While we attempted to imitate her technique, she prowled the room, observing and offering advice or corrections.

"The objective is to lay down a thin coat of graphite, which lodges in the tooth of the paper. If you use too much pressure, or indent the paper with the point, you're doing damage and won't get the desired effect."

When she got to me, she said, "You're using a lot of pressure. Try again with a lighter touch, like this." She took my pencil and demonstrated, barely brushing the paper. "This isn't the time for working out your tensions."

She moved on, crisscrossing the room and addressing individuals or occasionally the entire class.

"When you finish the first box, move an inch down the page and do another one, using the same pencil. This time use a little more pressure, so your sample is just slightly darker. Let's make six or eight or ten boxes, each one a little darker, until the final one is as dark as you can make it."

Nita was bent over her work. It looked good to me.

The task took several minutes, and then we repeated the process with the softer, HB pencil.

Then Katherine noticed the time. "Go to the rest room. Get a drink. Check your messages. And be back here at..." She looked at her watch again. "Ten thirty. The grass should be dry by then. We're going for a short hike. Everyone has walking shoes?"

Eloise Levine didn't. I could've told Katherine that.

"I can't walk in the woods." She smiled prettily at Katherine. "But I'll be here for all the classroom instruction. When should I come back?"

"We have box lunches coming," Katherine said. "They'll be here when we get back and we'll eat then. Say, eleven thirty? Eleven forty-five?"

"I'll be here." Eloise sang out and batted her eyes.

She was in her seventies, still glamorous, and I loved her bubbly personality. But she always made me think of a female impersonator. Bless her heart.

* * * *

I'd been in Fairhope long enough to learn that, in this rainiest spot in the country, a network of deep, semi-wild gullies provided drainage to Mobile Bay for floodwaters. Raccoons and possums and foxes, and occasionally a homeless person, lived in the gullies.

I'd heard all about the gullies and seen them as I passed by, but I hadn't been down into one until Saturday morning.

We left our drawing materials in the studio, visited the bathrooms, checked our phones, and then we formed an amoeba-like blob and meandered past the community vegetable gardens, through a semi-open area of knee-high shrubs and weedy grasses, and into the woods.

The packed-earth path was just wide enough for Nita to walk beside me. She held my arm with one hand and her cane with the other, and the younger people clustered together at a lengthening distance ahead of us.

Birds called all around. A pair of chickadees fluttered in low branches beside the path and scolded us.

"Hush, little birds," Nita scolded back. "Do you think they have a nest already?"

"Mid-March? Yes, I think so. Babies by now, probably."

The path curved and the gully appeared beside us. I'd been here a few months ago, when a group of women collected holly and seedpods and other natural materials that we used to make holiday arrangements. After another fifty yards, we stopped beside a section of rickety fencing attached to a handrail that sloped downward, into the gully. Katherine waited until Nita and I had caught up with the group beside the fence.

"This is a gentle slope," she said, "and a fairly wide path, but if you're afraid to try it, you can stay right here." She looked at Nita.

"I'm going." Nita craned her neck to look over the rail. "I want to see it."

"Just watch for loose rocks and don't turn an ankle." Katherine gave me a warning glance and I nodded back. Adult protective services, on the job.

Nita hooked her cane over one arm, grasped the handrail with her right hand, and clutched my arm tightly with the left. "Not too fast, now."

"There may be splinters on that rail," I cautioned. "Don't slide your hand or you'll pick up one. We should've brought gloves."

"I'll put them on my supply list for next time." Katherine was keeping a watchful eye on us.

I was looking at a concrete retaining wall, about thirty feet long, constructed on our side of the gully and positioned to deflect the rush of water as it rounded the nearby curve.

Chapter 11

We were the last of the class members to reach the bottom of the gully.

"This is what we've come to see." Katherine stood at the foot of the ramp, facing a section of the wall.

At head height, a face had been sculpted into the gray concrete. Larger than life size, and protruding slightly from the flat wall, the face was stained by age and weather. Numerous black dots the size of a pinpoint, and several hemispherical dents about as big as a pencil eraser, spotted the face. The cheeks were rounded, the nose was shaped like a small light bulb, and the bulging eyes were half hooded. The rest of the wall had sprouted crusty colonies of lichens, in shades of brown and tan, but the face was spared such indignities.

"I've wanted to draw this face since the first time I saw it," Katherine said. "Now we're all going to do it together."

She had both hands on the face, caressing the cheeks. Then she pinched the nose and brushed a little dirt off the brow. "Notice that the concrete is almost the color of graphite."

"What is graphite, exactly?" one of the teenagers asked. "Lead?"

"A type of carbon," Katherine answered without looking at him. "Lead is a misnomer. Ask me when we get back to the studio. Right now, I want everyone to concentrate on this face. Come up and feel it. It's gritty. It's rough, and that texture is what you'll be drawing, as much as the features."

Her admiration for the face was oddly sensuous and sincere. I looked again, trying to see what inspired her. She ran a finger over the shadowy, almost invisible curve of the mouth, and then stepped back to allow us to take turns exploring the face with our hands.

Nita couldn't quite reach the eyes.

When everyone had filed past, feeling the texture and features and snapping a few photographs with our cell phones, Katherine returned with a yard-long length of cotton cord.

"This is how you'll get the proportions for your drawing, whatever size you decide it will be."

She held the cord against the face and made knots to mark the exact top and bottom of the face. Then she folded the cord in half and made another knot at the midpoint.

"We'll put in two more knots and then make a photo, lining up the facial features to the quarter, half, and three-quarters marks." She spent a couple more minutes measuring the lengths of cord, making knots, and then adjusting the knots until she was satisfied. Then she held the cord in place while most people took photographs. "You'll reproduce this with a cord sized to fit your drawing paper. If you like, you can draw a grid over a photo and match it to a grid sized for your paper."

"I'll use your photographs, if you don't mind," Nita told me. "If I drew from my perspective, I'd be looking up his nose."

Katherine was repeating the knotted cord process, working in the horizontal direction this time with a second cord. Then she had another person help her hold both cords in place while we took more photos. "You can stay here and repeat this process yourself, if you like, just for the experience. Or you might want to examine the sculpture in more detail. But if there are no more questions, I think we're ready to go back to the studio."

The kids commented among themselves, giggling, and Katherine waved us toward the ramp back to ground level.

"I'm glad I came," Nita told Katherine while we waited for the others to go up the path ahead of us. "It's nothing like I imagined."

I took the opportunity to look at the gully.

Taller trees kept the entire area shaded. Except for the short section of retaining wall, the sloping sides of the gully were covered in native vegetation, mostly of the low-growing variety. A few big rocks stuck through the greenery, and dozens of long, skinny saplings had grown straight through the mat of plants. About six feet in height, they leaned at a steep angle into the gully, reaching for a narrow strip of sunlight, their tops sprouting heart-shaped green leaves.

When Katherine came back to walk up the ramp with us, I pointed to one of the saplings growing near us. "That looks like the leaf in your drawing."

Katherine examined the closest leaf and agreed. "I collected botanical samples here last fall. Some of the leaves were really huge. They turn bright yellow before they fall. Does anyone know what this tree is?"

Jacques was the only other class member still attending to our conversation. "You're not from here, I take it. Are you testing us, or do you really not know what it is?"

"I don't know," Katherine said. "Do you?"

"You have to be careful, going around collecting stuff you don't know. It's tung oil. Now you know it, don't you?"

Katherine looked puzzled. She shook her head and he laughed. Then recognition dawned.

"You mean tung oil like artists use?" She sounded incredulous. "A base for oil paints?"

Jacques laughed again and nodded. "It dries faster than linseed oil and gives a hard finish when applied to wood. I used it on my pencil rack. But the fruit's poison. Don't eat it. And watch for snakes when you're down here. Flat rocks like these are their heating pads." He pointed to the rocks I'd been looking at.

"Are they poisonous?" She cast a quick look at the ground around our feet.

Nita caught my gaze and smiled. Jim had cautioned us about snakes last night.

Jacques signaled for us to precede him up the trail. "Venomous, you mean. I've seen rattlesnakes here, but they're rare. No coral snakes, but they're up on the Tensaw, for sure. Rat snakes, corn snakes, racers—we've got lots of those, but they're harmless."

"I'll remember that." Katherine sounded properly concerned. She didn't allow Nita to pause for a rest but kept her moving up the ramp. I followed right behind them.

Jacques stayed in the gully for a longer look at the face, or maybe to water the daisies, but he was a fast walker and caught up with us soon after we made the U-turn toward Harbor Village.

"Do you know the tung oil flower?" he called after us. "There are some on the ground here if you want to see them."

He borrowed Nita's cane and raked a few white flowers out of the litter beneath a big azalea. "They're pretty, I think."

I looked for snakes before I picked up two flowers. I handed one to Nita. The flowers were large and very white, trumpet shaped, with a dark maroon throat. "Five petals." I counted.

"They're beautiful," Nita and Katherine agreed.

"I'll take them, if you don't want to keep them," Katherine told Jacques.

For a painting, I assumed. Nita and I handed over our blooms and Jacques gave her several more.

"I'll make photographs before they collapse."

"Well, remember what I said," Jacques warned. "Wash your hands after handling them."

"Venomous," Katherine said.

"No." He laughed. "Poisonous, in this case."

"Is the poison an alkaloid?" I asked.

He looked at me quickly, and then his gaze dropped to the ground. He nodded and smiled shyly, rearranging brown leaves with the toe of his shoe. "I know what you're thinking. Twinkle Thaw, right?"

"Right," I admitted. "Did you know her?"

"Virtually, you could say. We had an online debate once, years ago. On the subject of morality."

I heard a little sniff as Katherine exhaled. "We'd better get back. I need to remind everyone to wash their hands before they eat."

"You go ahead," Nita said. "We'll be right behind you."

"Remember, I have to miss the afternoon session," I told Katherine. "Prior commitments. But I enjoyed the morning session very much."

"I'm sorry you can't stay, but do some drawings. And show them to me. And take your materials and box lunch with you. It's all covered in the class fee."

"Thanks, I will." I thought Dolly might like to have the drawing materials, and I'd enjoy the lunch. All the walking and standing had developed my appetite.

Katherine and Jacques walked on together, chatting, and Nita and I followed behind them.

"You know, we've been here before," I said to Nita as we crossed the clearing. The raised garden beds weren't far ahead.

"Yes." She seemed pleased that I remembered. "I realized it when Katherine talked about the leaves turning yellow. This is one of the places we cut plant materials for the holiday wreaths."

I agreed. "I got some of those bright yellow leaves. The stems were at least a foot long and the leaves were huge."

"Such a beautiful, clear yellow. Did Jacques say they're poisonous?"

"Something is. Fruit, maybe. Wonder what kind of fruit tung oil has. I didn't see any."

"It's the wrong time of year, probably."

"We got some branches from that native holly, too." I pointed some distance away, to a tree at the edge of the clearing. The pyramidal tree was twenty feet tall and had pale gray bark.

"And we got magnolia leaves, somewhere..."

I looked around. "Right there." I pointed.

The magnolia was the darkest green in the woods, almost black, and the tree sent out horizontal branches that began not far above ground level. Beneath the lower branches, leaves and seedpods created a grass-free area that looked like a perfect spot for children to hide and play.

"I wonder if magnolias are poisonous," I said.

"We can ask Jacques. Do you remember the sasanqua?"

"That white flower that I thought was camellia? What did you call it?"

"Sasanqua. It's a cousin to camellia. Don't you love the way Ann pronounces that word? *Ca-may-ya*. Those were pretty wreaths we made. And that huge arrangement in the lobby—oh, so pretty. Let's do it again this year. And this time, I'd like one of those trees for our porch."

"The Norfolk pine? The one we did for my building?"

She frowned. "It wasn't on the porch, was it?"

"No, it was in the lobby. We had a couple of parties while it was decorated. A Sunday afternoon reception for everybody, sort of an open house. I'm sure you and Jim came. It was the Sunday after Thanksgiving. Riley and I came back from Savannah in time to attend. And there was another little party a week later, just for the residents of our building."

"Well, of course your building would have wonderful parties, with Ann doing the baking and Georgina decorating. *Our* building has Dolly and me and a few other inept people. You know how accomplished *we* are."

"I'm sure Ann would bake for your building, too."

She stopped abruptly and when I looked to see why, I was shocked to see a frown on her face and tears in her eyes. She reached out and grasped my hands in both of hers. My heart raced. What was wrong?

"Cleo, you know how fond of you I am. And I'm just worried…" Her lip quivered.

"What's wrong, Nita? Do you need to sit down?"

She blinked and shook her head. "Has Riley talked to you?"

"No. Don't tell me there's something wrong with him." I clutched my throat.

"He wouldn't like me saying this." She frowned, put her fingertips over her lips and pressed, like she was trying to hold something in. She was blinking back tears.

"Oh, Nita. You're scaring me. Don't tell me he's sick."

"No. It's not that." She was shaking her head. The threat of tears passed, but she still looked terribly worried. "You have to talk with him. Just the two of you. Can't you make time today?"

"Tell me. I won't be able to think straight until you do."

She shook her head. "I shouldn't have said anything. I told him I wouldn't."

"Oh no! If he's sick, why hasn't he told me? There's treatment for everything today."

"He's not ill. It's not that." She looked as miserable as I felt, but I saw her gathering her resolve. "He came back to the apartment last night, after you left. He's had a phone call."

"From his wife." I have no idea why I jumped to that conclusion.

"His wife?" Nita appeared startled and now her worry seemed to refocus and target me. "He doesn't have a wife. You know that. You really aren't thinking straight. Poor Cleo. I've upset you."

I laughed and hiccupped. "Excuse me!" Another hiccup. "Nita, I'm having a nervous breakdown here. What's wrong with Riley?"

"He's had a job offer. Now don't panic."

I stared. Then I exhaled so much air I nearly crumpled. And then I laughed again. "A job offer? A *job* offer? What's bad about that? I think I'm getting one myself. Oh, Nita! You don't know how panicked I was." Tears of relief came to my eyes, but I was on the verge of a giggle fit. I searched my pockets, found a tissue, and used it.

"He'd have to go away for a while. Months, maybe."

"Go away? And he thinks he's sticking me with that house? No way. Not gonna happen." I shook my head.

"He wants you to go with him."

"He wants—Oh my god, Nita. Where?"

"Were you serious about having another job offer? You're not really considering that, are you? I can't believe you'd leave Fairhope and all your friends."

"I didn't say I was leaving. I said I got a message. I haven't even…"

"And you haven't told Riley?"

"There's nothing to tell yet."

"Is it in DC?"

"No, it's in Tuscaloosa. Why do you say DC?"

All at once, she was mad. "Cleo, don't you and Riley ever talk? I swear, young people don't know how to communicate." She clenched her hands into tiny fists and shook them.

"We're not young. We've already retired once."

"Look. Katherine's coming for us and we're standing here arguing. We have to get back. I do, I mean." She tipped her chin up defiantly and picked her feet high as she walked through the weeds, using her cane but not waiting for my arm.

I stood still for a moment, my thoughts a jumble involving Riley, DC, the house….

I was about to catch up with her, just passing the raised beds, when I realized the person walking toward us from the arts and crafts studio wasn't Katherine, but Patti. What was she doing here on a Saturday?

Patti stopped beside Nita. I could hear their voices but not the words, and when Nita talked, her hands waved toward me. Patti glanced in my direction and shook her head sympathetically before she took Nita's arm and walked with her toward the studio.

I paced myself to arrive before they went inside and caught up just as they stepped onto the covered walkway. The entire drawing class could, if they chose, look out the windows and see us.

"Nita, I'm sorry," I said. "I just freaked out."

"No, I'm sorry." She was shaking her head. "It's all my fault, me and my big mouth." She gave me a hug. "Let's just let Riley take care of everything. He's good at that, you know. I'll have to apologize to him."

For what, I wondered.

"Are you guys coming in?" Katherine was holding the door open.

I went inside and got one of the remaining box lunches and all the art supplies stacked on the table where I'd been sitting. The stack was bulky and hard to carry.

"Here, let me get that." Patti took the drawing materials out of my hands.

I told Katherine how much I'd enjoyed the morning session, and then Patti and I departed, giving Nita little waves as we passed her. I waved to Jacques, too.

"I'm glad you showed up," I told Patti.

We went through the back doors of the big house, into the lobby. The new painting was hanging right where Michael Bonderant had imagined it, above the seating area.

"Look at this," I said.

"OMG!" Patti squealed. "What is that?"

She ran across the lobby, shoes clattering on the hard floor, to stand behind the couch and look at the painting. I joined her.

Michael had been right about the location, I saw immediately. The painting dominated the lobby and, displayed high on the wall, looked even larger than it actually was. It drew my attention upward, to the painting and beyond, to the heavy beams that supported the chandelier, and on to the small wooden ceiling at the top of the room. I brought my focus back to the painting. As I admired it, I wondered what made it art. There was no doubt that it was. Perhaps Katherine could tell me. "What do you think?"

Before she answered, I looked around and saw Solly Roka's ceramic piece, on a big black pedestal in front of the window wall. I walked over for a close look. The koi pond fountain provided an appropriate background, but the work needed a spotlight. I'd tell Stewart. "This was done by Emily's father."

Patti went into rhapsodies based on the word *awesome*. "That's the only word for it. You bought it yesterday? Cleo, it's…I don't even know what to say. The painting *transports* me, right to the bay. Is it a real place? Where? And what do you call this…thing?" She looked at me. "I thought he made pots. What do I call it when I tell Emily how awesome it is?"

"I don't know. Patti, what are you doing here on Saturday?"

She gave me a blank look that lasted a long second, then clasped her hands tightly. "I almost forgot, when Nita was upset. Stewart's being questioned again. Isn't that bad? Shouldn't we be worried? I could go down there."

"He's at the police station?"

She shrugged. "I guess."

"Have you had lunch?"

She shook her head and twisted her hands together. Her fingernails were still peach colored, but her curls didn't bounce today; instead, they trembled. "I don't think I could eat."

"Let's go to the dining room."

She was looking at Solly Roka's ceramic sculpture again. She ran a cautious finger over the glaze. "What's it supposed to be? A castle? I know! Hogwarts!"

"A piano, I thought."

Patti frowned and shook her head. "No, I don't see that. It looks all bent and wizardy." She pulled her gaze away slowly. "The dining room's full of people. I don't think you want to go there. Not when you've got a lunch already." She indicated the box in my hands. "We wouldn't be able to talk in there."

I looked at the cardboard box I was holding. "You want to share it?"

She shook her head.

"Then let's go sit on my porch. You can tell me what happened while I eat. My walk has worked up an appetite."

Chapter 12

The parking lots at both ends of the big house were full of cars, people, and shuttle buses. Our usually quiet community buzzed with distant conversations, laughter, traffic noise, and bustle.

We went to my apartment. I left the box of food on the porch and Patti took the drawing materials inside, to the bookcase beside the TV.

"You want 7-Up? Or water?" I went to the kitchen.

"7-Up." She reached into the fridge while I washed my hands. "This is the last one, unless you've got more someplace else."

"I'll have water," I shook my hands over the sink and reached for a towel. "I have to do some shopping this afternoon."

"No, I'm not taking your last drink. You have it."

"I prefer water." I got a glass, walked around her, and opened the freezer to get ice cubes.

"Well, okay."

When I opened the upper cabinet to get out paper napkins, she spotted the blue can of Spanish peanuts.

"Can I have some peanuts, too? Just something to nibble."

I handed the can to her. "Get a bowl and pour some into it. You want a glass for your drink, don't you?"

"Oh, no. I don't want to be any trouble."

"It's no trouble. There's a dishwasher."

"Well, in that case, I'll take some ice, too."

I got a feeling about how things were going to go and put a couple of salad plates and forks on the tray with our drinks and napkins. Patti got the bowl of peanuts, and I carried the tray to the porch.

I pulled the chair closer to the love seat, while Patti opened her drink and poured it over ice cubes in a short glass. I was hungry, and lunch smelled good. There was a bag of chips on top and, beneath it, a curried chicken salad sandwich on dark, whole wheat bread, the sandwich sliced into two triangles. A dill pickle spear had oozed a little juice, dampening one corner of the sandwich. "Pardon my fingers." I used fingers and a fork to transfer half the sandwich to each plate.

I divided the chips evenly. "What happened with Stewart?"

"Well—" Patti stalled to chew and swallow peanuts and then sounded evasive. "He…" She waved a hand vaguely. "He had some things to do here this morning. He told me to pick him up at eleven."

"He didn't have his car?"

"I had it. It's a long story. Don't ask. Anyway, I got here at eleven and no Stewart. I thought he might be at the new house, and I walked over, but the decorator—Michael? He thought you'd sent me to spy on him, and shut me out. Fortunately, Riley was there, and Michael remembered Stewart had been there, but Mary Montgomery sent somebody to drive him to the police station. The police station! Again! I've tried to call him for the last hour, but he doesn't answer his phone." Her emotion meter swung all the way to depressed. "I just know they're trying to blame him."

"For Twinkle's death?"

She nodded.

I scoffed. "And why would they do that?"

"Look at it." Her voice sounded so sad. "He sat beside her at dinner, he delivered the food from the kitchen, and he cleaned up afterward." She looked at me in a sly manner. "And she's his old girlfriend. Did you know?"

"An old girlfriend? I hadn't heard that."

She closed her eyes and shivered. "She stayed at his place sometimes, when Georgina was in Greece. He says they were just friends."

"Wasn't Stewart just a kid then? Twinkle's too old for him."

"You think he's too old for me."

I didn't disagree, but she seemed reassured.

"He says she was crazy."

"Eat your lunch." I pointed to her plate.

"Do you think I should worry?" She took a bite of the sandwich.

"No. Who else is Montgomery going to talk to? Georgina is grieving, Michael is working on the house." I grimaced and glanced at my watch. The hour of the reveal was drawing closer. "Solly Roka and Fran Beck are busy with the festival."

"Do they pay for those tent spaces? I'd be mad if I paid a lot of money and they made me miss my customers."

"That's what I meant. How many shows do they attend in a year? A weekend like this could make up a big chuck of an artist's annual income. Montgomery wouldn't want to interfere with that. Stewart's the only one available. It sounds routine to me." I ate a chip and sipped water and hoped to heaven I was right.

"I hope so. If he hadn't admitted to taking the leftovers home, this wouldn't have happened."

I could tell she blamed me. "If he hadn't taken the leftovers home, there would've been nothing to admit."

"Right," she admitted grudgingly. Her gaze drifted back to my plate. "Are you going to eat that pickle?"

I held my plate out. She took the pickle and bit off half of it. "What was wrong with Nita?" she asked, her mouth full.

I'd been so successful at putting the episode out of my mind that I winced when Patti reminded me. "What did she say? Was she upset with me?"

"Upset with herself, she said. Why?"

"I can't remember."

"Of course you can."

"Well, yes, I do remember what happened, but I don't understand why. We'd had a nice walk down to the gully and were almost back to the studio when all at once she got upset. Emotional, I mean. I thought something was wrong with her, but she said no, and then I thought she was saying something was wrong with Riley, and I got upset."

I kept talking, thinking out loud. "He said something yesterday about being called back to work on a project, but it didn't sound like a big deal. I gather it's happened before, and he hasn't agreed to anything."

"I hope you don't plan to call me back to work after I retire." She rolled her eyes and giggled, the first sign her normal disposition was returning.

I thought about Ken Ingram's phone call that morning. Should I tell Patti? No, I decided immediately. Izzy might not call, and I didn't know that I'd take another academic job, even if he did. But it was depressing to have exciting news and no one to share it with. I'd have to wait until I saw Stephanie.

Patti asked, "What kind of work did Riley do, exactly?"

"Banking." I knew a little more than that, but he didn't like to talk about it, and I'd gotten in the habit of giving the same terse answers he did.

Patti was satisfied. "What did y'all do in the gully?"

Dessert was a large cranberry pecan muffin. I cut the muffin into two parts with the plastic knife from the lunch box. "Remember those big yellow leaves we collected last fall?"

"They were gigantic. And we decorated that little pine tree for your office. Where is it now?" She looked around the porch.

"It wasn't mine. It just sat in my office for a day or two, until Stewart could move it back." I dropped the knife back into the box. "I burned my fingers, gluing that skinny green ribbon with a hot glue gun."

"Everybody who ever used a hot glue gun got burned. Where's the tree now?"

I was examining my fingers, wondering if the fingerprints had come back. The burn had lasted a few days, but I didn't see any permanent marks.

I nodded toward the apartment. "It's up front, in the lobby. I never took the berries and seedpods off, but surely someone did. Georgina waters it. She probably undecorated it."

"Or changed it to a Mardi Gras theme."

That rang a bell, once she said it. I must've seen it sporting a new theme.

"Purple, green, and gold. But that was a month ago. You could use it out here, you know." She looked around at my sparsely furnished screened porch. "Why don't you get one? Put it in that corner. Stewart knows this plant place in Loxley with really good prices."

"Tinkerbelle would probably eat it."

"Or climb it. I think I'll get two for my next porch project, and some of those yellow leaves, too. I'm calling it a lanai now, did you notice? That sounds more elegant than *screened porch*." She signaled air quotes.

"You know the leaves aren't yellow now, don't you? They're green in the spring."

"Well, *duh*. Why didn't Katherine just bring some leaves to the studio today and save Nita that walk? Lots of people would've preferred it. Eloise, for instance."

"Katherine took us down there to see a face that's sculpted into the retaining wall."

"He's a weird thing, isn't he?"

"You know him?" I was surprised.

She nodded. "Georgina took us down there when I was a senior in art class. Seven years ago. They'd just built the wall then, after a big washout."

"Who made the face? Georgina?"

She wrinkled her face. "No. Not Georgina, but you know what? It might've been her sister."

"Twinkle Thaw?"

Patti shrugged. "Does she have another sister? I don't know. I'll have to ask her."

Her phone rang and she nearly turned the table over in her haste to stand up and pull it out of her pocket. It was Stewart.

"Okay!" she said, after listening a minute. "Now where?" She listened again then pushed the phone back into her pocket, grabbed up two handfuls of dirty dishes, and sped to the kitchen.

"It's Stewart. I have to pick him up. Then I've got a million things to do." She burst back onto the porch. "Thank you, Cleo. Thank you, thank you, thank you." She grabbed me in a bear hug, tried to involve me in her happy dance, and finally dashed out the screen door. "See you tonight!"

"Tonight?" I said.

She waved both arms, erasing invisible words. "Oops! Not tonight. Later. I don't know when. Bye." And she galloped off down the sidewalk. A single chortle echoed back as she disappeared around the garage.

I leaned back in my chair, drew a deep breath, and closed my eyes for a minute. Riley's fine, I told myself, just thinking about a temporary assignment. No problem there. *I* was the one who might get a real job offer. I hadn't even thought about returning to university life. But I couldn't deny I'd enjoy working with a graduate program now, after my time at Harbor Village. I had a dozen ideas for curriculum additions. The realization almost frightened me, like I was running short of time.

I hopped up and busied myself. I pulled the porch furniture back into place, stacked the last of our dishes and trash, and took the stack to the kitchen. I pressed the garbage in the already-full can, added dishes to the dishwasher, and pushed its buttons.

The day was slipping away. I needed to shop for groceries and visit Georgina, and I was meeting Riley at the new house at four. I looked at my watch. Stephanie and her family were probably in town by now, along with a hundred thousand other festival visitors, give or take. Maybe two hundred thousand since Saturday was the busiest day. Our parking lot, one of several dotted around town, had been full all day, with a steady stream of shuttle buses coming and going.

I changed out of the clothes I'd worn to the gully, into my usual black pants, this time with an aqua shirt and a knotted scarf. Then I checked my phone to see if Stephanie had left a message. Nothing. And the charge was low. I plugged it in at the desk charger, got my keys, and walked through the interior hallway to Georgina's apartment.

There was no answer when I knocked. I checked my mailbox and found one oversized, matte black envelope with gold lettering. I assumed I was being invited somewhere elegant, but it was just Capital One, snooping around to see what was in my pocket.

As I walked past the kitchenette bar, I thought about the pine tree and glanced toward the window beside the fireplace, expecting to see it there. Zilch. It wasn't anywhere in the lobby. Someone must've moved it into an apartment.

I went back to my apartment, dropped the black envelope into the empty recycling basket, got my shopping list and bags, and walked to the garage. I was backing out when I realized I hadn't picked up my phone. I felt uneasy when it wasn't in my purse or pocket, but this was a short trip, and it wouldn't be fully charged yet. I didn't go back.

I went to Publix every Saturday, and it was always one of the highlights of my week. The carts were new—still silent and maneuverable. I got a wipe from the dispenser beside the door and cleaned the handle.

The sale bins came first, and I scanned them on the way to the bakery. A box of cranberry scones caught my eye; Stephanie's husband was always looking for snacks. The vegetables were fresh, plentiful, and colorful. As usual, there were two or three people handing out tasty samples. I was always on the lookout for something new to try. This time it was almond milk popsicles, covered in dark chocolate, from the freezer. I knew Boyd would like them, to combat what he thought of as our unbearable heat and humidity. He had complained even at the New Year's celebration. Riley would probably be around later, too, which would make five of us. I got two boxes of the popsicles. And while I was in the freezer aisles and thinking about Riley, I picked up a couple of frozen Mexican dinners for Sunday night, after the big weekend was over.

When I drove back down Harbor Boulevard, two people were sitting on the front porch of my building. One of them was Georgina, I thought. I lugged my shopping bags from the garage to my kitchen, put away the frozen foods, and did a hurried job of washing fruits and vegetables. Once they were laid out on towels to dry, I went to the building's front porch. Georgina and Ann were still there.

"Georgina, I've been missing you." I bent over the rocking chair and gave her a hug.

Ann sat with her back to the boulevard. "We just had a late lunch, and I'm relaxing for a minute before I go back to the shop. Boy, we've been busy. Can I get you a glass of tea?"

I declined and pulled up another white rocker, creating a triangle for easy conversation.

"How are you?" I asked Georgina.

She smiled sweetly. "Adjusting."

"She's doing well," Ann said. "Everything we can think of is done."

"It wasn't like I saw her every day," Georgina said, "but I expected her to be here long after I'm gone."

"Will there be a service of some type?"

"At the Methodist Church on Friday. The cousins are coming." She signaled to Ann. "Make a note to reserve the guest suite. Somebody may want to stay over."

"Patti handles that." Ann added a note to the list resting on the arm of her rocker.

Georgina talked briefly about Twinkle, beginning with her childhood. "She was the usual bratty kid, but I went off to college before she started school. Then I was in Europe for a while, and back to New York. By the time I came home, Twinkle was a teenager and didn't hang around much."

I didn't want to be obvious, but I was still working on Twinkle's Thursday agenda. She hadn't been here for a year, which made me think that, somewhere in those few hours Thursday, someone decided Twinkle needed to die. I wanted to know who, and why.

"I expected her today," Georgina said, "but she liked to keep people guessing. Showed up Thursday without even a phone call, and me with a million things to do for the party. I knew right away she was going to ruin it."

"Ah, Georgina," I sympathized.

She shook her head quickly. "No, it's true. You didn't know my sister."

"Did she look like you?"

Georgina was big and pudgy and pale. If I had to describe her with one word, it might be fluffy.

"Maybe like I looked twenty years ago."

Ann disagreed. "Georgina was always prettier."

She waved the compliment away and complained about taking Twinkle to the dining room. "I thought it'd be the fastest way to get some lunch, but she had to talk to every person in there. Total strangers she'd never see again. Told them about her travels while I kept looking at my watch, thinking of all I needed to do."

Ann agreed. "She picked at her food till everybody else was gone."

"You were there?" I asked.

Georgina hadn't said that.

"Not with them, but in the dining room." She glanced at Georgina. "We were making sheet cakes for this weekend, and Carla wanted to get the lunch dishes cleaned away before we started. We didn't like to rush Georgina, not with her sister visiting, so we waited, and waited."

"I *do* wish you'd said something." Georgina closed her eyes. "I'd have gotten her out somehow. She made a wreck of me, playing with her food, and talk, talk, talk about her travels and her commissions and her reviews."

"Was she always a light eater?" I tried again to lighten the mood.

Georgina nodded. "Always. You saw—well, no, I forget you didn't see her. But she was scrawny, her whole life." She looked at Ann. "I was never scrawny."

I asked, "What did she say when you told her about the party?"

"At first she had other plans. I thought *yippee*, maybe it would work out. But later, after lunch, she went to see the Bergens, and when she came back here, she said set a place for her, too. She'd canceled her plans."

"Did she learn something from Jim and Nita that made her change her mind?"

She snorted. "What would they talk about? The portrait she was supposed to paint? Harbor Village? Food? Twinkle wasn't interested in any of that."

I'd already talked with Jim and Nita. If Twinkle learned something from them, they weren't aware of it. "What were her original plans?"

"Originally, she was arriving Saturday afternoon, just about now." She looked at her watch. "And going to the festival. Then Sunday, tomorrow, she was going to paint all day on the sidewalk in front of Fran's gallery. Fran sent out announcements and framed some old work to sell, and Twinkle was going to be the big attraction." She looked at me. "People will stand and watch for an hour if you hold a brush and dab a little paint now and then."

"Did she need money?"

Georgina snorted. "She had money. Plenty. She wanted me to follow her up to Daphne while she turned in the rental car. I told her I didn't have time, but she kept after me. She finally got huffy and said she'd work it out. That was just before Katherine came. I told her Twinkle was here and coming to the party, and she said we didn't need to rearrange the table. Twinkle could have her place. Not a ruffled feather, but no discussion, either."

"Can't blame her for that." Ann's mouth snapped tight and she glanced at her watch.

"Maybe she already knew Twinkle was here." I was thinking about the immediate decision, the lack of discussion.

Georgina shook her head. "No. They'd come from Ocean Springs, two hours away. Solly dropped her off here and went into town. I'm not saying I blamed Katherine. I was wishing I could waltz off to an anniversary party myself. No, not really. I wouldn't have done that. I was excited about my party until Twinkle got here."

She was sounding stressed. I steered the conversation in another direction. "She turned in her rental car. How'd she get back here?"

Georgina looked surprised. "I don't know. She was gone a couple of hours, maybe more. How long does it take to drop off a car?"

"She had to fill the gas tank," Ann said.

"Right. And get somebody to pick her up. I don't know which rental company it was."

"They're all close together," Ann said. "Say twenty minutes to drive up there, ten minutes to get gas, another ten for paperwork. Even waiting for a ride to town, you're talking an hour, more or less."

"To town?" Georgina asked.

Ann nodded. "Isn't that when she went to Royale Court?"

"Went to—?" Georgina looked blank. "Why would she go there?"

"Looking in her storage locker, I understand."

"Her storage locker?" She blinked slowly, not quite synchronized. Like an owl.

"I guess I forgot to tell you," Ann said. "She's been renting a storage locker for years. I just heard about it."

Georgina was still frowning. "Right. That one."

"Do you have her keys?" I thought there'd be one for the storage locker, and wondered if we might discover what Twinkle kept there.

Georgina shook her head. "The hospital gave me her bag, but the detective took it."

"Okay. That's something we can look into later." Ann added another note to her list and looked at her watch again. "I need to get back to the shop. Prissy panics if I'm gone too long."

I was prioritizing my questions about Twinkle's afternoon, but Georgina began talking without prompting.

She'd taken a shower after Katherine left with me, at five. "Twinkle was back by the time I got dressed. Then Stewart brought the food and we were all busy for a while, warming the oven, getting the lasagna and bread in there and the salad chilled, and bringing the plates back in to be served. Stewart and Twinkle stayed out in the courtyard, lighting the fire and catching up on each other."

"Green salad?"

Georgina shook her head. "No, what do we call it, Ann? Tastes like dessert, but the dining room calls it salad. Strawberries and cream cheese, remember?"

"Our strawberry salad?" I thought I'd made a discovery. Had Hunter known what kind of salad he'd been looking for in the garbage? "Does it have nuts in the crust?"

"No," Ann said firmly. "Brown sugar, butter, and ground pretzels. That's the name…Strawberry Pretzel Salad. But now that you say it, walnuts might be good. We'll have to test that."

"There weren't any nuts," Georgina insisted. "And no green salad. The police keep asking, but they sifted the crumbs. They should know. They would've found nuts if there'd been any."

She told us more about the party. Solly and Michael had arrived on time, both of them bringing red wine, convinced theirs was best. "Everybody had to taste both and compare without knowing which was which. We went to the courtyard and sat at the table for that, with extra glasses, everybody laughing and talking. That's when we served the salad."

"Who did that?"

"Fran and Stewart helped me, I believe."

"And Twinkle ate hers."

Georgina nodded. "She asked for a small serving at first and that's what I gave her. Then she told people I was trying to starve her and I gave her more. Other people got seconds, too. I don't know who, but it was all gone at the end. Nothing left but crumbs."

"And when did she get sick?" Ann asked.

"Her system had forgotten what to do with food. She went to the apartment for antacid, but it got worse. We served the lasagna after a while, but the smell of food set her off."

We sat quietly for a minute, watching a shuttle bus glide slowly down Harbor Boulevard, bringing festivalgoers back to their homes or cars. Ann checked the time.

"Where did Twinkle live?" I asked. "Not just on a cruise ship, surely."

Georgina rocked. "The hospital asked that. Her driver's license gave the old family place on Oberg Road, but nobody lives there. It's an old house, not really livable, and there's an outbuilding where she paints sometimes, when she's here. Her mail's delivered to her agent."

"Fran Beck," I said.

"Right."

Ann said, "If there is any mail. Mine's all junk."

"Why did she go to see Jim and Nita? Do you know?"

Georgina rocked for a minute before she answered, staring into the distance and sounding almost bitter. "She sat here on the porch and went over the reference photos, laughing like there was something funny about

them. Then she asked which apartment was theirs and took off over there."
Georgina waved toward the Bergen apartment, directly across Harbor
Boulevard from where we sat.

"They told me she visited," I said. "Was it just to refresh her memory?"

"Is that what she told them? I don't know."

"How did she and Solly get along at the dinner?"

"They spoke, they hugged, nothing special. She asked where Katherine
was and Solly gave a vague answer. I wondered if he even knew."

I rocked for a minute. "What kind of problem did Solly help her with,
do you know? I guess it was a few years ago."

"Two thousand thirteen."

I thought I might be asking too many questions, but she started talking
again, with Ann hanging on every word.

"I think her name jinxed her, right from the start. She sang that little
nursery song and thought she was a star. Even signed her name with a star
over the *i*." Georgina had a little smile, and I thought she was imagining
Twinkle as a child. "Twinkle was talented, but portraits take time. She
wanted to be one of those big-name artists with an assembly line, and she'd
come along and add the Twinkle magic."

"She got rich," Ann said.

Georgina's smile went away. "Cleo asked about the Solly business." She
turned to me. "It started with this guy in Hattiesburg, a creditable painter
but with no training, no market. Dewey Square, that was his name. She
bought up some of Dewey's paintings and he thought she loved them. But
what she did was take them to that shed at the old place and fiddle with
them. Enhanced some features, added a wash, painted in more people,
altered some colors. Then she painted out his name and added her own.
Presto! Twinkle Thaw originals. She could finish two on a good day."

"She bought them, you said?" Ann asked. "What's wrong with that? It
might be unusual, but she can do what she wants, once it's hers."

"Right, but she can't claim it as her work. There's such a thing as
copyright. Twinkle had collectors lined up to buy her paintings, and she
started selling Dewey's pictures for a lot of money, passing them off as
her own. She entered one in a contest sponsored by a fancy art magazine.
Thick paper, high gloss, entries judged blind." She looked at Ann. "That
means the judges didn't know whose work it was. Then they wouldn't be
influenced by a big name. Anyway, the thing won."

I laughed out loud. "She really did have a magic touch."

"I guess. They ran photographs of the winning entries in the magazine,
a big spread. And some urologist in Jackson was a subscriber. Dewey

Square was sitting in the waiting room and picked up a magazine, and there's his painting, close enough that he can still recognize it. He reads on and learns the painting's won a blue ribbon and a cash prize, and, of course, he has his lawyer contact the magazine. Then he comes here, looking for Twinkle."

I nodded. "And that's how an artist gets into a professional bind."

Georgina nodded in slow motion. "Hattiesburg has some good attorneys, let me tell you. But good ol' Solly came running to the rescue."

"What did he do?"

"Dewey Square got a solo exhibit at the Magnolia Art Institute. Sold a few pieces, probably to Solly and his friends. Twinkle turned over the magazine prize money, not admitting anything, of course, and paid his legal fees. He had to agree not to sue. The whole thing got hushed up. The magazine printed a correction, saying the winning entry was a collaborative work by Dewey Square and Twinkle Thaw. Dewey must've been happy. A few months later he sent her a message suggesting they continue their collaboration. But she'd learned a little, finally. Or maybe his prices had gone up too much, now that he was a prize-winning artist."

Georgina laughed, a bitter sound.

We rocked and listened to a mockingbird, and I thought about Twinkle being a cheater.

Did these events somehow contribute to her murder? Would the cops dig up old history? I needed to go, but I had another question. "What are reference photos?"

Georgina scowled. "The photos artists work from, showing a person in a variety of poses. You combine features to make the most flattering representation. That's what makes it art, and not just a copy of a photograph. I took the reference photos of Jim and Nita after Twinkle left last year. They got dressed up, Nita in blue with her pearls and lipstick and that pretty white hair." She chuckled. "He was a lot more concerned about how he looked than she was."

"I'll bet," Ann said.

I smiled. Nita would've been more concerned about him, too.

Ann reminded me. "It was supposed to be a fiftieth anniversary portrait. The reference photos had to get them at the right age. Too bad." She shook her head.

"You'd have thought the party was in her honor," Georgina said. "Fran gets paid to take it, but Stewart, he's such a gentleman." She looked at Ann. "Wasn't there something between them once?"

Ann shrugged. "Twinkle got around, you know."

"Wasn't there an age difference?" I asked.

Ann shrugged again. "She was older and glamorous."

I had another question. "Was Twinkle one of your students?"

For the first time, a real smile lit Georgina's face. "From the day she was born. Or maybe age two, to be accurate. She forgot all that, the time I spent teaching her. Just thought she was born gifted."

"And Fran paints, too? Or just runs the gallery? She must've been one of your students."

Georgina rocked and reminisced. "She wanted to be an artist more than anybody I ever saw. Instead, she wound up running a gallery."

"That's a talent, too. I was in there yesterday, looking at Twinkle's work. And I bought one of Fran's prints a few months ago. A gift for Stephanie."

"You remember what it was?"

"A street scene. The Fairhope clock. Lighted trees along the street, with a few snowflakes in a black sky."

Georgina was smiling and nodding. "That was a book cover, on the best-seller list for months. Artists never get credit. I've got a copy here somewhere."

"By the way, we have a new painting in the big house. I want to know what you think."

"I already heard. I'll take a look."

Ann clapped her hands against her knees and stood. "We need some good news around here, Cleo. I've got to get back to the shop and do an early close. Prissy's staying open, but late sales can carry over to tomorrow."

I remembered my own plans. I got up and pulled my rocking chair back to its original position. "We see the house this afternoon. Or I do. Riley's already had a preview."

"And what did he think?" Ann asked.

I shrugged. "He wouldn't tell me anything. But he's not making plans to move in. That tells me something."

"I just hope you're not going to break his heart," she said.

I groaned. "I do have one more question, Georgina, if you don't mind. What kind of poison was it? Did the police say?"

Georgina shook her head. "They keep asking what she ate between four and eight. She wasn't even here half that time. And maybe she was allergic, but I never heard it." She looked at Ann. "She went to Royale Court, you said?"

"To her storage locker. I'll ask Usher if she ate anything there."

"And she saw Usher, did she? Did she tell him anything?"

"I can ask."

"Ask if he picked her up after she turned in the rental car," I said.

"I'm guessing he did, but I'll ask." Ann sat down again to make another note on her pad.

I turned to Georgina. "Do you still have those reference photos?"

She took a full minute to answer. "I gave them to Twinkle. They'd be with her things. The cops took all that."

Ann and I hugged Georgina and went through the building to our apartments at the back.

Ann said she wasn't stopping but going straight to the knit shop. "I'm already late. Prissy's going to be in a state."

Chapter 13

When I got back to my apartment and took the phone off its charger, it beeped to let me know I had messages.

Stephanie had called to say they were at the festival and would see me later. Much later. I heard a band playing in the background.

The second message had arrived an hour ago and was from Travis. He was standing outside my apartment, he said. Where was I, and where was this cedar swing Stephanie called him about? He'd understood it was on my porch, but he was there and didn't see it. He waited a minute like he thought I might pick up the phone. "Well, I'm going to the motel now and then I'll rendezvous with Steffie and see you later." And he clicked off. I had no idea what swing he was talking about. He must've gotten his messages scrambled.

Riley's message was third. "Hey, Cleo. Got a little change of plans. Don't come to the house until I call you. It'll be after four. Michael's having a meltdown."

I almost wanted to go to the house immediately, just to see that, but I didn't.

Instead, I went to the kitchen and made a pitcher of tea. I was thirsty and should've taken Ann up on the offer of something to drink. My cheeks felt tight from dehydration, and I could just picture the creases setting in place.

While I waited for water to boil, I bagged up the veggies that had been drying. Cauliflower and pepper and grapes went into the fridge. I dried the countertop, put out a clean towel, and took the wet ones to the laundry room, thinking all the while about Twinkle. She had arrived two days early, Georgina said. Had she known Georgina was having a party? Was she offended that Georgina didn't invite her?

As I filled a glass with ice cubes, I imagined Twinkle laughing when she looked at the reference photos of Jim and Nita. What would have amused her? What was the reason for her sudden visit to Jim and Nita's apartment? Wouldn't she have preferred to avoid them rather than explain that she hadn't finished their portrait? Hadn't even started it, in fact.

I took a small sip of still-warm tea and left it on the counter while I cleaned the floor around Tinkerbelle's dish.

Twinkle had gone to Daphne to return a rental car. Someone, probably Usher, had picked her up there and delivered her to town, where the festival wasn't yet in full swing. But artists were beginning to arrive, socializing, planning their setups. Had she gone to see Solly? Or Fran Beck? Had Fran, like Georgina, expected her on Saturday? And what had Twinkle done at her storage locker?

I took another sip of tea, carried the glass and a paper towel to the desk, and opened the laptop.

I hadn't checked email since Thursday and there was a ton, most of it junk that could go right into the trash. There was a message from an old friend, chiding me for retiring to play dominoes. "I can't believe you're really enjoying that. There's more to life than dominoes, you know."

I was indiscreet in my first reply but deleted it and wrote another note that leaned in the other direction, almost boasting that I'd been contacted about a deanship. It was true, mostly, but I knew it was petty. And I sent it anyway.

There was a note from Stephanie, dated yesterday, with links to half a dozen condos on Zillow. I flagged it to look at later.

I had consigned a dozen items to the great cyber landfill before something caught my attention. A message from the provost's office at the University of Alabama, also dated yesterday. The message was terse. Would I like to be considered for the vacant position of Dean of Social Work? Perhaps I could come for lunch and a tour of the campus?

The *oh-my-god* chorus burst into full-throated song, and I almost flew across the room and away from the laptop, tea glass in hand.

I inhaled half a glass of icy tea, then got a refill and leaned beside the kitchen window while I sipped.

Dean Mack.

Dean Cleo Mack.

It had a nice sound, didn't it? A no-nonsense name denoting a no-nonsense administrator. And professor. I enjoyed teaching. I wouldn't want a strictly administrative position. I assumed that would be an option— teaching one course a semester, supervising internships, pursuing grants, representing social work within the university. I wondered when the curriculum was last revised and if I could preview it online.

I hated to admit it, even to myself, but my engines were revving at the prospect of returning to the academic setting.

But you love Fairhope. I agreed.

You've got a great job and good friends here. I agreed again.

And there's Riley.

A few hours ago, I'd been envisioning the rest of my life entwined with his, debating the residence question, even marriage. Now I was swooning over a challenging job two hundred miles away that might not be offered. When had I become so flaky?

I thought about my life at Harbor Village. Was I missing something? Young people, maybe. And ideas. Enthusiasms. Riley had brought up the critical element last night, when he spoke of intellectual curiosity. Those were the very things that defined a campus.

My pulse was pounding and tears were stinging my eyes when I realized I wanted to go for the interview. Whatever repercussions it might bring.

I got a tissue from the box on top of the fridge and stood beside the full-length window, drinking tea and drying my face. I'd miss Nita if I left, but she'd want what was best for me. If only I could figure out what that was. She certainly wouldn't want Riley hurt, but wasn't he about ready for a little adventure himself? He always wanted to take trips. Would he consider moving if I did? I had no idea. Nita was right. Riley and I didn't talk nearly enough.

I'd been looking at something white outside my window and finally I put aside the dithering and tried to figure out just what it was. A plastic bag, caught up on one of the pink azaleas. I had no idea where it had come from, but it was definitely an eyesore. I stuck my tissue into a pocket and went through the dining area and out to the courtyard, intending to retrieve the bag.

It was easier said than done.

I'd noticed on several occasions, with some surprise, that the protected courtyard wasn't free of wind. More than once, I'd seen a little whirlwind spiral in the open space, whirling dust and leaves and whatever debris had accumulated there. That must have been what happened to the plastic bag. It was knotted tightly around branches and leaves and fat, unopened buds, looking like a white jellyfish intent on strangling the plant. I had to go back to the kitchen for scissors.

When I returned to the courtyard, I got on my knees, crawled under branches and into the azalea, and snipped at plastic. When I'd reduced the bag to numerous pieces, each one had to be worked free. The process took several minutes but eventually, all the jibbles and strips were loose and collected and stuffed into a still-usable corner of the original bag.

I stood and brushed debris off my knees, then picked up the plastic and scissors. I was about to go inside when I noticed the chiminea, still full of ashes after Thursday night's party. I walked toward it, wondering what equipment I'd need for the cleanup job.

Would my dustpan fit through the opening?

I was measuring mentally, about to head for my apartment again to equip myself for the task, when something else caught my eye.

The little Norfolk Island pine stood near the glass doors to the lobby.

The tree was at least three feet across at its widest point and over five feet tall, if I included the pot, and still decorated. But just as Patti had predicted, the color scheme had shifted from Christmas to Mardi Gras. Holly berries had been sprayed gold, and the little seedpods were shiny purple with a sprinkle of glitter. Strands of Mardi Gras beads, in purple or gold or green, hung in swags and swoops from branch to branch, and musical blow-out toys and glittery noisemakers echoed the same color scheme.

The yellow leaves I remembered from the woods were gone, if they'd been used on this tree, but near the ends of the branches, I counted three little loops of narrow, lime green ribbon, the cause of my burned fingertips with the hot glue gun. The nuts we'd found near Big Mouth Gully were gone. The ribbon loops that had suspended them dangled limply.

I forgot about the ashes and went back inside, to my glass of tea. I had an uncomfortable, tingly feeling. I was too suspicious.

But the nuts were definitely gone. Did we have a mouse? Maybe I should let Tinkerbelle into the courtyard. I still didn't know what the nuts were. Chestnuts? Or black walnuts? They were the right size, two inches in diameter, with thick olive-green husks that would've turned black by now. But they were definitely gone. Should I call Montgomery?

It seemed rather silly, but I'd rather have her laughing at me than subjecting me to one of her deadly stares, which was what I'd get if I failed to report something important. I got the phone and left her a message.

Then I filled the tea glass again, took the phone and the cat brush, and let Tinkerbelle onto the screened porch.

She loved the fresh air but didn't get to enjoy it often during the week when I was at work. I expected her to sit with me on the love seat, but she headed instead for a patch of sunlight in the corner, where she assumed her sphinx pose, looking exotic, ears turned sideways to monitor me.

I hadn't brushed her today. I hoped Katherine would follow through and put her in a painting. "You're a pretty girl."

She looked at me, blinked once, and then leaned to look toward the corner of the building. I heard someone sneeze and Debra Hollen came into view, on the back sidewalk.

I was looking at her when she noticed me. Her eyes widened and her step faltered.

"Hello, Debra," I said. "I'm Cleo Mack, Executive Director of Harbor Village. Won't you come in and have a glass of tea with me?"

Chapter 14

As someone in the communication business, Debra Hollen must've been acutely uncomfortable for the next minute. She knew my name, she said, and repeated hers as if I hadn't just said it. She stammered out the words and glanced around as she talked, almost desperate in her efforts to locate a means of rescue or escape.

I stopped her. "You're the health reporter for the *Washington Post*, I know. I've liked your TV work. I'm guessing you're not here to find a home for your aunt. Why don't you come in and tell me what you're learning about Harbor Village. Perhaps you have some questions I can answer."

I left her on the porch while I went in to fetch a glass of tea for her. I hadn't expected her to be so meek and wondered if I'd been overly obnoxious. When I came back, in a minute or so, Tinkerbelle was standing on her lap.

"She's a beautiful cat," Debra said. "I say she. Is it true all calicos are female?"

"That's what I hear. Are you a cat person?" If my cat liked her, maybe I could cut her a little slack.

"I wish I could have one, but I travel too much."

I put her glass and a napkin on the table beside her but said nothing about Tinkerbelle's shedding. It was obvious, if she wanted to know. But Debra Hollen didn't seem concerned about cat hair.

I pulled my chair closer to the love seat and sat facing her. She was an attractive woman, athletic looking and at least ten years younger than me. Her thick hair was already turning a steely gray, and she wore only a trace of makeup. Something about her made me think of a politician—a mayor or congresswoman, perhaps. She was too young, too sporty, for the senate, but her demeanor was serious enough.

I got a faint whiff of fragrance when she reached for her glass, something floral and delicate. No wedding ring but a large amethyst on the middle finger of her left hand.

"Are you enjoying your stay in Fairhope?"

Local residents were proud of our town and always gave visitors an opportunity to say how impressed they were by this little slice of paradise.

"Did you go to the arts and crafts festival?"

She smiled. "I thought it was going to be a little street fair, but what a production! I spent half a day and still didn't see everything. What a special little town."

That was what we liked to hear.

I told her about the Harbor Village purchase prize. "The pieces are already in the lobby, if you'd like to see them. This was my first festival, and I would've had no idea how to proceed without an artist friend to steer me through the selection process. Now we have two beautiful pieces and Harbor Village can say it supports both the arts and the community."

We were sparring. I'd gotten in a plug for Harbor Village, but we still had the real topic to discuss. I glanced at my watch.

"I'm expecting a phone call soon and when it comes, I'll have to leave. Let's talk business first, in case we're interrupted." I smiled. "You've been here since—when? Thursday? I assume you're researching some aspect of retirement communities and hoping to uncover misconduct on our part, either management or our employees. Are you finding what you wanted?"

Oops! There I was, being obnoxious already. Debra Hollen hesitated but finally smiled.

She told me about visiting retirement communities in Virginia and New York. "My editor wanted me to branch out, and I found Harbor Village because of the murder last summer. And now I'm here and there's another *suspicious death*, I believe you're calling it."

"That's the police term."

"As for what I hope to find, I'm ambivalent about that. A reporter doesn't win any prizes for describing an idyllic little village with a perfect retirement community. I look for something newsworthy—abuse, neglect, fraud."

"It's in our history. But not today."

She dipped her chin and looked at me from beneath her brows. "I'm especially fond of the misuse of government funds. Something I can get my teeth into."

I laughed. "We do get government funds, and there was financial mismanagement in the past, but the corporation took that hit, not government. I'll give you contact info for our corporate financial officer."

Debra Hollen had a sweet smile. "If that checks out, maybe there'll be a positive side to my story."

"And what would that be? Happy residents? No Pulitzers there."

She shrugged. "Maybe you have innovations of some sort. I've heard about classes and lecture series, voter forums, resident committees. Anything can contribute to a good story."

"I wish you'd come by the office a few days ago. We could've set up the ballroom and provided refreshments, and you would've been swamped with people and stories. How much longer will you be here?"

"I leave Monday."

I shook my head. "Too late to do much now. But if you've discovered anything we need to work on, I'll look forward to learning about it."

"I do have a few questions you can answer. Naturally. What can you tell me about the woman who died yesterday?"

"Twinkle Thaw." My gaze drifted from the reporter to the yard on the other side of the fence, where birds were gathering on the ground beneath a feeder.

"I never met her but she was visiting her sister, who lives here. I understand she was a well-known portrait artist."

"And she was poisoned?"

"Lieutenant Montgomery's handling the case. She can tell you more about it."

"I've already heard about the collection of food samples."

I winced. "I hate to hear that. I hope you won't get Hunter into trouble. He's a freshman interning with the FPD, and he was warned not to talk about it."

"He seems like a good kid. I'm not saying he told me anything, but I always protect my sources. Is there any connection to the murder last summer?" She smiled. "I read about the embezzlement online, but my source told me a few things I didn't know."

I smiled. "He's a good kid, a technology wizard, and lives in Robertsdale, which is Tim Cook's hometown. But his grasp of confidentiality may be a little weak."

"*The* Tim Cook?"

I nodded. "Harbor Village had big problems when I got here. We instituted tough screening practices for employees, began drug testing, raised their pay, and added in-service training. We try to be a good employer as well as a good place to live, and we stay ahead of problems now."

"Did you know that research says one in three nursing home residents is a victim of abuse?"

"I've read that. First, Harbor Village isn't a nursing home, and second, there's no abuse here. All our residents are here by choice and most of them are fully functioning. Independent living means just that. We do have an Assisted Living program—have you visited it?" I gave her directions. "But I'm quite sure you won't find abuse."

My phone rang. I answered and Riley asked if I was ready.

"On my way," I said.

Debra Hollen took a last sip of her tea and set the glass back on the table. "I've enjoyed our talk, Cleo. I think we would've been friends if we'd met under other circumstances."

"Thank you, Debra. I don't see why we can't be friends anyway. Let me give you my phone number." I fished a card out of the phone case and she gave me one of hers in exchange.

"My daughter will be in town until noon tomorrow, but I'll be free after that if you want to get together."

I held the door for her and took our tea things to the kitchen. Tinkerbelle followed me inside and went to her food dish. When I set out for Riley's new house, my stomach was full of butterflies.

I went down the wide sidewalk and passed the end of the garage, thinking as I walked about my list of suspects. Who poisoned Twinkle Thaw? Anyone at Georgina's dinner party, although no one had an obvious motive. She was Georgina's sister and a pain in the butt, but they were rarely together. She was Fran's business partner and no doubt the primary contributor to the gallery's bottom line. She was old friends with Michael and Solly and Stewart, and perhaps an old flame, too, although I hadn't heard anything specific about Michael. It was pointless to include the kitchen staff on the list of suspects, but they'd prepared the food, so I added Carla and Lizzie. Pointless to include Stewart, for that matter. Katherine had been there for the party prep and had as much motive as anyone, but she wasn't present after the food arrived. Twinkle had visited Usher Slump in the afternoon, and it sounded like they had a history together. Debra Hollen didn't appear to know Twinkle, but I'd keep her name on my list anyway. That made—what? Nine people?

I was about to turn left, toward Andrews Street, when I noticed Jacques, the architect from Katherine's drawing class, in the parking lot ahead. His arms had been full of drawing materials and now they were eluding his grasp, sticking out at hazardous angles. He clutched clumsily, raised a knee to take some of the weight, and teetered as if he were about to fall.

"Let me help!" I hurried to his side.

"Take the pencil pack." He turned his side toward me. The wooden box was clamped under his arm, tilted at a precarious angle, and sliding.

I grabbed it.

"That's the important thing. Got it? Okay, I'm letting go." He released his elbow from his side and turned to face me.

"I'll take these papers, too," I offered.

"Just don't drop the pencil case. Everything else will survive."

We got things sorted out and under control.

"My car's right here. I was trying to get the key out of my wallet and things went amiss. Here." He handed me the little bag of art supplies Katherine had given each student. "Hold this."

"Can I look at your work?" I asked.

He was unlocking the car. "Just hold on a minute. Let me…" He reached in to click a button on the armrest and then opened the back door and began arranging things on the seat.

I got a quick glimpse of a big drawing of the face from the gully. The largest sheet of paper was no longer white but a smooth, soft gray all over. "Did you get gray paper?"

He laughed. "Of course not. Just hold your horses and I'll show you."

The back of the page was white. He turned it over again and I saw solid gray. "This is powdered graphite, laid in with a brush. A pencil's going to take forever. I can't imagine why she recommended that."

I was looking at the image centered on the gray field. The concrete face was taking shape inside a dark oval. The proportions looked right, the color was still pale, but the image itself already had a three-dimensional look, with shadows in the corners of the mouth and at the creases around nose and eyes.

"Jacques, this is looking good."

"It's not good yet, but it will be. Very good. Powdered graphite is the only thing to use on a work this size. Katherine agrees now. She doesn't like to use it because the stuff's messy, she says. But art is messy. And it's not bad if you make your own as you go."

"I wish I knew what you're talking about." I was holding the drawing at arm's length and examining it.

He'd put details into a little section of the brow, black specks and a startlingly realistic little bowl-shaped dent that looked like a concrete air pocket had burst. I was tempted to stick a finger in.

He took the drawing and turned away from me and bent over, adding it to materials already in the back seat. "You make powdered graphite with pencils and a knife, of course. Then a mortar and pestle and a soft filbert brush, number ten for background and number two for details. I'll show you sometime if you're really interested."

"Jacques, you know a lot about everything. I have another question about trees."

"Go ahead." He didn't turn around.

"A group of us went into the woods a few months ago to collect plant materials for holiday decorations. Holly and magnolias and seedpods, some nuts. I think they were black walnuts. Is that likely?"

"In Big Mouth Gully?" He straightened up, backed away from the car, and reached for the back door.

"Not in the gully, but in that vicinity."

"This big?" He made an open circle with thumb and middle finger. "Leathery texture, sort of a brownish green? Or had they turned black already?" He slammed the car door.

I was nodding. "Blackish brown but with a little green, if I remember. Not hard. Leathery, like you said."

He frowned. "Black walnuts don't grow this far south. Not unless someone's planted them, and that's not likely, out in the woods."

"Do you have any idea what they were?"

"You're as bad as Katherine. You shouldn't go around collecting things willy-nilly. Good way to get poisoned. I'm serious."

"Well, I won't do it again. Especially now that I know there could be a rattlesnake out there."

"Tung oil," he said. "It's not native either, but there were plantations here at one time and there are still little colonies of the trees here and there. Stay away from them. The flower's pretty, but the nuts are messy and poisonous."

"But I thought you said tung trees have fruits, not nuts."

He gave me a look I'd employed myself, dealing with a particularly unpromising student.

"What do you think nuts are? Did you ever take a science course? Botany maybe?"

"I don't remember anything about nuts being fruits, if that's what you mean."

"Botanically speaking. Fruits, nuts, seeds. Review that sometime."

"And this poison that's in tung nuts…or fruit. Whatever they are. Do you happen to know if it's an alkaloid? I don't really know what that is, either, but I've heard the word."

He looked at the ground and shook his head. "I'm not really sure either. Seems like it's a glycoside rather than alkaloid." He looked up abruptly. "But you'll have to ask a chemist. I've got to go. You need a ride somewhere?"

"No thank you. I'm just going around the corner." I pointed. "I'd like to see your drawing when it's finished."

"Give me a week or two." He got into his car and slammed the door.

I hurried on my way, feeling late now. Jacques wasn't the easiest person to deal with, but he sure knew a lot.

The jelly palms rattled in the breeze as I walked by, a dry, scratchy, lonely sound that put a catch in my throat. I hadn't seen much of Riley this week. Stephanie and her family would stay with me tonight, but they weren't coming for dinner. Maybe Riley and I could go somewhere after we looked at the house. How long did it take to walk through a house and thank Michael Bonderant? And I must remember to thank him, whatever I thought of the finished project.

I reviewed the items on my to-do list. Riley wanted me to look up the Gardner Museum and its art heist, and now there was the chemical Jacques had mentioned. And the school of social work at the University of Alabama.

Oh-my-god, the chorus whispered.

Chapter 15

I turned the corner onto Andrews Street and saw Riley walking toward me. He had dressed for the occasion and looked debonair in a black turtleneck and gray trousers, with a brushed-nickel belt buckle peeking into view. His beard was short and attractive, in spite of his frown.

I waved and walked faster. "Sorry to be slow getting here. Someone in the parking lot needed a hand."

"Let's get this over with." He turned around.

Crabby, I diagnosed. I took his arm. It was nerves, I knew. I suffered from the same problem, but for me it manifested differently, usually in a private performance by my Ave Maria mental chorus.

"There's something I need to talk with you about." I was thinking about the possibility I might be getting a job offer. "This may not be the best time."

"Not if it can wait," he groused. He looked at me again and forced a smile, like a peace offering.

This house business had been tough on both of us. I squeezed his arm.

Our destination was the eighth house on the left side of the street. One level, no longer yellow but a soft dove gray, still with a porch across the front. "Looks better already." I tried not to sound skeptical, even though there wasn't a lot of difference in what I was seeing.

We walked onto the porch and all familiarity ended. The storm door was gone. The front door was different—aged wood now, with a divided glass panel that began about waist level and went as high as I could reach. Riley turned the doorknob and the door swung open into what appeared to be an art gallery. A very upscale art gallery.

"Michael calls this the salon." He cocked one brow and drew out the word as if it had a bad taste.

The room felt larger, and smelled—well, maybe it didn't smell at all. Just a faint aroma of fresh bread. We stood on a creamy tile floor that looked like river rocks in the mountains. I looked around. And up. There was a large, square skylight, flooding the room with bright white light. Around it there remained a strip of the old low, flat ceiling, now dotted with recessed lights. Underfoot, a thick, plush carpet with a geometric design in cranberry and gray and black staked out a conversation area in the center of the room. I pointed to it. "Beautiful. And it's red." Michael had baited me about my aversion to reds.

The furnishings included Riley's leather couch and a pair of chrome and leather chairs I didn't recognize, positioned neatly around a stone table on a short, inset pedestal. No stubbed toes there.

On the back wall of the salon, a thick shelf ran full length and displayed a group of ceramic pots at one end. I assumed they were more of Solly Roka's work. The Jeanine Lawrence painting Michael and I had selected for the house was mounted above the shelf.

"Did you like the painting?" I asked Riley.

He smiled and nodded. "Perfect."

There were flat cushions along the shelf, too, suggesting it could function as additional seating. I made a quarter turn and saw, not the old brick firebox, but a white wall, sliced horizontally with a black and copper fireplace that resembled a long, skinny TV. It glowed with a straight line of flames, burning silently behind glass.

"The fire is ethanol." Riley stared at it in a way that implied he didn't quite trust it.

I felt someone watching me and jumped when I saw Carla and Lizzie, Harbor Village's cook and her young assistant. grinning around a doorway that had previously led to the disgusting kitchen.

"Hey, guys!" I said, as Ann appeared behind them. What was up?

Carla and Lizzie waggled fingers at me and looked as if they might burst with glee.

"What's going on?" I looked at Riley. "You have guests." I made a move to join them, but he touched my arm, pushing me in a different direction.

"Come this way."

We continued across the living room—salon, I meant—toward what had been, and apparently still was, the master bedroom.

I was thinking about Ann and Carla and Lizzie, but the large, low platform bed—the epitome of inviting—snared my attention. It was covered with a gray duvet and had a darker gray, bumpy throw folded across the foot. There were rows of puffy pillows, which Riley probably hated. And in place of a headboard, a carpeted wall and another wide, full-length shelf, holding modern, black, adjustable lamps and an electronic box of some sort.

"The carpet's for soundproofing. The HVAC and driveway are right outside. And this control box runs the whole house. I'll have to go back to college to master it."

I looked at it, feeling the same distrust he'd displayed toward the ethanol fireplace. When I turned, I saw the fireplace was visible from this room, too. "That's nice." I stooped to look through it to the salon. "Like vacationing in the mountains."

The master bath was next, and totally redone. The floor had the same river-rock look as in the salon.

"But it's textured." Riley rubbed it with his toe. "Nonslip. We don't want any falls."

The shower was large and bright, with tile on two sides, glass on one, and was completely open on the fourth.

"It's designed so it doesn't need a curtain, Michael says. We'll see. Supposed to be low maintenance. That's a heat lamp above."

"Nice." I was using that word a lot.

The tile counter had a pair of round hammered-copper sinks with unique faucets, shaped like something you'd see at an old water trough. I tipped a handle and saw a wide stream of water flow out, almost soundlessly. A reflected row of small lights twinkled in the mirror, and a row of square baskets filled the open shelf beneath the counter. Fluffy rolled towels stuck out of one. The walls that weren't tiled were painted cranberry.

There was a big closet beside the bath, fully equipped with racks and shelves and drawers, a big mirror with a padded bench in front, black and white carpet, and a blingy little chandelier like Patti might select.

"It's beautiful, Riley," I said, "the whole house. Why aren't you delighted?"

He looked at me with narrowed eyes. "You like it?"

I pressed both hands against my mouth, looked around again, and nodded.

"Come on." He gave me a half-smile. "Let's see the rest."

We went back through the salon and into the kitchen, where Carla and Lizzie and Ann were busy setting out food. The wall where the pass-through had been now housed refrigerator, ovens, and a tile countertop above an array of drawers. Above the counter, rising almost to the ceiling, glass-fronted cabinets were softly illuminated.

The aromas were wonderful and the heat radiating from the oven felt good. A line of trays holding additional food waited under wraps on the countertop.

The primary kitchen equipment—sink, cooktop, and dishwasher—had been pushed together in a little octagonal area with butcher-block countertops. I stood in the center and turned slowly, finding everything within easy reach. I'd never imagined a kitchen could be cozy and inviting. Its window came down low, right to the countertop, and looked out on a birdfeeder and a few pots of blooming plants.

"What are you doing?" I asked the kitchen crew, as if it weren't obvious. We were having a party. I looked at Ann. "I thought you were going to the shop."

She laughed. "Just to be sure Prissy had things under control. You didn't suspect a thing." She shot an accusing look at Riley. "We weren't allowed to see a thing. Come in the back door, he said. Stay in the kitchen."

He tried to look innocent. "A couple of people may stop in." He glanced at his watch. "There's been a lot of curiosity about this house. Your friends are referring to it as Igor's lab. Let's move along."

I wondered if the people he referred to might be the same ones who'd worried that I was going to reject the house and break his heart.

Lizzie giggled as she took a tray out of the oven and began transferring little appetizers onto platters. The round breakfast table was arranged for buffet service. A kitchen cart stood nearby, loaded with bottles and pitchers and glasses.

Even the humble pantry had received a facelift, in the form of a reeded glass door, a fancy light fixture, and artistically arranged foodstuffs on shelves.

"Very pretty," I commented.

"Come on," Riley rushed me. "We need to see the rest before people get here."

We went back through the salon to what had been two bedrooms at the end of the house. The smaller one was now set up as Riley's office, with the desk from his apartment, a leather chair, and a matching credenza that must be new. The Jack-and-Jill bath was still there, but now it had dark colors, a pedestal sink, and a tiled, walk-in shower where there had been a tub.

"I told him we take showers, not baths."

I nodded. "And where is he? I thought he'd be here." I stepped back into the hallway, opened a door, and found an empty linen closet. Next to it was an empty room.

Riley shook his head. "Stressed out. He didn't want to be here when you saw it for the first time. Just thinking about it gave him hives. This is the guest room. I thought you'd want to bring Barry's bed and...whatever fits."

He was envisioning my grandson visiting here. Sweet and thoughtful, but I wasn't quite at that point yet.

"Riley, I think the house is…a total success. Light and bright, good smell, streamlined. And it suits you perfectly. But…I don't know…I'm not sure I see *me* living here."

He smiled, and this time his eyes crinkled charmingly. "Just wait. We haven't finished the tour. We could go through this door, but let's take the long way and get maximum effect. That's Michael idea. Thinks he's Scorsese."

He led back through the salon, past the kitchen, and into what had once been a long, skinny, dining room with a mirrored wall. The mirror was gone. A love seat upholstered in soft fabric with huge yellow flowers sat in the center of the room on a plush gray carpet, with tables and lamps and a modern recliner from Riley's apartment. I gasped and clutched my heart.

"Is it too much?" Riley asked.

"Oh, no. It's…perfect. No wonder you aren't making plans to move in. Your stuff's already here."

"The essentials, anyway. Your TV goes here, or mine. Now, come here…watch." He went to tall, louvered, bi-fold doors and swept them open. "This is your office."

There was a long wooden desktop with a stack of drawers at each end, wall-to-wall shelves above, task lighting, a chair. On one end of the desk, a wicker basket held a puffy cushion.

"For Tinkerbelle. He thought of everything. She'll love this." I patted the soft cushion.

"All the outlets and chargers and surge protectors are in this drawer." He pulled a drawer open and poked at the contents, but I barely looked. I'd just noticed the pair of glass doors that opened to a screened porch.

I squealed and went out into the light breeze. Hanging at the end of the rectangular porch, facing me, was the most beautiful red cedar swing, complete with contoured cushions and pillows.

"Oh, Riley! This is *beautiful.*"

I ran my hand over the cedar, which was utterly smooth and sealed with what looked like an inch-thick, clear, protective coating. "Like a work of art."

I sat in the swing and pushed it into motion then patted the cushion beside me.

Riley timed its motion and dropped down beside me. "Thank Stewart for this."

"Stewart? He made this? Goodness. I just learned that he's a real artist with wood."

"Patti and Stephanie hatched the idea."

That was what Travis's confusing phone message had been about! The swing might be Stephanie and Patti's idea and Stewart's work, but it wouldn't have been cheap, and I suspected Travis had paid for it. And misunderstood which porch it was for. I hadn't told him about Riley's house, or the possibility I might be living here, too.

I pushed the swing into motion again and noticed a narrow shelf mounted between posts, to serve as tables for glasses or teacups. Near the doors I saw a two-seat bistro set.

"For breakfast on the porch, I guess."

"I thought your heron lamp would go there." He referred to one of my most treasured possessions, purchased when I moved to Fairhope.

"What do you think?" He took my hand and lifted it to his lips. "In case you don't know, you're supposed to find the package irresistible and be willing to share it with a grumpy old guy who holds you in the highest esteem."

"You're not grumpy." I rubbed his cheek. "Shall we finish the tour? I assume there's still a laundry room and garage? And maybe I should help in the kitchen. Who's coming to this party?"

"There's one more thing before we go." He changed positions and reached to his pocket. "You can't have it yet, but you can see it." He brought out a little blue velvet box and, even at a glance, I was pretty sure what it was.

Oh-my-god, I thought once and then a second time, and then Michael Bonderant appeared in the doorway.

"Dare I show my face?"

I slapped a hand over my mouth and hopped to my feet. "Michael!"

I hurried to give him a big hug. "The house is wonderful! I hate to admit just how perfect. I know people always say this, but I really can't imagine how you did it. You barely know me."

He clutched his chest and slumped against the doorframe. "The relief! You can't imagine."

He lifted the back of his hand to his forehead in a gesture of swooning then fanned his face dramatically. "I'm so pleased you like it. And Riley is pleased, I know, if not with the house then just knowing he's finished with all my little peeves and quirks. Have you set a date to move in?"

Riley answered. "Not yet. We're talking about that." He gestured toward the rest of the house. "Come on, let me introduce you to people."

"Just a minute." He stalled Riley with a raised hand. "We have a couple of punches left, Cleo. We didn't get the glass shelves for orchids yet, but that's okay, you don't have the orchids either. And I'll be here until noon on Monday. If you discover any problems, Riley's got my number."

"Michael, I'm in awe." I looked at the den again. "I can't imagine anything I'd change. I wouldn't dare." Not even the yellow flowered love seat.

"Mom?" Stephanie stood in the doorway, peering at me. She turned and shouted over her shoulder. "Here they are!"

"You're early!" I went to her. "Eight o'clock, you said."

She smirked and gave me a hug. "You are *so* gullible. How do you like them?" She giggled and held up fingernails that looked like Patti's. Hot pink with white daisies.

She had another hug for Riley. "And the house is beautiful. But you'd better come inside, all of you. Your guests are arriving."

Nita and Dolly were just coming through the kitchen, all dressed up and peering around excitedly, more eager to learn what I thought than to see the house for themselves. They congratulated Riley and told me how much they loved everything.

"When are you moving?" Dolly asked.

I stole Riley's line. "We're still talking about that."

"What's this room?" Nita looked around and her voice dropped to a level just above a whisper. "Cleo, it's lovely. And a screened porch? Riley, you thought of everything, you sweet man. And Michael..." She reached back and gave his arm a squeeze. "You're a true artist. Not like those people in our class this morning." She looked at me and shook her head.

"When are you moving?" Dolly asked again. "I'm not just being nosy. I've been thinking I might want your apartment when you give it up. I told Wilma to put me on the list while I decide. I'd like a screened porch, although I hate to move off and leave Nita."

Jim was there, too, ignoring me to talk with Michael Bonderant. "Will you have some free time tomorrow, Michael? I need to take down that print in the niche and nobody can figure out how to disconnect its lamp. I can't remember if it's wired in or on a plug. Stewart would know, I guess, but he's been tied up all week."

"I'll come by," Michael promised him.

I found Patti and Stephanie in the kitchen, helping Carla and Lizzie rotate trays from oven or microwave to the table. I put my phone and a tissue in my pocket and Ann showed me the base cabinet where she'd left her bag. I dropped mine beside it and heard Wilma's laugh ring out from the salon.

The aromas were intoxicating, and my half-sandwich lunch was barely a memory.

Stephanie was getting her own drink and a plate of food and didn't care that she was blocking my path to food.

"Mom, did you suspect anything? Did you believe I'd really forgotten this was arts and crafts weekend? I think I deserve an Oscar for that performance. And that line about having dinner plans and not getting here until late? All that was made up on the spot. Did I always have a talent for acting or is it something new?"

Patti had a plate, too, stacked with goodies, and she wanted to participate in the complaints about surprising me. "What about Thursday, when I had to make calls and send emails inviting everybody, and swear them all to secrecy, and you would *not* leave the office? It was *so* exciting, just like being an undercover agent. Don't you think I'd be good at that?"

Carla looked at me, rolled her eyes, and handed me a paper plate with spinach pinwheels and mini tacos in puff pastry. "Try these. They're really good."

"The paper plate will be good if I don't eat something soon. Especially with these appetizing aromas."

Other people were filling plates with what Carla identified as kielbasa coins in spicy peach glaze. "And these are yummy. Zucchini Parmesan crisps."

"I'll come back." I escaped to the laundry room, set my full plate on Riley's new dryer, and took a sip of ginger ale. As I ate, I took a few deep breaths. I'd never been good with surprises. The laundry area, I saw, was full of shelves and cubbies and a hanging rack for clothes, all very organized and efficient. And in the corner a new litter box waited beside a bucket of litter. The man—one of them—had thought of everything, even Tinkerbelle.

I was about to peek into the garage when Eloise Levine joined me.

"The food is fantastic," she said. "Cleo, you are the luckiest woman alive. That sweetheart Riley Meddors, and now this beautiful house, and all that storage space. It's like a romance novel come to life."

"A romance novel," I repeated. Who thought about storage in a romance novel?

Travis McKenzie's face appeared at the window of the outside door. He peered in, grinned when his gaze landed on me, and opened the door.

Eloise threw herself at him like he was the romantic lead in the novel she'd just been imagining. "Travis!" She reminded him of the fall lecture series on antique automobiles, when her old friend Reg Handleman had presented a series of talks.

"Yes, yes," Travis kept saying, with that devilish smile and a twinkle in his eye.

Eloise went on and on. I hid a smirk and Travis shot me a dirty look. Finally, Eloise went back into the house, calling to her husband, Charlie, telling him Travis had arrived.

"Hello," I greeted him and licked a blob of salsa off my knuckle.

Travis had been good looking as a young man. Now, with a tan and a mane of dark hair just getting a few streaks of gray at the temples, perfect white teeth, and expensive, well-tailored suits, he looked like a celebrity. And knew it.

"Your message confused me," I said. "I didn't know anything about a cedar swing until a few minutes ago. It's on the screen porch at this house. And it's beautiful. In case you had anything to do with it."

"Yeah, lucky you weren't home, right? Stephanie was afraid I'd spoiled the surprise. Any word about the reporter?"

I popped the last mini taco into my mouth and leaned against Riley's new dryer while I chewed. "You want something to eat? It's right there." I pointed through the door to the buffet table.

He shook his head. "Later, maybe. We're going out tonight, aren't we?"

I frowned. "I doubt it. I was told not to expect anyone for dinner and with all these people in town, restaurants will be packed. This is probably it for the day."

"The motels are full, too. So...you were saying. About the reporter."

"Yeah, right. I had a talk with her this afternoon. She's looking into the abuse of seniors. She's already visited two facilities elsewhere. She picked us because of..." I gestured vaguely. "Our problems last summer. Her research must've turned up the news stories."

"And? Has she found anything here?"

"I guess I haven't told you..." I hesitated.

"Now what?" He bumped me to one side and leaned against the dryer, too.

I told him about Twinkle Thaw's death. "She wasn't a resident and she died at the hospital from...uh...something she ate, but she was at a dinner party here right before she got sick. The reporter was already in town, so she's on all that."

Riley appeared in the doorway from the kitchen. "Cleo, do you—oops!" He spun around. "Sorry. Didn't realize you were busy."

"We're not," I said.

He was still a little uncomfortable about Travis.

"We were talking business, but we're finished now. I was about to look at the garage. Anything new out there?"

"Let's see." He stopped to shake hands with Travis, and I went on into the garage. The back wall was outfitted with shelves and cupboards and cubbyholes and a long, brightly illuminated workbench.

Travis followed us. "Nice. I need something like this. Where'd you get that food, Cleo?"

I pointed back to the kitchen and he headed off in that direction.

"Did we finish our talk?" I asked Riley when we were alone. I was thinking about the ring box.

He gave me a grin, but low-wattage. The week had been a strain on him. "Let's save it for later. Tomorrow, maybe, when everyone's gone and things get back to normal."

"Weren't you going to make a toast to Michael?"

He raised his brows, sighed, and turned to the door. "Let's find him and get it over with."

We returned to the house. I refilled my drink cup, and we went in different directions, looking for Michael Bonderant. I walked past the pantry, heading for the fireplace end of the salon, and was nearly flattened when a woman with a blond, Dutch boy haircut burst out of the powder room.

"Jeanine!" I called after her. "Did you see your painting? What did you think?"

The artist looked back and smiled when she recognized me. "Cleo, you have such a lovely home. A perfect place for receptions. But the question is, what do *you* think of the painting?"

We walked together to the front of the salon and looked across the seating area. Nita and Dolly and a few other people were in the room, everyone doing their own thing.

"Friends," I announced loudly, "if you haven't met her already, I'd like to introduce Jeanine Lawrence, the artist who created this lovely painting, and also the new work in the lobby of the big house."

There were oohs and aahs and a smattering of applause. People moved closer to talk with her.

"I love it," I heard from multiple sources. "Gorgeous."

"Where is that location?" someone asked, pointing to the painting. "Weeks Bay?"

Jeanine answered coolly. "Well, it's actually more impressionistic than—"

Someone cut her off. "I know I've been there. It's on the causeway, isn't it? Across from the Blue Gill?"

Jeanine smiled at me and shrugged. She was wearing a flowing tunic and wide-leg pants, with a diaphanous duster that looked like a watercolor painting. She laughed when I complimented it. "It's from the thrift shop in Gulf Shores. Do you ever shop there?"

"I never shop anywhere if I can avoid it. Thrift shops must've changed since I went to one."

"Go with me some time," she said.

"Sure." I ignored how much I hated shopping. Maybe she'd take Stephanie.

Jim Bergen was standing near the painting, examining it from various angles. He looked around, spotted Jeanine, and called out, "Where's your signature, Jeanine?"

She sniffed and went around the couch to join him. "At the Art Institute, we weren't allowed to sign our work. It was supposed to be distinctive, so there'd be no doubt who did it."

"Really? Very interesting." Jim grinned at her. The man had an amazing curiosity about everything. I heard him begin the story of his loaner painting and moved away.

I found Michael with Stephanie and Patti in the empty room, discussing the size and placement of guest room furniture.

"I can have it moved next week," Michael was telling them, "but I won't be here to oversee its placement."

"We won't be here, either," Stephanie said.

"Patti can do it," Michael said.

"Are you by chance discussing my belongings?" I gave them what I hoped was a warning look. I should at least have some time to consider a life-changing decision. "Where's Barry? I haven't seen him."

"He's at your apartment," Patti said, "with Emily."

I was really annoyed now. "Good thing I never leave anything confidential lying about in my *private* quarters."

Stephanie laughed. "Emily knows all your dirty little secrets. How do you think I find out things?"

I hoped she was kidding.

I took Michael back to the salon, looking for Riley, but Katherine and Solly Roka were just arriving with a woman who used a cane and looked familiar to me.

"Do you know Joanie Ross?" Katherine asked. "The new pots are hers."

Michael gave her a hug and talked pottery, and then we all went closer to admire her glazes, which varied from smooth to rough, chalky to a burlap texture. One slick beige pot with a cranberry interior resembled the chiminea in my courtyard.

"They're really beautiful," I said. "Joanie, don't I know you? Do you live here?"

She laughed and nodded. "I was in Assisted Living for a few weeks, when I got my knee fixed. Remember the kitten that hid in my bed? But I'm back at home now."

"And still making pots?"

She nodded. "But very carefully."

"I hope so," Katherine told her. "That clay gets heavy. Solly's got arthritis in his wrists and shoulders."

"Me, too," Joanie said. "Do his fingertips tingle?"

I patted Joanie's muscular arm and looked around the room. Michael had disappeared again. Maybe he was with Riley.

Mary Montgomery came through the front door, still in uniform and towering over the other female guests. She came through a crowd like she was breaking up a field of sea ice, greeting people, pausing for a little handshake or the choreographed routine she always did with Jim. "Mr. Bergen," she said, formally, even though they were good friends on a first-name basis. "It's good to see you. Mrs. Bergen. I hope you had a happy anniversary."

I moved in her direction. When we met up, and after Nita finished telling about our dinner at Jesse's, Montgomery lowered her voice. "I went to your apartment. Your grandson's a cute kid. He told me there was a party going on over here."

I squinted at her. Barry didn't say more than a few words to anybody, and I couldn't imagine him chatting with a stranger in uniform. Maybe the shiny bits and patches appealed to a child? Even so, he certainly didn't pass along any messages.

"Are you sure you saw Barry? He's not three yet."

"That's him," she said, nodding. "I made up the part about the message."

"Come see what Michael Bonderant's done to the house and get some food. I assume you've met with Michael by now?" He'd been at Georgina's party and therefore was on Montgomery's list of people to interview.

"Point him out to me." She hadn't talked with Bonderant yet.

Maybe he'd begged off while he finished work on the house? I scanned the room but didn't see him in the salon.

"Maybe in the kitchen. And so is the food. Get a plate for yourself while I find Michael."

"Is there some quiet place where you can tell me what you called about?"

I nodded. "I'd forgotten, with all the people and partying. But I know more now than I did then. Get some food and follow me."

I bent over the cooler and fished out two cold bottles of water. When I straightened up, I was facing squarely into the laundry room, where

Travis stood with his back to me. He wore a dark suit and was gesturing with great intensity. Riley leaned against the dryer with a drink in hand, legs crossed at the ankles, facing me and nodding to Travis occasionally. It was nice that they had something to talk about for a change. I wiggled my fingers at him but he didn't seem to notice.

It struck me finally, as I led Montgomery to the screened porch, just how out of character it was for Riley to host a big gathering like this. He must be beyond ready for everyone to leave. Come to think of it, I was, too. There were still a few people standing around the table, but most of them were making up little bags of food to take with them.

Montgomery and I sat on the swing. Twilight was descending and the breeze was brisk, the temperature ten degrees lower than when I'd walked to the house. I pulled my shirt collar tight, but there wasn't much warmth to be gotten from a thin shirt. Montgomery looked snug in her uniform jacket.

"Not the safest place to eat." She planted a foot firmly on the floor to keep me from pushing us into motion. "Go." She took a bite of kielbasa.

"Okay. They may not be what you're looking for, but I've found some missing nuts."

"And where are they?"

"No, no. I mean, the nuts are missing. They should be on a little Norfolk pine in the courtyard of my building, but they're not."

She seemed more puzzled than intrigued. "What kind of nuts does a pine tree have?"

"I'm not too sure what they were. I thought black walnuts when we picked them up in the woods, back before Christmas. We used them in holiday decorations. But Jacques the architect—a man I met at art class today—he says black walnuts don't grow here. He thinks they're from the tung oil tree, which does grow here and is poisonous. At least some part of it is."

While she ate, I told her about decorating the Norfolk Island pine, tung oil plantations, and Jacques the architect's knowledge of poisonous plants.

"I saw him again as I was walking over here and clarified a few things. He's very precise about what he says, but I haven't looked it up yet. Why don't I do that right now?"

I pulled the phone out of my pocket and saw the house had Wi-Fi already. "Michael Bonderant thinks of everything." I keyed in the passcode for Riley's apartment and, after a moment's hesitation, it worked.

While I typed in the name of the tree, I told Montgomery, "Jacques the architect thinks the chemical is *glyco...glyco* something. He told me to ask a chemist. Here's a likely site."

I clicked on a link to agricultural science at the University of Florida and up popped photographs of leaves and blossoms.

"'Tung is the Chinese word for heart,'" I read. "'Each nut contains several seeds within a hard outer shell...a number of industrial uses... paints, linoleum, brake linings.'" I scrolled down and gasped when I saw a warning printed in big red letters:

All parts of the tung tree are poisonous. The seeds are most dangerous. One seed can be fatal to a human.

I turned the phone and showed it to Montgomery.

She read silently for a few seconds, then aloud. "'Severe stomach pain, vomiting, diarrhea, impaired breathing.' A bunch of chemistry stuff, alkaloids and glycosides. Whatever that is. Sounds like antifreeze." She handed the phone back. "Go back to that part you just read. About paint and stuff."

I accidentally hit a hot link and a different page appeared, but with similar content. Montgomery gave me the evil eye, but I ignored her and began reading aloud, skipping from paragraph to paragraph:

"'Tung oil comes from nuts...If you're allergic, exercise caution... Excellent for finishing wood...doesn't darken as it dries from within... Chinese oil paints are made with tung oil and Western oil paints are made with linseed oil. Choose one or the other. They can't be mixed.'"

"Send me all that."

I did and backed up to send her the University of Florida page, too. I added my own address for a copy of both.

She watched. "Now ask it who's responsible for Twinkle Thaw's death."

I shook my head. "That's a different app. But don't worry. You won't be obsolete for a few more years."

"I'm still missing something here. I thought you started out saying these nuts were on a pine tree." She popped a pinwheel into her mouth.

I explained how we'd decorated trees and made wreaths for the holidays. "The tree was one of those Norfolk Island pines, growing in a pot. And the materials were collected from the field and woods behind the big house—seedpods and berries, dried flower heads, some little tendrils off vines. All of it was left natural for Christmas, but someone sprayed them purple and green and gold for Mardi Gras. That's customary, I guess. I don't know. We didn't have Mardi Gras where I come from."

"You had a deprived life. You know what I'm thinking? Every person at that party Thursday night was an artist. Probably every one of them knew tung nuts were poison."

I didn't agree. "Katherine's an artist, and she didn't know anything about them until Jacques told her this morning. And Stewart's not a painter."

"He paints apartments. And works with wood, too, I hear. You just read that this stuff's excellent for finishing wood, doesn't discolor when it dries, is waterproof..."

"But that's the *oil*. It's *nuts* that are poisonous, and nuts that are missing. Or seeds. Listen to this. 'Every nut contains several seeds. And one seed is enough to kill a person.'"

"Yeah. So?"

"There are three nuts missing. Three times several is what? Ten? A dozen? How many did Twinkle ingest?"

"More than one. It's safe to say that."

"No wonder she died."

"Now think about the people at the dinner party. How many of them would recognize the tung nut if they saw one?"

"I'm not sure anyone would. Did you ever hear of a tung oil tree?"

Montgomery shook her head. "I'm not much of a tree person. I'm more into evil."

She got to her feet and moved around the porch, stretching and twisting, popping her knuckles, while I described the lime green ribbon loops still hanging on the tree. I told her about burning my fingers while I attached the ribbons to the nuts.

"Or fruits. Jacques says technically those terms refer to the same things."

"And where exactly is this decorated tree? In the courtyard of your building, you said? Who has access?"

I shrugged. "Everybody. It may have been out there for weeks, for all I know. And the nuts might've fallen off and rolled away."

She sighed and changed the subject so fast I got whiplash. "The detective got Twinkle Thaw's cell phone from her sister. Any idea why she was calling Usher Slump in the afternoon?"

"Why are you asking me?"

"Because people tell you things."

I sighed. It was true. "I heard she needed someone to pick her up when she returned a rental car. Or maybe she was making arrangements to go to the storage locker she rents from him."

Montgomery's eyes widened. "Uh-oh. A storage locker? Where is it?"

"At Royale Court. Where Usher's the manager."

She nodded slowly, looking thoughtful. "Well, thank you for the food and information. You know how to contact Jacques the architect?"

"No, but I can find out."

She said she'd check back later. "Right now I've gotta go take a tree into custody."

"Before you go," I stopped her before she could open the door to the den. "I've been wondering. *Why* was Twinkle killed?"

Montgomery scowled. I couldn't tell if she was reluctant to tell me or actually didn't know, so I kept talking.

"She'd been in town no more than a few hours, after an absence of more than a year. I never even saw her. Was there an old grudge we haven't heard about? Something from the past? Or did something happen Thursday to inspire murder?"

"Don't get involved in this, Cleo. Leave it to the professionals."

I gaped at her. "You were just asking me for information. Now you want me to butt out?"

"You can't help it if people tell you things, and you can't resist putting two and two together. But you live alone, and you don't know who did this."

"I've heard that poisoning is a woman's crime. Is that true?"

"I know you suspect Fran Beck. I suppose you just happened to run into her somewhere, and she happened to mention tung nuts."

My cheeks burned. "I saw her yesterday, but she wasn't talking. Wasn't very nice, either, even though Twinkle was her client, and maybe her main source of income. Michael Bonderant thinks Fran has some of Twinkle's paintings ratted away and says they'll bring a big price now."

She sighed and shook her head. "It's okay to listen, but don't get involved. I'd hate having to arrest you. No, that's a lie. I really wouldn't."

She smirked, and I followed her into the house.

Chapter 16

We gathered in the salon and Riley made a short statement about Michael, expressing appreciation for his talents and congratulations on a job well done. He ended by thanking everyone for coming. It sounded like *thank you and good night*, and people took the hint and began to depart. The skylight was dark and the house suddenly had that feeling like *the party's over*, a settling down for the evening.

As soon as the toast ended, Montgomery corralled Michael near the front door. They talked in low voices for a couple of minutes before she handed him a card and left. I assumed she was making an appointment with him. Michael saw me watching and gave a big shrug and a head shake.

"Cleo?" someone called from the doorway behind him. It was Vickie Wiltshire, the flashy, feisty, local real estate agent with her own office in the shopping center next to Harbor Village. She'd been the listing agent when Riley bought the house. I heard her telling Jim and Nita and Dolly good night and promising to visit with them soon, but all the time she kept one finger in the air, like she was pressing a button to hold me in place.

"I was driving by and saw the big crowd." Vickie joined me. "What's going on? God, look at this place. Riley!"

She squealed and trotted over with quick baby steps, arms in the air and stiletto heels clicking on the river rock tile. She gave him a hug and an air kiss, while standing on one foot, the other leg bent at the knee and a stiletto heel stuck out like an old movie siren. "It's like a museum in here. I love it. Why haven't you called me to come see?" She clung to his arm and was tugging him off for a guided tour.

I went to the kitchen, where Carla and Lizzie were cleaning up and repacking their boxes.

"Ann took some party food to Georgina. There's not a lot left," Carla told me, "but we've put it in the refrigerator. Just give it a minute in the microwave if you want to eat again tonight."

"I can't imagine anyone being hungry again. Well, Boyd maybe. The food was fantastic, by the way. Did you really not see the house earlier? I'll give you a tour if you like."

They had sneaked out of the kitchen during the party, they said, and seen everything except the screened porch. "You and Lieutenant Montgomery were out there. We didn't want to interrupt."

"Then come see it now." I led the way.

They loved it and opened all the drawers in the office closet of the den.

"If I move here, that porch will be the reason," I said. "And Riley, of course. Tinkerbelle would love it, too."

Lizzie giggled.

Patti and Stephanie popped in at the doorway, with Stewart and Boyd behind them.

"We're going to the apartment, Mom. We promised Barry that Patti would stop by."

"We'll be there soon." I watched until they turned the corner toward the salon and front door. "Has Stewart been here tonight?" I asked Carla. "I don't remember seeing him until now."

Carla didn't remember. "I barely looked up. I'm going home and putting my feet up."

"He was here early," Lizzie said. "He was afraid your cop friend was invited."

"Montgomery?" I didn't know if she'd actually been on the guest list or not, but Patti probably knew and told him. "Carla, the salad served at Georgina's party the other night—did it have nuts, or not?"

She smiled and shook her head.

Lizzie giggled. "We keep saying no and people keep asking."

"Too many dentures," Carla explained. "If you'll notice, on the rare occasion when we use nuts, there's a nut-free version, too. It was a small group Thursday night, and they didn't need two salads, so it was nut-free."

They returned to the kitchen and I went to the salon, looking for Riley. Instead, I found Travis, and he was in Vickie's clutches.

"Why didn't you tell me your ex was looking for bayfront property?" she complained prettily. "You know that's my specialty."

I looked at Travis, who grinned back at me. He had a specialty of his own.

"I guess I must've forgotten." I gave her a big smile.

Could it possibly be true? Would Travis be looking for property in Fairhope? No way. He had a corporation to run and it was based in Houston. But the mere idea made me wary. More likely he was looking for the next Mrs. McKenzie. What would she be—number four? Five?

A minute later, Vickie abandoned Travis with a flirty little wave, moved stiffly to my side without making eye contact, and spoke softly into my ear. "Do you really not have a decision about the house? That's what Riley says, but I don't believe it. Just remember, I can sell this place in a minute if that's the plan. Okay? You'll call me? Or I'll call you. Tomorrow."

I promised to remember and excused myself to tell a few people goodbye.

The porch was dark, but there was a row of white rocker switches and one of them operated the porch light.

The house had emptied out, except for a few people helping Carla and Lizzie take pans and platters and boxes out the back door. Riley was standing alone in his office, leaning against the desk like he was on the phone, only he wasn't.

I went to stand with him. "Well done. The house is amazing and the party was nice." I was expecting a hug, but there was a hint of a chill in the air.

"It had to be done, I guess. Now everybody's seen it and that's over."

I leaned against the desk beside him. "We need to talk."

"Yes."

Travis was seeing Vickie off at the front door. Both of them had their phones out, keying in contacts.

"Talk with you tomorrow," Vickie called out when she noticed me.

I gave her a wave.

"Is something wrong?" I asked Riley.

He smiled and I laid a hand on his arm. Our connection was remote and impersonal.

"Let's save it for later. You need to visit with your family, and I want to clean up here. I'll walk you home and come back."

"I'm going that way," Travis volunteered from the doorway. He looked at me. "If you don't mind. I haven't seen my grandson yet."

"Well, that's settled." Riley stood up straight. "Thanks for coming." He took a couple of steps and shook Travis's hand again, but there was no hug for me until I initiated it.

"I'll see you tomorrow. Want to go to breakfast with us?"

Finally, he smiled. "Enjoy your family. We'll talk later." He gave me a quick kiss on the forehead and a little push toward Travis.

Something felt very wrong. I was leaving my lover with a ring in his pocket and walking home with my ex.

"You liked the house, I assume," Travis said as we hit the sidewalk. "I did, anyway. So why is it for sale?"

"For sale? It's not for sale. Why do you say that?"

"Well, Vickie hinted at it, and Riley didn't seem very excited. Things not going well with you two? He didn't seem too excited about Tuscaloosa, either."

My heart stopped first, followed immediately by the rest of me, frozen in place on the sidewalk. "Tuscaloosa? What about Tuscaloosa?"

Oh-my-god, oh-my-god, the choir burst out.

Travis stopped, too, and turned to look at me. "Didn't you get a job offer? I gave you a glowing reference."

I could barely hear him over the roar in my ears. Blood flow, probably, but the choir was doing its part, too. My mouth had gone dry and my voice sounded unfamiliar.

"Did you tell Riley I'd gotten a job offer?"

"Well, it's true, isn't it? I can't believe you didn't tell him."

"There's nothing to tell."

"You turned it down? My god, Cleo! Come on. Let's go."

"What did you tell him?"

"Nothing. Give me some credit, please. I saw he didn't know and did some fancy footwork. He didn't suspect a thing. But the dean of social work! That doesn't mean you have to dump him, not necessarily. This job *he's* looking at might be more of a problem."

I looked around for a place to sit but there was just the sidewalk and the lawn beside it. I took a deep breath and then another one, and still saw spots swimming before my eyes.

"Come on." Travis jerked his head. "Let's go. What's the matter with you?"

I made it home. Barry was a doll, of course. He came running to give me a big hug, already dressed in his jammies and feeling super snuggly. I picked him up and squeezed until he giggled.

"Keebee!" He pointed to the bedrooms but I wasn't sure what he meant.

I chatted with Patti and Emily for a bit, until gradually my knees quit shaking and I could think about something other than my problems with men. It was a minor matter, I told myself, an overreaction on my part. Things would be normal again in a few days, when all the excitement about new houses and parties and festivals and unsolicited job offers was over. I didn't know where I'd gotten the silly idea that I could control anything.

"Keebee," Barry told me again, pointing toward my bedroom.

"The kitty," Emily said. "He loves her." She looked at Barry. "Tinkerbelle's tired now, Barry. Taking a nap."

"Where's Stewart?" I asked, and Patti's face contorted.

"Mary called him out to the courtyard ten minutes ago. More questioning, I guess. I'm beginning to understand this police harassment thing. I thought she was a friend of ours. Come with me. Let's go get him."

Boyd, Stephanie's big, red-faced husband, laughed at Patti, but I followed her out the garden door. Stewart was coming toward us when I stepped into the courtyard, and I heard him tell Patti he'd been helping Mary move a tree.

"Where is it?" As the words came out of my mouth, I saw the tree, still in the corner, but now a few feet closer to the doorway.

"I went to get a hand truck, but that thing's bigger than it looks. She's going to get her evidence people to come here and do their thing. What's it all about? Do you know?"

I was relieved. It was a good sign if she was letting him help.

"I thought she was grilling you again." Patti cast a hostile glance toward Montgomery. "Maybe we'd better get out of here before the idea occurs to her."

"Don't wait for me." I put a hand on Patti's shoulder and turned her toward the apartment. "Go in. I'll be right back."

Then I went to talk with Montgomery. "You saw the ribbons?"

She nodded. "Just three?"

"I don't remember for sure. Any husks stuck to the glue?" I bent over and got my eyes close to one of the loops before she warned me.

"Don't touch it. Did you touch anything earlier, when you found it?"

"I didn't get within six feet of it."

I left her with the tree, waiting for her evidence technician, and went back inside where Patti and Emily and Stewart were standing in the middle of the room, making a to-do about telling Barry good night. Stephanie got hugs from Patti and Emily, but the rest of us had to settle for waves.

"Well done on the party," Stephanie told them. "We're going to leave early in the morning, right after breakfast."

Relief. I could cope for a few more hours, especially if we'd be sleeping for most of them.

I smiled and saw them out through the porch and, when they'd gone, helped Boyd find some snacks in the kitchen. He'd already discovered the new dark chocolate popsicles on his own. Then I made a pot of decaf at Travis's request, while he sat on the floor with Barry.

"Anything wrong, Mom?" Stephanie asked when we were alone in the kitchen. "Are you tired?"

"Long day," I said. "I think I'll get my shower and turn in, if you'll entertain your father."

"He has a name, you know."

It always annoyed her when I didn't use it. I delivered his mug of coffee and found they'd moved to the dining table. Barry sat on the booster seat, between his father and grandfather, eating and talking like one of the big boys, but in his own language.

"Any news on the suspicious death?" Stephanie asked when we were back in the kitchen.

I told her what I'd learned about tung nuts. "I'm going to read it again later."

She dissed the idea. "Chinese nuts? Who'd know about such a thing? I think you'd better look for opioids. Or maybe heart meds or insulin, in a place like this."

I didn't say good night but told everyone I was getting my shower and headed for the bathroom. I took my phone with me. Once I was alone, I turned on the exhaust fan and called Riley. The call went to voice mail, and I didn't bother leaving a message, just got into the shower and washed the anxieties away.

I thought about the new house, handsome and spare, yet with charming little features like that gem of a kitchen and the pantry. And the den. Especially the den, and the screened porch. And I loved that Riley had wanted to please me. We'd be back to lovebird status in a few hours, I was sure. Wasn't I? And there was that little blue velvet box.

I was both happy in the moment and excited about the future, whatever it might bring. But I did wish I'd had an opportunity to tell Riley that.

The apartment was dark and silent an hour later, after I'd dressed for bed and dried my hair and puttered around in the closet for a few minutes, getting things organized after the busy week. I was tired but not yet sleepy, and thought Stephanie might come out of the guest room for a mother-daughter chat if I stayed up a few minutes. And if she didn't, it was a good opportunity to do some internet surfing. I'd sent myself links to the articles about tung nuts, to read at leisure, and there was still the Gardner Museum heist and Debra Hollen. And there was always email, which could bring exciting proposals, I knew now.

I padded out barefoot and went to the laundry room to scoop the cat box, then to the kitchen, where I flipped the light on, washed my hands, filled Tinkerbelle's bowl, and looked around. Stephanie must've tidied up. Everything looked fine, except the garbage can was full. Too late to take it out tonight. I turned the light off and went silently across the living room carpet to the desk at the front window.

Stephanie had left something on the couch. In the dark it looked like Barry, but she wouldn't leave him out there on his own. Must be his blankie, or toys. I sat at the desk, opened the laptop, and touched the space bar.

The screen lit up.

"Thanks for letting me stay," Travis said.

I jumped and screamed. Not loud, but a scream. I whirled around. He was lying flat but propped up on one elbow, looking at me. "Did I scare you?"

"What are you doing here?"

"Stephanie was supposed to ask you. Every motel between Pensacola and West Mobile is full. She thought you wouldn't mind."

I sighed. "You didn't tell Riley you were staying here, did you?" That might explain his emphasis on *my family.*

He snorted, pulled his pillow higher, and propped his head. "Don't tell me he's the jealous type."

"No, he's not," I lied. "But things are a little tense right now. The house and all." I was glad Riley couldn't see this scene.

"Tell me about the job offer."

I bent my knees, pulled my feet onto the chair seat, and wrapped my arms around my legs. "I haven't told Stephanie yet. Did you?"

"No. Any reason why not?"

"I just got the email this afternoon, asking me to come for lunch and a tour."

"I thought you were keeping secrets from me. Will you take it, if it's offered?"

I shrugged. My eyes had adapted to the dark, and I could see him clearly now. He was wearing a dark T-shirt. Stephanie must've raided the linen closet to provide him with pillows and sheets and a thin blanket, which he'd folded double.

"It was kind of exciting initially, the idea of returning to a campus. But I haven't gotten much beyond that point. Did you say Riley told you about the assignment he's considering?"

"Just that there is one. You two should try talking without intermediaries."

"Yeah, people tell me that. But it's been a busy week. Seems like all my weeks are busy. How come you're the CEO and have all this time for traveling around to festivals? Do you take part in every community like you do here?"

"Only where my grandson's involved."

"Well, that's nice to hear. Is Stephanie your only child?" I'd wondered ever since he reemerged in our lives last summer but hadn't asked. I talked with him frequently, but it was never about personal matters.

"There's a stepdaughter I haven't seen since the memorial service."

I knew about her and knew Stephanie had liked her. I asked about his sister-in-law, and he complained about the cost of defense attorneys.

"Does your grandson explain your sudden interest in bayfront property? Would you move your headquarters here to be near him?"

There was a pause before he chuckled. "Vickie's a cute girl. I might let her show me around, but I can't afford a retreat. Still getting my finances straightened out after Lee's death. Did you hear Reg Handleman's going to France to research that Bugatti? He's been asked to write something about it." That was a spinoff from the antique car show Fairhope had hosted last fall. "I might go along if I had somebody to go with me."

"Ask Vickie." I swiveled around and unplugged the laptop. "I'll get out of here and let you sleep. Are you warm enough?"

"I think so."

"I'll bring you another blanket."

"Good luck, Cleo. Riley's a good guy. Too serious for you, maybe, but a decent fellow."

"Yes, he is. Thank you for the good wishes. That means a lot to me." Well, maybe not a lot, but a little at least.

I took the laptop to my bedroom, went in the closet for a lap quilt Ann had given me, and took it back to Travis. "In case you get cold."

Tinkerbelle was curled up beside his feet. She looked at me with big yellow eyes, and I swear she winked.

I went back to my bedroom but left the door partly open. Sleep wasn't in the picture yet, not after that discussion. I sat up in bed, propped against pillows, and reread the two articles about tung nuts.

Then I looked up the Gardner Museum. It looked like a fantastic place and had an intriguing history.

The art theft had occurred in 1990. Wikipedia had a long article, complete with photographs of the missing works. One stolen painting, titled *The Concert,* by Vermeer, matched the print in Jim and Nita's apartment. I leaned back and stared across the bedroom. If Jim didn't know already, it was going to be fun to tell him the story. And I was looking forward to hearing Fran Beck's explanation.

There was a photograph of a stolen seascape, too, but it wasn't something I could imagine Jim liking. A dozen men were depicted in an old sailing vessel on rough seas, with patches of blue sky visible through threatening clouds. *The Storm on the Sea of Galilee,* Wikipedia called it, by Rembrandt.

I was getting sleepy by that point. I put the laptop on the nightstand and turned the light off. A minute later Tinkerbelle hopped on the bed, purring.

* * * *

The apartment was a madhouse Sunday morning. I was up and dressed early, as usual, and then Stephanie and Barry took over my bathroom, leaving the hall bath for Boyd and Travis.

"That's lipstick," I heard Stephanie say. "Boys don't wear lipstick. Put it back where you got it." I didn't want to know more.

Tinkerbelle had no patience with the change in routine and followed me, meowing, as I delivered the laptop to its usual spot on the desk. The sheets and blankets and pillows were in a tidy stack on the couch.

"We're going to Julwin's, aren't we?" Stephanie asked.

Travis came out of the bathroom smelling of toiletries. "Julwin's? I love that place."

"You know the festival has taken over town," I reminded them. "The shuttle buses won't start for a couple of hours. If we drive, I don't know where we can park or how full Julwin's will be. The exhibitors may eat there."

"We asked yesterday." Boyd was still in PJs but had his toothbrush in his hand. "Dave said come early. How soon can you be ready?"

I looked at my clothes and shoes. "I'm ready." I stuck the phone in my bag and hung it on the doorknob.

"How many cars do we need?" Travis asked. "Is Riley going?"

"I don't think so." I hadn't talked to him. "I'm going to take the garbage out while everyone finishes up."

"I can do that," Boyd said.

"You need to dress, and I need the fresh air."

I added some used litter to the kitchen trash, tied the bag, and, since it was heavier than usual, slipped it into a second bag, just for security. Then I went out through the porch.

There was a Sunday morning newspaper in the wicker chair. How many people would feel a surge of relief at the sight of a newspaper? I looked around for Riley, but he was nowhere in sight.

The sun was still below the tree line, but the morning was bright and clear, and Ann was cooking. I smelled bacon and sweets as I passed her apartment, spinning the bag as I walked.

I reached the garage and walked around to the front, where garbage containers were spaced between the doors. I usually went to the closest one, but today it was too full for my liking. I walked on to the second container and found it almost full, too. Garbage pickup must've taken a holiday. They never came on weekends, and Friday had been out of the ordinary, too, with the downtown area impassable and Harbor Village full of visitors' cars and a stream of shuttle buses.

I went to the next container, lifted the lid, and was about to drop my offering in, when something caught my eye.

The uppermost bag was made of thin, translucent plastic. Plastered against the plastic, on the inside, was a photograph of people I recognized.

I set my bag of garbage to one side and pulled the photograph around so I could see it. Then I poked a finger through the plastic and enlarged the hole enough to extract the photograph. Jim and Nita Bergen stood side by side, Nita wearing a blue sweater and Jim in suit and tie. There were more photographs behind the first one.

These must be the reference photos Georgina had made a year ago, for Twinkle to use as a guide when she got around to painting their portrait.

I kept at it until I'd retrieved eight photos that were clean and dry. Some were a little wavy, but there were no creases. Georgina had given them to Twinkle, she said. And Twinkle had thrown them away. In Georgina's apartment? Or in the lobby? I considered examining the bag to determine its origin, but only for a moment. Dumpster diving wasn't my style and certainly not when I was dressed to go out. Nita would be delighted with eight photos. Georgina was an excellent photographer, and these might be the only memento of a fiftieth wedding anniversary.

I stacked the photos, dropped my garbage bag into the container, lowered the top, and went back to my apartment.

"What'cha got?" Boyd asked when I went in. He was trying to squeeze a wiggling boy into a cardigan.

"Photographs."

I went straight to the kitchen, laid out a strip of paper towels, and arranged the photographs on top. Then, with another towel, I blotted the fronts, in case there was invisible moisture. When I was sure they were dry, I sniffed each one but didn't detect any odors.

"What'cha got?" Stephanie echoed her husband, looking over my shoulder. "Nita and Jim. Didn't they look great yesterday?" She picked up a photo and examined it. "Were these made on their anniversary?"

Suddenly I felt embarrassed about retrieving them. "Yes." I said nothing about which anniversary, or that I'd just dug them out of the garbage.

"You about ready?" She dropped the photograph and wandered out of the kitchen.

"Be right there." I folded the photos into the paper towels and stuck the packet inside an upper cabinet.

Travis was coming back in when I got to the front door.

"I'll ride with you, or vice versa. Their car's full of stuff. And mine's still over at Riley's house."

"I'll drive," I said.

I got my bag and locked up. The morning newspaper was still lying in the chair. I didn't like the look of that, like it had been ignored, or not appreciated. I picked it up and stuck it under my arm.

Chapter 17

"I've been thinking about this reporter," Travis said as we walked from the apartment to the garage.

Stephanie and Boyd had left a minute ahead of us and were already at their car in the parking lot, settling Barry into his car seat.

"I think I'll have a talk with her."

"Why's that?" I didn't like the idea, especially after I'd established a degree of rapport. "Wouldn't it suggest we're running scared? That I called in the boss because she's sniffing around, about to expose something? Or maybe she'd think you don't have confidence in me."

I clicked the remote and the garage door rumbled to life. He followed me to the driver's door and opened it for me. Riley did that, too. They were both from an earlier era, older than their years.

"Or she might be flattered you called in the boss," he said smugly, and closed the door.

I dropped the newspaper in the back floor while he walked around the car. My phone jingled and caller ID said Harbor Village.

"Hello," I said, and Nurse Ivy from Assisted Living answered.

"I'm just letting you know Pat Moon is being transported to Thomas Hospital. She's got a tummy ache, but her family's here and they heard about the poisoning. They want the doctor to see her."

"You're sure it's minor?"

Ivy spoke softly. "They brought her a bag of sugar-free chocolates yesterday, and they're gone today. You know what that does." She laughed. "But the family's concerned, so we'll let the ER check her out."

I thanked her and clicked off.

Travis buckled up and resumed his conversation about Debra Hollen. "I can say I heard she was here and wanted to be sure we're providing any information she needs."

"And what do you say if she tells you she's talked with Mary Montgomery and thinks we have a poisoner working in our kitchen?"

He laughed like the answer was a simple one. "Well, I might mention Mary Montgomery's age and the nature of cognitive problems, and…"

"Mary Montgomery's our friend with the FPD. There's a detective working on Twinkle's case, too, but Mary's the one I know."

"Well. Yeah." He tugged at his collar. "You'd need to brief me first, of course. Or be there, to keep me from stepping in something."

I drove in silence for a few minutes, around the curve and past the post office. The white tents ahead came into view, in the middle of Fairhope Avenue.

"I think you can handle Ms. Hollen," Travis said. "I need to head for Houston after breakfast."

Whew!

There weren't many cars on the streets at that hour, and I was able to do a U-turn and park on Bancroft Street, a short distance from Julwin's. Boyd had followed us and parked nearby. The restaurant was almost full but, after a short wait, we got a big booth in the back room and put Barry on a booster seat between Stephanie and me.

"Pancakes," he announced plainly when the server came. He was really a cute kid, and I didn't say that just because he was my grandson. Of course.

We ordered and then talked about Stephanie's quilt shop, Boyd's current investment advice, and Barry's daycare friends and the teacher who thought he was a brilliant child.

My blueberry-pecan pancakes arrived, showing their own signs of brilliance.

"So, Mom." Stephanie cut Barry's pancakes into bite-sized pieces. "Who's responsible for the Twinkle thing?" She cut her gaze to Barry then back to me, signaling something. "Adult vocabulary, please."

"*A duck caberry,*" Barry echoed, or something like that. Imitating his mother.

When we laughed, he repeated it and looked around for more applause.

"Eat your pancakes." Stephanie tucked a napkin in the collar of his shirt and handed him a salad fork.

"Okay. About Twinkle's, hmm, situation." I reviewed the facts for them, from Carla and Lizzie's preparation of the food through the dinner guests.

"Twinkle," Barry said.

I looked at him and then at Stephanie. "Did I say something?" I shared her concern that he shouldn't understand the topic of our discussion.

She shook her head. "Twinkle, twinkle," she sang to him. "You like that song? That looks like a good pancake."

He smiled at her and forked up another bite.

"Go on," Boyd said. "I haven't heard any of this."

"Okay. The victim plus five guests at dinner, and some of them we can rule out. Michael Bonderant?"

"The designer?" Boyd asked and then answered, "No. Not him."

"No," Travis agreed.

"I agree with Dad."

"Why?" I asked them.

"What was she going to do?" Stephanie asked. "Blackmail him? He wouldn't care. A little scandal in his life would just enhance his reputation."

Travis nodded. "I agree. Nothing would matter to him."

Boyd ate and listened.

I looked around to be sure we weren't being overheard.

"You know Emily's father, Solly Roka?"

"We met him last night," Stephanie said.

Travis gave her a questioning look.

"The muscular guy with the pretty wife," she said. "You talked with her."

"Katherine? Yeah, I know now. He's a cold fish."

"I hope he's not involved, for Emily's sake." Stephanie looked at me expectantly, waiting for me to rule him out.

"I don't know about him, one way or the other." Travis bumped Boyd with an elbow. "What do you say, Boyd?"

"Naw. He reminds me of me."

Ouch, I thought to myself. A cold fish who played around on his wife? Stephanie asked him, "How so?"

Boyd shrugged. "Conventional, no drama—but wait—he's an artist?"

"A potter," Stephanie answered.

"And an administrator at an art school," I said.

"Yeah, okay." Boyd did his bobblehead routine. "No, he's definitely not a poisoner. Next candidate?"

I felt the same way about Solly. "I'm going to rule out Georgina and Stewart. She's a cupcake and he's the rock our whole operation depends on." I glanced over my shoulder again, all the way to the front window. The people at the nearest table were talking with each other, oblivious to us. I turned back to the table. "That leaves Fran Beck."

Stephanie dipped her napkin in a glass of water and wiped Barry's fingers. "And she is...?"

"Another artist. Lives here and has a gallery right down the street. A cat sleeps in the window. Your Christmas present was a print of her work."

"Was she at the party last night?" Boyd asked.

"No. I don't know her well, and I doubt Riley ever met her."

Stephanie signaled to interrupt. "Wait—what was that about my Christmas present?"

"The street scene, remember? It's a print of one of Fran's works. Georgina says it was the dust jacket design for some best seller."

"Really? I love that print. Do you know what book?"

I shook my head. "Georgina has a copy. She's going to find it, just because I was curious."

"I need a copy to go with the print. An artist who's also a murder suspect? That's an interesting combination. Do you think anyone's ever done a collection of art by murderers? That could be my next project."

"Good idea," Travis said. "In Texas, prisoners draw on white handkerchiefs with ballpoint pens. They have big exhibits."

"That sounds so cool, Dad. Can you get me some? It's what I want for every birthday, from now on."

I felt my eyes flutter. *From me she wants condos? And her dad gets away with handkerchiefs?*

"They're not cheap," he said. "Lots of people collect them."

"Nobody I know," Stephanie said.

I had another cup of decaf while everyone finished breakfast, and then Travis paid the bill and we walked out onto a busy street. Many of the tents were already open and doing business.

"Anybody want to see Fran Beck's gallery?" Stephanie asked. Clearly, she did.

"I was just there on Friday," I said.

She might have Twinkle Thaw originals, as Michael suspected, but I didn't think she'd be displaying them yet.

Boyd looked at his watch. "How far is it?"

"A block or so," I said.

"Let's don't, Steph. You get down there in those booths, talking to people, and we'll be here until noon."

Stephanie hesitated but relented, and we walked to the cars. She hugged her father and me while Boyd swung Barry into the car and let him climb into the car seat on his own.

"Tell Granddad bye," Stephanie prompted.

He waved at Travis.

"Did you give Grandma a kiss?"

I closed my eyes and shivered, just hearing the word.

She snapped, "If you don't like it, tell me what you want him to call you. And not Cleo."

We'd had this discussion several times but never come to agreement.

"I'm just not fond of...that word."

She turned to Travis for support. "I suggested Nana but she doesn't like that, either."

"Mimi," he suggested. "That's what all my elegant friends are called."

"Mom's not that elegant." Stephanie turned back to Barry without even a smile.

"Bye, sweetheart," I told Barry.

"Bye, *swee-har*," he said, using a foghorn voice.

Boyd hugged me and shook hands with Travis. "Thanks for breakfast."

"Drive safely," I said, as I always did.

Travis and I stood waving as Boyd backed out, turned left, and went toward the four-lane highway. Barry was scowling, watching us and looking like he might cry.

"My car's at Riley's house," Travis reminded me as he held the driver's door. He went around the car and got in. "But my stuff's at your place."

"Then I guess we go back there."

He buckled up. "Made a decision yet? Are you going to move to the house?"

I looked over my shoulder, backed out of the parking space, and flipped the turn signal. "I haven't had time to think about it. It's a big step."

A maroon shuttle bus idled at the barricade on Fairhope Avenue. I got into the turn lane.

"You want some advice? Get a prenup." He laughed.

"Who said anything about *nups*?" The light changed and I turned. "Well, what's your advice? Not that I'd necessarily follow it."

"Door number three."

I glanced at him but didn't detect any clue. "What does that mean?"

"You're not ready for retirement. Playing dominoes? Jeez, Cleo, you'll be a zombie in another year. If you want to work, come to Houston. We've got a VP slot right now. You can build new facilities. And that dean's job? You've done the academic thing. This is your opportunity to go big."

"And big is...Houston?"

"Ha! No. Big is Washington. HHS." He swiveled as far as the seat belt permitted. "Develop some sensible policies. I've got good contacts.

I can put out feelers today if you're interested. You could be up there by September. What do you say?"

Oh-my-god, the chorus crooned. Like I needed more options.

We turned onto Harbor Boulevard in silence. I was trying to imagine Washington. Traffic, Jim had said, and the threat of terrorism. And what about Barry? He was at the cute age now, making big changes. I wouldn't see much of him if I were in Washington. Right away it occurred to me that a mountain condo in North Carolina might be the halfway point. And what about Riley? I swung into the garage, got the newspaper out of the backseat, and we walked to the apartment.

"What do you need for your drive? Snacks? Bottled water? A mug of coffee?"

"All of the above. But don't go to any trouble. I can stop."

While he gathered toiletries from the bathroom and packed his bag, I made coffee, sliced an apple, and poured some walnuts into a sandwich bag.

He popped through the doorway, bumped against Tinkerbelle's dishes and splashed water, swore, and disappeared again.

"Did you know walnuts don't grow here? We had them in Georgia, but there's a line somewhere." I wiped up the spilled water and then took him a shoebox filled with fruits and nuts, a few chocolates, paper napkins, and beverages. "This can sit on the seat where you can reach it safely."

I picked up the linens he'd folded before breakfast, took them to the laundry room, and left them on the washer. When I came back into the living room, he was juggling the shoebox and trying to get the pull-handle on his bag to click in place.

"I'll walk with you." I took the box.

"What's the deal about walnuts?"

I told him about tung nuts as we walked down the sidewalk to the garage, then along the drive to Andrews Street. "That's what poisoned Twinkle Thaw. And I may have provided them, inadvertently." He listened intently as I told him about the decorated tree.

"I've never heard of them. Where do they come from?"

I nodded toward the big house. "The trees grow wild back in the woods."

"Who did it? And why?"

I shrugged. "I'm working on it. Fran Beck, I think, but the why is a problem. Seems to me she needed Twinkle."

His car was parked in Riley's driveway. I put the shoebox on the front seat and walked around to the driver's door.

"You think about what I said. Washington. I'm pretty sure about this one. And I could use a friend there."

"I'm already thinking about it. But I don't know yet. Thanks for the advice. You drive safely, too."

He lowered his window, shifted to reverse, and began to ease backward. "What's your immediate plan about the reporter?"

"I've got her contact information. I'll give her a call later."

He nodded but still seemed reluctant to depart. "Do you hear from Handleman? He's getting serious about bringing an antique auto museum here."

"That would be nice."

"I think I'll invest."

I nodded and waved. "Be careful."

"Investing? Or driving?"

"Both."

The blacked-out window went up, but I waved again when he reached the street, shifted gears, and moved away. He had a new car since his last visit.

I stood in the driveway and looked across the back of Riley's house. Screened porch, birdfeeder, flowers, all very nice.

I walked onto the grass, leaned against the breakfast room window, and put my hands alongside my face, blocking the glare. I still couldn't see much, but I heard bees buzzing in the flowers. I walked back to the driveway and around the end of the house to the front porch.

There was glare on the front door, too. I blocked it and looked inside. The Jeanine Lawrence painting was the focal point, but my gaze followed the hallway that led to the den. Too bad I couldn't get another look at that love seat.

I walked back to the corner, past the jelly palms, and up the sidewalk to my apartment, which held a stack of laundry and a Sunday newspaper.

Forty minutes later, the buzzer on the washer sounded. I went to the laundry room and moved sheets from the washer to the dryer. When I finished and stood up straight, there was the broom, the dustpan, and my gardening gloves and trowel, all hanging side by side on a row of hooks. The trowel's rounded end looked like the perfect tool for cleaning ashes out of the chiminea.

I got the tools, stopped in the kitchen to put a couple of clean bags into the empty garbage container, and went to the courtyard. It was quiet and empty, with a damp, humid feeling. The sky was vivid blue straight above, but puffy clouds were mounding to the southwest. I knelt on the cold tiles in front of the chiminea.

A clay chiminea got quite hot when there was a fire inside. It consumed a pile of twigs and sticks in no time, converting them to soft, powdery, gray ashes. The trowel made a raspy sound as I slid it into the mound and scooped up ash. I waited for the swirling to settle before bringing it back through the opening and deep into the garbage can, where I watched the powder slide off. There was something shiny in the powder. My second scoop brought more objects, some dark and some shiny.

I used the trowel to pick out a sliver for closer examination. I took it with my fingers and blew lightly to remove ash. It was hard and curved, dark on the concave side with a few fibers attached, slick and gold on the other side. The painted shell of a tung nut.

I got to my feet and, in a quick movement, picked up the garbage can with the trowel inside and zipped across the courtyard and into my apartment. I stopped to rinse my hands, then got my phone and called Mary Montgomery.

"Don't tell me," she said, instead of hello.

"You'd better come, or send somebody. I'm at my apartment."

"Lights and siren?"

"Stealth mode. No need to get everyone involved." By that, I meant Jim Bergen. "I found the nut shells. Come to my screened porch."

It took her an eternal fifteen minutes to get there, during which I leaned against the wall beside the kitchen window, keeping watch over the courtyard like I expected someone to slip in and steal the rest of the ashes.

Montgomery arrived wearing blue jeans, black Nikes, and a black T-shirt. Anyone would know at a glance she was a cop. The leather holster sticking out below the T-shirt was one giveaway.

I met her at the door. "Sorry to interrupt your off day. I already handled this, before I knew what it was." I handed her the shell segment and led her across the room. "There's more in the garbage can, mixed in ashes from the chiminea. And most of the ashes are still outside."

"They didn't burn, so they went in after the fire was out." She used the trowel to poke around in the ashes.

I agreed. "Sometime in the last two and a half days. Maybe someone meant to have another fire."

"Let's take a look."

We looked at the chiminea but didn't touch it. Montgomery talked into her radio and then we sat at the table, watching clouds and chatting.

"They'll need your garbage can. I hope you're not attached to it."

I shook my head.

"This place is wide open all the time. You see anybody out here since the party?"

"Just your people, Friday. It's been cool this weekend." I leaned back to watch a little wisp of cloud moving across the open sky.

A minute went by.

"You and Riley getting married?"

I sat up straight and sighed. "I don't know about marriage for people our age. It's not like we're going to have children. We've already got some, and they might not like us shaking things up."

She chuckled and there was a long, comfortable silence. "But you might get sick. Hospitals are strict about that stuff now. HIPAA, you know."

"We need to talk about it. But he's unhappy with me right now."

"What'd you do?"

"Travis told him I had a job offer somewhere else."

She scowled. "And you didn't tell Riley?"

"I didn't see him except at the party. I haven't talked with anyone yet, just got a message."

"That would mess up the little love nest, I can see."

"He's got a job prospect, too. Temporary, I think."

"I thought you guys were retired."

I grinned and shrugged, and just then Berly McBee came through the lobby door and into the courtyard. Hunter trailed after her, looking sleepy and carrying the sample case.

Montgomery showed them the chiminea, and I let them into my apartment. They took my garbage can and the trowel.

I washed my hands again and returned to the laundry. The sheets were ready to fold, and the beds in the guest room were waiting. Stephanie usually left the sheets on top of the washer, but not today.

I was stripping cases off the pillows when my phone rang. It was Nita.

"Michael's coming to get the print down. Can you and Riley help?"

"He's not here. I haven't heard from him today."

"I tried him first, but he didn't answer." She sounded concerned.

"Maybe he went to the festival."

"I'm sure that's it." She didn't fool me. She was still worried. "Everything's okay with you two, isn't it?"

"I hope so."

Someone knocked loudly at the courtyard door. I walked toward it as I told her, "Someone's here. I'll come when I can."

"It's not Riley, is it?"

"Mary Montgomery, I think."

"Oh. Well, we're going to the dining room at eleven thirty." Click.

Montgomery was peering through the open blinds. "I thought you'd left." She held out a plastic evidence bag. "Know anything about this?"

I looked at a pair of pliers.

"No. Why?" As soon as I said that, I realized the significance. The husks I'd found might peel off with finger pressure, but if tung nuts were really like black walnuts, there'd be a hard inner shell around the edible part—the poison part, in this case. And it would require cracking.

"Where'd you find it?"

She tilted her head toward the lobby. "In a cabinet in the kitchen."

I drew a breath and squinted at her. "Show me."

I pulled the door closed behind us and followed her through the courtyard. Berly McBee was busy near the chiminea. One uniformed officer was with her, taking photographs, while another searched around azaleas and the remains of banana trees. Hunter waited in the kitchen, near the bar.

Montgomery looked at him and spoke softly. "Show her."

He pointed to one of the base cabinets in the bar. The cabinet door and handle looked like they'd been dusted with ashes. I assumed he'd tested for fingerprints.

He watched me but kept a blank expression.

"Can I see inside?"

It was the cabinet with cookie sheets. I looked at Montgomery. "We checked every cabinet and drawer Friday, when Hunter looked for food samples. Most of the cabinets were empty. There were definitely no pliers, not anywhere."

She pursed her lips and nodded.

"That's what I told her," Hunter said.

"Is that the only thing you found?"

She nodded but motioned with a thumb toward the courtyard. I was about to follow Hunter, but she tapped my arm and pointed, silently, to the bookcase beside the fireplace.

When we got there, she stuck out her arm to keep me from getting too close, and pointed to a portion of the weathered wood surface. I saw a streak on the wood but however I leaned, I couldn't tell anything about it. Montgomery jerked her head toward the courtyard.

McBee intercepted us there. "We're finished."

"Go ahead," Montgomery answered. "I'll be another minute." She handed Hunter the pliers in the plastic evidence bag, and he put them into his case and followed McBee.

"What were you showing me on the counter?" I asked.

"They pretty well cleaned it up getting samples, but there was a streak. Probably where the nuts were cracked, then later the shells were brushed up and dumped in the ashes, after the fire burned out. The pliers have flecks of gold paint and little pieces of nut fiber in the teeth. That pretty well locks it down."

I imagined the events unfolding during the party. Fran must've seen the tung nuts and left the table long enough to crack them, chop them, and add them to Twinkle's salad. Other guests might've noticed her absence, but this was Sunday, almost three days later. Memories fade quickly.

"If there were nut shells on the bookcase, why didn't someone notice?"

Montgomery never looked happy, but the look she gave me held an abundance of displeasure. "That's the sort of thing that happens when a little police force gets stretched to cover a big festival. We didn't know anything about tung nuts on a pine tree until last night and the shells were already in the ashes then. Nobody was looking for a smear."

She was annoyed with both of us—with herself for not finding the shells or the smear, and with me for noticing.

"You didn't see it, but there's a name etched on the pliers."

"Oh?"

"S. Granger."

I drew a deep breath and shook my head. "No. Not Stewart. They're his pliers, but he didn't poison anybody."

"I have to talk with him again."

"Talk all you like. Stewart doesn't have anything to do with this. I'm sure."

She was on the verge of exploding. "I didn't say he did. I'm willing to bet the pliers are wiped clean, and he's not an idiot, he wouldn't wipe off the prints and leave his name in plain sight. But I don't know if the poisoner overlooked his name or hoped to implicate him."

"He always has his tools with him. I saw his belt coiled on the bottom shelf of the food cart when he left Thursday night. He keeps it handy in case he gets an emergency call."

"That's good to know, but I still have to talk with him." She turned to depart. "There was one whole nut in the ashes. Any idea where Stewart is today?"

"I can call him if you like."

She shook her head. "No. I'll take it from here."

"Have you talked with Fran Beck?"

She grinned and shifted to cop-talk. "The murder investigation is ongoing. We have no comment at this time."

Chapter 18

Riley was sitting on my screened porch.

I shot through the living room and jerked the door open. He stood up and turned toward me, distracted and still talking on his phone. "Here she is now." He gave me a smile.

I zipped to his side and gave him a hug, resting one hand against his chest. I could feel his heart beating. Maybe that was an omen? Maybe romance was still alive, too?

"Two o'clock? Isn't that nap time?" he said into the phone. He cocked an eyebrow, put one arm around me, and ruffled my hair. He kissed my forehead absently, said "okay" a couple of times, then ended the call and dropped the phone into a shirt pocket.

"Nita and Jim are going to the dining room for lunch. Bonderant's with them."

"I'll bet the dining room's full, with the festival in town."

"Then let's go somewhere else. I've had enough socializing for a while."

He drove us to a steakhouse near the interstate, and on the way told me about his conversation with Nita. "I said we'll come by later and get the print down. Did you read about the art heist?"

"I did. Very interesting. Must've been a lot of copies made over the centuries."

"Did you notice anything odd about this one?"

"Apparently not. What?"

"I didn't notice at first, but I've been back for another look. The entire perimeter's missing."

"What?"

He grinned and nodded. "Just like the original would look today, after being cut out of its frame."

"Now why would anybody...?" I had a sudden thought and gaped at him. "It *is* a print, isn't it? It couldn't be the original?"

He laughed happily as he braked for a traffic light. "I expected Jim to ask that, not you. It's not *impossible* that it's the missing painting, but what we know for sure is that someone wanted people to *think* it was."

I felt a sudden resentment toward Fran Beck. "She might've called it a print, but she should've said a *fake*, meant to deceive. She was Twinkle's agent, you know."

"Twinkle painted it, but Jim and Nita got it from Fran? I didn't quite follow all that the other night." He gave a signal and slowed to turn into the parking lot.

"They really weren't too clear about it. Maybe we can get it straight today. I hope we find her signature on the receipt. One thing I'm thinking is it's an awfully fancy frame for a print, but I guess it was intended for their portrait."

We parked and walked into the restaurant and almost immediately were seated in a quiet booth. The server brought hot, crusty bread and took our orders, and finally Riley changed the topic.

"I'm sorry about the house."

"I like the house." I had dreaded this conversation, but I was ready to get it over with.

He fiddled with forks and spoons. "It was wishful thinking. I thought we'd have more room, more privacy, more time together. And you'd realize how irresistible I am." He looked up and grinned.

It was his most fetching pose. I reached across the table to take his hand. "The house is amazing. I've had trouble thinking logically about it. I love it, you know."

"Love it so much you want to leave town."

I withdrew my hand. "That's an overstatement. I'm curious about the deanship. That's all, so far. Would you go with me?"

He gave me a quick, startled look, and then glanced away, shaking his head. "I haven't recovered yet. My hearing's playing tricks. I thought you said something about me moving to Tuscaloosa."

"Haven't recovered from the party?"

He nodded. "It went on too long. Too many people. And more socializing this morning. You think you had a math block when you got here? You should see Bonderant. We settled up this morning. The man can't add. He guesses at percentages. I don't know how that happens."

"I tried to call you."

"We were in town and we walked through part of the festival before it got crowded. Phone service is spotty, you know. Then I went by the house for a final look."

I was shocked. "A *final* look? Oh, Riley. No."

He corrected me. "A final look before Michael leaves. I wanted to see it in the cold light of day, with no distractions."

The server brought our food and extra napkins, refilled our drinks, and said she'd check back soon.

Conversation suffered for several minutes while we ate. I was first to break the silence. "I went to the house this morning, too."

"You don't have a key." He laid his fork aside and took out his keys.

"I looked in windows."

He removed a key and slid it across the table to me. "And? What did you think?"

"I thought it seemed lonely without you there." I got out my key ring, but he took it from me, forced the ring open with his thumbnail, and added the new one.

"Tinkerbelle would fix that. Just imagine it's summer, you're sitting on the porch with your cat and a glass of tea, the fan is turning." He looked cheerier, just saying the words.

The server returned to check on us, breaking the spell. As we ate, I told him the little I knew about the dean's job and that I'd learned I was under consideration when an old colleague phoned. We ate in silence for a minute.

"I don't dislike Travis, not really. But I hated the idea you'd told him something that important without mentioning it to me."

"I didn't tell him anything," I protested. "Someone called him to inquire about me. Travis should've called me immediately, but he didn't. And by the way, he offered again to find me a VP slot if I want to move to Houston. That's strictly a business offer."

"Right." He didn't believe it. "Is it something you're considering?"

"Of course not. Even Travis doesn't think I should do it."

"He thinks you should stay here?"

"No." I hesitated. "He thinks I should go to Washington, of all things."

There was another pause, followed by another grin. "You'd do that? What if it's not in Washington?"

"It?"

"My job offer. If I take it."

I threw my hands into the air and let them drop to my lap. "You haven't told me anything about it. Is it definite? Is that why you've lost interest in the house?"

He denied it. "I haven't lost interest. I'm just not pushing it, not with… other things going on. My offer is like your dean's job—a possibility if I want to pursue it."

"I thought you called it a command performance."

He relented slightly, shrugging. "Only if I want to stay in the good graces of the department. If I've really retired, that's not important."

We'd finished our meal when he reached out and covered my hand with his. "I'm always half afraid you'll go back to him."

I laughed. "Get over it. It's been twenty-five years. He's not my type. But he is Barry's grandfather, so we're stuck with him. Did I think about that when I was twenty-two? Nooo."

He grinned. "And what is your type, Ms. Mack?"

I smiled and squeezed his hand. "He's not a type. He's one of a kind."

As we walked to the car, I told Riley about Twinkle's misuse of Dewey Square's paintings and how Solly had come to her rescue. "Do you think she'd fake a stolen painting and offer it for sale, after having one narrow escape already?"

He chuckled. "Isn't that precisely who would—someone who's ethically challenged?"

"I suppose. I read about a chemical test that tells the age of a painting from a tiny chip of paint. She knew a replica wouldn't fool the experts."

"If she put a big enough price tag on it, there'd definitely be experts involved, but there's a lot of financial incentive before the alarms are triggered." He walked to my side of the car and held the door for me.

"This isn't necessary, you know. I can open doors."

"I'm just letting the heat out before I get in." He laughed, closed the door, walked around to the driver's side, and got in. "Jim's not out any money, is he?"

"Just the deposit. It was substantial, but they'll probably get it back."

We headed for Harbor Village, and I continued to think about the replicas.

"Twinkle and Fran made the perfect team. Twinkle had the artistic skill and the proclivity, Fran had the contacts and found buyers. But I'm beginning to wonder if the replica business worked that way. Remember what Georgina said? Twinkle saw the photographs and laughed hysterically. I think that's important."

He slowed to feather into traffic at the traffic circle and drove in silence for a few minutes. "You do think Fran poisoned Twinkle, don't you? What was the reason?"

"I wish I knew. She'll profit from Twinkle's death." I told him what Bonderant had said about the value of Twinkle's paintings doubling immediately. We rode in silence for a minute and then I admired the afternoon. "Wish we were going to the pier."

"We can, as soon as we get this picture down and take a look at it."

I brought him up to date on tung nuts and pliers and reminded him who had attended Georgina's dinner. "I just wish the cops would get beyond Stewart and focus on Fran Beck."

"What about the guy you named—Solly Roka. Do you know him?"

"He was at the party last night. He's Katherine's husband and Emily's father, remember? You retrieved him from Georgina's party Thursday night?"

"Right. Bit of a dud, wasn't he?"

I shrugged. "People seem to think so. I thought he was nice."

We parked in his usual spot in front of his building and walked across the street to Nita and Jim's.

"I'm thinking it's going to be a paint-by-number," I said. "Did you ever do one of those?"

We were laughing when we got to the Bergen apartment.

"Here they are!" Jim boomed as he let us in at the front door. He got right to the business at hand. "Michael's here. And Dolly, of course. Ready to tackle the job?"

Michael Bonderant got up from the couch, shook Riley's hand, and gave me a hug. "You still like the house? Found any problems yet?"

"I like the house very much."

"Did you stay there last night?" Dolly snickered.

"Stephanie was here, with her family." I hoped I wasn't blushing. It had been the bane of my life, and Dolly would pounce if she noticed.

Nita stepped forward and took charge of the conversation. "We were waiting for you, Riley. Jim can reach, but I don't want him climbing. At our age, hurt is forever."

We moved to the dining room. I stood with Nita near the table.

Dolly pulled out her usual chair and sat. "Let's get the show on the road."

Michael fumed as he examined the picture. "I specified exactly how the lamp should be done, then Fran sends in some jackleg who thinks he knows better. Let's see if we can't do this without moving the buffet. It weighs three hundred pounds."

The men discussed who would be on the ladder, who would remove the lamp, who would disconnect the plug, what shape bracket they were likely to find, and how to remove the picture from it.

"We'll need to go straight up," Michael said, "but the plug…I just hope it's not hard-wired."

"I hope the lamp's secure," Nita fretted. "It's brass, so the corners are sharp. Be careful. It may be heavy."

"If it's not attached, we can just lift it off," Michael said.

He couldn't quite reach it, with the buffet taking up so much real estate.

Riley wanted to remove the lamps from the buffet, but that left the area in shadow.

I turned away. This simple task was taking forever.

There were scuffling sounds and muttered oaths about top-heavy frames and tippy lamps.

"Stewart put it up there by himself?" Dolly asked.

"No," Nita said. "Stewart wasn't here. Fran's electrician brought his own helper. No, that was the seascape, wasn't it? We should've waited for Stewart. Maybe we should wait for him now. Michael, can you take the lamp off first?"

I looked again and saw him prodding the brass lamp. It didn't move.

"Then let's hope it's secure." He changed directions and tugged at the lamp, and all at once it was loose and sliding. He grabbed it.

"Look out!" Jim said.

"I can't put it down," Michael warned. "The cord's too short. I'm stuck. Riley, can you and Jim get the frame? It won't be heavy now."

Riley was already on the ladder. He grasped one side and the bottom of the gold frame and lifted the picture up and off its bracket. "Jim, can you reach it?"

He could, by stretching across the buffet.

Riley backed down the ladder, still holding one side of the frame, and they moved a few feet away and leaned it against the wall. There was a big sigh and the giddy laughter of relief. Dolly clapped. Nita checked on Jim, and Riley went back up the ladder to unplug the lamp and pass the cord to Michael.

And just like that, the deed was done. The wall looked stark, with just a metal bracket and a single electrical outlet centered high above the buffet.

"What a production," Riley grumbled.

"I think the electrician was fooled by the seascape," Jim said. "He got the outlet too high. That picture was twice the size of this one."

"Okay, what's next?" Dolly asked.

"The seascape," Riley repeated to himself.

"You remember," Nita prompted. "The first painting Fran loaned us?"

"I know nothing about any seascape," Michael fumed. "Twice as large as this? I certainly hope not. This niche was designed for a portrait exactly this size. Why would she put some monstrosity in here?"

"It was available," Jim said.

"Jim liked it," Nita said.

"I remember it," Dolly said.

Riley was busy with his phone. After a minute, he held it out to Nita. "This isn't it, is it?"

Nita looked at the phone, frowned, and grabbed at her husband's sleeve to get his attention. "Jim? Look at this."

Jim took the phone, stretched out his arm for a distant view, moved it back near his eyes, and repeated the sequence. "Any way to enlarge it? Remember that patch of blue sky, Nita? That always looked a little odd to me." He tapped the phone screen and the display changed.

"Oh, Riley. We lost it." She took the phone from Jim and passed it back to Riley, who clicked around, recovered the image, and held it out for them to look at.

Jim avoided touching it but bent forward, nodding. "It's close. I can't say for sure, but it's close."

Riley passed the phone to me.

I looked at the image, did a double take, and looked at him. "*The Storm on the Sea of Galilee.* Another one?"

"The only seascape Rembrandt ever did." Michael reached for the phone. "I don't believe it. Let me see that."

"Stolen from the Gardner Museum of Art in Boston," Riley said, "in nineteen ninety. Just like the Vermeer."

Dolly screeched. "Stolen? Is that what you said? Jim, what have you been hiding? Let me see!" She scurried around the table.

Michael had the phone by that point, and held it so Dolly could look.

Jim looked from one of us to another and then staggered backward toward the wall. Nita grabbed for him.

"Stolen?" He hit the wall with a thud but stayed erect.

I couldn't take the drama. I went to the side of the dining room and knelt in front of the Vermeer.

Michael joined me. "Like a zoo."

"Welcome to my world. How do we tell if this is a print?" A dean's job was sounding better and better.

"It's not always easy." He straightened the frame. "It's Vermeer, we know that much. Now, is it a print?" He tipped it various ways. "I don't see pixels, but they use that giclée process and print on canvas. Wrap the edges, add a gloss finish that looks like varnish…they can even tint it to make it look old. Add a few layers of dust and grime and…*voilà*. A new thing I've read about is this powder you mix into paints, so the chemical spectrum looks old." He patted my hand. "But don't worry about the pieces you just bought. They're originals. I vouch for them personally."

"I'm wondering about this one. Is it a print? Or an original?"

"Definitely not *the* original." He stood up, groaned, and bent over to rub his knees. "I don't even have to look to tell you that much. The original was done by Vermeer."

Jim had joined us. "How do we know this isn't the original, if it's missing?"

Michael laughed and took my hand to help me up. "Because the original's worth a hundred million dollars. Actually, I don't know what it's worth or where it is. But I know a few places it's *not*, and one of them is Harbor Village." He looked at Jim. "Stolen, you said? No, wait, that was the seascape, wasn't it? Now I'm getting confused. It's contagious." He looked to Riley for clarification.

"Both the Rembrandt and the Vermeer were stolen," Riley said, "almost thirty years ago. Part of the biggest art heist in history."

"Whoa now!"

"Don't get excited, Jim," Nita said. "This is a print, not the original."

Riley raised outstretched hands as if to calm them. "Not *the* original, I'm sure, but it may be *an* original. That's what we're going to check. I should've brought a magnifying glass."

"Use this." Jim pulled a little black plastic box from his pocket. He snapped it open to reveal a small but powerful magnifying glass.

Riley used it to examine the surface from various distances and angles. "No printer dots." He looked at Michael. "You know how to take this thing apart?"

"Take the frame off? That should be easy enough." He leaned the frame forward and examined the back. "There's no paper cover, just a backing against the canvas. Foam core or something like it, to prevent punctures." He looked at Nita. "Do I have your permission to disassemble it? We might need professional help to get it back together."

"What tools do you need?" she asked.

"A screwdriver."

"And pliers," Riley said. "And a big towel. We'll lay it face-down."

They worked several minutes and finally separated three parts—the gold frame, a black metal filigree that Jim called a spacer, and the image itself.

Michael peeled the backing away. "Well, it's on canvas, not a board."

"We'll look through it from the back, see if there's thick and thin spots. Overlap, chipping—anything of that nature." Riley looked at Nita. "We need a strong light."

Nita turned to Jim. "Your new lamp."

"Right." He stood. "I've got an adjustable LED reading lamp, boys. Come this way." He led them to his recliner and swiveled the gooseneck lamp around.

"Tilt it up," Riley said. "We want to look at the light through the canvas."

Nita, Dolly, and I stood to one side, where we weren't looking directly into the bright, glittery light. Jim was close behind Riley and Michael, looking over their shoulders. Minutes dragged by.

"See this?" Michael's voice was soft, as if he were talking to himself. "A seam."

"And here." Riley pointed to a different spot. "All four sides."

"The original was cut out of the frame?" Michael asked.

"Right," Riley indicated another spot. "I saw this cracking the other night. Think the canvas might've been rolled?"

"And look at this." Michael rubbed another spot.

They examined nail holes and canvas thread counts and finally seemed satisfied.

"What are you finding?" Jim asked.

"What's it worth?" Dolly asked.

Michael waved for Riley to take the lead and he did, speaking slowly and deliberately. "It appears to be an original painting." He pointed to the seams. "Additional canvas has been grafted on to allow it to be stretched. There are no old nail holes…"

Jim interrupted. "But remember, the original had its border cut off."

They put the picture aside and we all sat down at the dining table.

"Let's get the timeline straight," I proposed. "When did you get it, Nita? July?"

She took a notepad and pencil out of the buffet and brought them to me. "We got the seascape first, on our fiftieth anniversary, which was a year ago Thursday." She looked at Jim. "The electrician brought it in his truck, remember?"

"It was too big for a car," Jim said. "Almost six feet high and over four feet wide."

"He had his helper with him," Nita remembered.

I jotted down the basic facts. Jim turned the pad around to read what I'd written then gave it back and repeated the painting's dimensions. I added them.

"We kept it for two months, maybe three, then she replaced it with this one. July, do you think?" Nita consulted Jim.

"About. She'd found a buyer." He looked at my notepad and signaled with writing motions.

"Wait a minute," I said. "The seascape arrived in March, brought by Fran's electrician and his helper. Was Fran with them?"

"No," Nita and Jim agreed.

Pooh.

"Georgina was," Jim said.

"She's always helped Fran." Nita looked from me to Michael. "Didn't she?"

He shrugged and nodded. "Yeah. Always the teacher."

I started to write, but Nita stopped me.

"Wait. Jim?" Nita held one finger to her lips then bounced it in midair, emphasizing her growing certainty. "She wasn't here when they put it up, but she came that afternoon to see the print in place. And that's when she took our photographs."

"Right." Jim drawled, slowly coming into agreement with her. "Right, Nita." He looked at me. "Color coordinated. I wore a clipper blue tie, and Nita wore her clipper blue sweater."

"And my pearls," Nita said.

They were doing a good job of describing the photos from the garbage.

Jim frowned. "Never even saw the pictures. Do you suppose Georgina could find them?"

I interrupted and steered them back on topic. "The seascape arrived in March and was here for how long?"

"Three months," they agreed.

I dated the first entry March and read my notes aloud. "The electrician and a helper installed the plug and hung the seascape, Georgina came later to look at it and take photos, and it stayed for three months. That would be late June." I printed the word June and underlined it. "Who took it down?"

"Who was it?" Nita looked at her husband.

"Stewart?" Dolly suggested.

"Fran?" I proposed.

Nita's eyes narrowed. Once again she pointed at Jim in time with her words. "Stewart sent a helper."

"Drew. He brought that six-foot ladder." He pointed to the wood floor in front of the buffet. "Remember? Got paint on the floor."

"I won't forget that. Stewart came the next day and cleaned it up."

"Drew got the seascape down and this one up and the lamp on it. Then he walked that big painting across the street." Jim pointed to my notepad. "To Georgina's apartment, where somebody was picking it up. He's a little guy, you know. A fresh breeze could've blown him over there."

"And the Vermeer stayed up until today." I wrote the date along with Riley and Michael's names, as the people who'd removed it. "You know, late June was when I visited you for the first time."

"I remember," Nita said.

"The seascape was up then." Riley was looking at me. He indicated the chair at the end of the table. "You sat there while we played Mexican Trains. Right in front of it."

"Oh, Riley," Nita cooed.

Dolly interrupted. "I feel like I've missed out, being sick. What's the point of all this picture business?"

Riley jumped right in, speaking like a trial lawyer wrapping up his case. "There aren't that many stolen masterpieces in the world, but this apartment has housed copies of two in the last year. Jim and Nita didn't ask for them, they didn't even like them especially—the paintings just appeared. I find that curious."

"When you put it like that..." Dolly said.

"Jim and Nita thought they were prints," Riley went on, "mechanical copies of the originals. But that's not correct, at least for this one. An artist painted it, duplicating the original, even to the trimmed canvas. I think a projector was used to get this painting as close as possible to the original, as it would look today."

"If it still exists," Michael said.

"Good point," Jim said. "Nobody's seen it for twenty-five years."

"Is that legal, copying a famous painting?" Nita asked.

"It's common practice," Bonderant assured her. "That's how students learn."

"So now what?" Dolly pressed. "It's a real painting, but you can't sell it. It's a fake. You don't even own it, do you?"

Jim scowled and asked Bonderant. "What would it bring at an upscale auction?"

Bonderant shrugged but named an eye-popping value.

I thought we should get the conversation back on track. "Dolly asked the right question. Now what? We have one replica of a stolen painting, knowledge of another one, and one murdered artist. What's the connection? I'm sure there is one."

"Nita, we need coffee," Jim said.

She moved immediately toward the kitchen.

I took the opportunity to move, too, but in the opposite direction. I'd just remembered something. "I need to run back to the apartment for a minute."

Riley volunteered to go, but I pleaded a need for fresh air and let myself out quickly.

The air was cooler. Shuttle buses were returning with passengers and going out again empty. I crossed the street behind one bus and waved to the riders, then waited on the median while an empty bus, followed by two cars, passed me in the outbound lane.

My building was quiet. There was no one in the lobby but, as I neared my door, I heard Tinkerbelle. I stopped to stroke her head. "Pretty girl. Did you miss me?"

She sashayed to the kitchen and meowed, telling me what she'd really missed. I added a little food to her dish, then opened the cabinet and pulled out the bundle of photographs. I talked to the cat as I removed the paper towel wrapping. Would she ever take food for granted, after her weeks of living in the woods? I was beginning to think it was unlikely.

The photographs were four inches by six inches, on glossy paper. I locked up the apartment and looked at the top photo as I walked through the building. Nita looked stoic and regal, dwarfed by the dressed-up, smiling Jim. Clipper blue was her color, all right. Behind them, and just even with Nita's shoulder, the lower edge of a dark painting came down behind the buffet lamp. It was too big to be the Vermeer and lacked the regularity of its black-and-white floor tiles.

Was it the seascape?

I failed to notice Georgina at first. She was standing at her apartment door, her back to me, a large tote in one hand and a thin wooden case in the other. She muttered and struggled, and the case banged against the door, bouncing it out of reach.

"Hi there." I held the photographs behind me. "Need some help?" What was I going to do with the photos if she accepted?

Georgina crouched over the items she held. "No! No, I've got it."

She pinned the wooden case against the wall with her body, leaned in to grab the knob, and closed the door with a bang.

The glance she directed over her shoulder was almost furtive. "Thank you." She gripped the wooden box again. But she didn't move.

I hesitated. The box was golden oak, streaked and smeared with every color in the rainbow. An artist's paint box. Twinkle's? It must hold emotional significance for Georgina.

I took a hesitant step. Georgina looked over her shoulder again, and I sucked in a quick breath. She looked terrible. Her eyes were swollen and her face contorted and gray. Grief had caught up with her.

I searched for words of comfort. "How are you, Georgina?"

She still hadn't moved. "Fine. I'm going out."

"Do you need a driver?"

"No. I want to be alone."

That was definite.

"Well, call if you need me."

She said she would, and I walked on, uneasy and still concealing the photographs. The festival would end at five, and Ann would be home soon after that. I would ask her to check on Georgina before bedtime.

Riley was waiting just outside the door.

"Everything okay?"

I nodded and looped my arm through his. "Georgina looks awful but she's going out."

We waited for a car to pass. "Let's don't let this discussion drag on," Riley said. "If we're going to the pier, I'd like to get there in time to see the sunset."

Chapter 19

Jim, Nita, Dolly, and Michael Bonderant were seated in the Bergens' living room when Riley and I returned. They fell silent when we entered, and everyone rotated slightly to face us. A cup of coffee steamed on the table beside my chair. I placed the photographs face down on the wide leather arm, sat, and picked up the cup.

"All right, Cleo," Jim said. "Who did it?" He waved for me to take the floor.

I began by clicking through the guest list for Georgina's Thursday night dinner and then summarized Twinkle's trip to the ER. "Montgomery said Twinkle consumed a toxin, at about the time of the dinner."

All this was background for most of us, but some of the details were new to Dolly and Michael. They asked questions about the food served at the party.

"Our kitchen staff prepared the meal, but they weren't there to serve. If they were involved, we'd need to ask a different question—not who killed Twinkle, but why someone delivered a random dose of poison."

Nita and Dolly and Jim knew the kitchen staff and agreed they weren't suspects.

"Tell us about Katherine." Jim consulted the legal pad resting on the arm of his recliner.

I drank more coffee before describing Katherine Roka's involvement in preparing the courtyard for the party. "She went to Jesse's with us and, by the time we returned, Twinkle was already ill."

"Okay." He put a checkmark on his paper. "Debra Hollen."

"Debra Hollen is a reporter from Washington—"

"Debra Hollen?" Michael interrupted. "I know her! She's here? In Fairhope? I should invite her to tour your house, Riley."

"She's been in town since Thursday," I said, "investigating retirement communities for an assignment. She knows about Twinkle's death and will probably include it in whatever she writes."

"I think we can rule her out." Nita looked to Jim for confirmation. "She would've left town immediately if she'd been involved."

Jim nodded. "Sensible girl. No motive. I'd mark her off."

"How old is she?" Dolly frowned.

"Forty?" I guessed.

She looked at Jim. "I thought you said girl. I was picturing a teenager."

"You're a girl, too." He gave the group an unapologetic grin. "Nita, do we have any cookies to go with the coffee?"

She got up. "Don't wait for me. Just talk louder. I can hear from the kitchen."

"Okay. There were six dinner guests. Five, excluding Twinkle."

"You think suicide can be eliminated?" Jim asked.

"I think so. She was in good spirits in the afternoon, visiting you, talking with old friends, taking care of business. She had plans to paint at Fran's gallery Saturday."

"Okay. Five guests with an opportunity," Jim said. "Do we have any motives?"

"No!" Michael exploded. "I object! Not five! How could I have poisoned her? I know *nothing* about poisons. And I had no quarrel with Twinkle. Take me off the list."

"We wouldn't include you in this discussion if we thought you were guilty," Riley assured him.

"We're not seriously considering Georgina or Stewart, either," I said, "except to clear them. There's really only one possibility, in my book."

"Means, motive, opportunity." Jim looked at Michael. "Five people with opportunity."

Nita came back with coffee refills and a plate of cookies that she passed around and then set within Jim's reach. I took a cookie and asked Michael to describe Georgina's dinner party.

"Whose idea was it, anyway?" Jim asked.

"Did anybody leave the room right before the food was served?" Dolly asked.

"I was just out of the room," Nita said. "That doesn't mean I was poisoning anybody."

Riley gave me a look.

"The rest of them got together at last year's festival," Michael said, "and thought it would be fun to organize something for this year. It was just good luck that I was going to be here." He told us that Twinkle had left the courtyard at least twice. "And Georgina was in and out all evening, heating the food, serving the plates, checking on Twinkle. Stewart helped her, just as a means of escaping." Michael did an eye roll. "Solly and I had each other to talk to, and Georgina when she sat down, but poor Stewart and Fran. They just sat there and took it."

"Took what?" Jim asked.

Michael rolled his eyes again and dropped his head against the back of the couch.

"Twinkle. She was putting on a real performance, patting herself on the back, belittling artists who didn't meet her standards. She could be such a jackass. I would've told her to kiss off but Fran..." Michael looked around then patted Nita's and Dolly's hands. "Pardon me, ladies. I meant to say Fran just sulked." He looked at me. "You saw her Friday. She was still in a snit."

"What was Twinkle saying, exactly?" I asked. "This could be important, Michael."

He shrugged elaborately and took a sip of wine, enjoying the spotlight. "*Patina, thread count, spectral analysis.* I tuned it out, really, except for her tone, which was egotistical, arrogant...needling. That's the right word. Needling."

"Needling whom?"

"Fran, I'm sure. One of Twinkle's pet peeves was projectors and the artists who use them. Twinkle was not a nice person." He took another sip of wine and a thoughtful look altered his face. "Things happened so fast. She went from needling to doubled over with pain—" He snapped his fingers with a loud crack, and Dolly jumped. "Just like that."

"After the food was served?" I asked.

He nodded. "Yes. We had the salad early, along with the wines. That required a lot of discussion. Then we took a secret vote. Mine won, of course. Four votes to Solly's one—his own, I'm sure. And I remember something else." He pointed to Jim. "She talked about your print. Am I right that Fran loaned it to you?"

Jim nodded. "Twinkle was impressed. She was here looking at it just a few hours before she died. Do I need to tell everybody about that?"

He knew how she'd been dressed, how long she had stayed, and that she'd had some tea but nothing to eat. "No nuts, I'm sure of that. And she really studied this print. It was interesting, seeing how an artist observes." He hesitated and frowned. "Seems like she might've called Vermeer an amateur. That's not true, is it?"

"No," Riley assured him.

"She used that word at dinner, too," Michael said. "Referring to Fran without using her name. Like we didn't know. Needling." He lifted his glass, as though he were toasting Twinkle's memory, then sipped.

I asked, "You said your wine won four-to-one?"

"Right."

"Who didn't vote?"

He gave me a blank look.

"Good call, Cleo." Jim looked at Michael. "There were six people there. Four plus one is five. Who didn't vote?"

"Ooh," Michael said, slowly. "Must've been Georgina, being diplomatic. Or maybe she was in the kitchen."

"By the way," I said, "We should quit referring to it as a print. It's a painting, we know now, a copy of *The Concert*, by Vermeer. We saw the perimeter is missing, probably to make people think it's the original. And this is the second painting Fran loaned to you." I looked at the note I'd written earlier. "You're sure she didn't deliver it personally?"

"No," Jim and Nita answered together.

"Georgina brought it," Nita said. "Stewart's helper took the seascape down and walked it across the street to Georgina's apartment. Fran was picking it up later. I remember we waited for a day when it wasn't raining."

Maybe Fran was smarter than I'd thought and had kept an intermediary between herself and the paintings. I moved on to another topic: money. "You paid a deposit for your anniversary portrait, but you didn't actually pay anything for either of the two loaned paintings?"

Nita confirmed it.

"Then we can't claim you were defrauded. Let's get back to Georgina's dinner. The first dish served was a salad. Strawberries and cream cheese." I looked at Michael.

"I remember. Very tasty."

"Did people serve themselves?"

"Stewart brought the plates in. Somebody said Twinkle was still eating like a bird, but she surprised us and asked for seconds. Georgina got it for her, I remember. She went inside after that but didn't stay long, not the first time, and when she came back, she wasn't very talkative. I see now she was getting sick." He shivered. "You know, that detective asked me all this, and I didn't remember half of it. Y'all should show them how to question people so they don't get nervous. Your memory works better when you're relaxed."

"Maybe they should serve wine." Dolly looked at the glass in his hand.

I steered him back to the subject. "And after the salad, the main course."

"Well, eventually. There was a lot of talk first. Twinkle was in and out. The food was served in the kitchen—Georgina did that, or maybe it was Fran. Stewart ferried plates to the table. He put a plate where Twinkle had been sitting and cracked a joke about there being more for the rest of us and him being closest to it." He paused to consider. "I guess we didn't see her again. She couldn't have eaten much of the entrée."

"Did you ever hear of tung oil trees? And the nuts they produce?"

He looked puzzled. "Of course."

I hadn't expected that answer.

"Why's that?" Jim challenged. "You don't strike me as the outdoors type."

Michael drew back with an indignant expression. "I use tung oil all the time. It makes a beautiful finish on concrete floors and countertops. Very popular right now. You've probably seen it, even around here."

All gazes shifted back to me.

I shrugged. "I know the oil has industrial uses." I looked at Michael. "If you didn't know, tung nuts are poisonous. There were some in the courtyard and they wound up in Twinkle's food."

"Tung nuts? That's what killed her?" Michael seemed stunned. He looked back at me. "Well, I hate to tell you, but all Georgina's students knew about them."

We stared at him.

Michael shrugged. "We might not recognize them after all these years, but Georgina drilled it into our heads when we stained gourds. We had to act responsibly or switch to choir. She didn't want to explain to parents if art students started dropping dead."

"People, we're making progress," Jim said. "It's one of five people, and they all knew about tung nuts."

Michael said, "My salad was crunchy, but I didn't get poisoned."

"Pretzels," I said.

"It's called strawberry pretzel salad," Nita told him.

They slewed off into a discussion about the salad, a favorite at Harbor Village and frequently on the lunch menu. I hated to tell them they wouldn't see it again soon, but there was bound to be resistance after the poisoning.

"Here's what I think." I looked from Nita to Jim. "Twinkle was here for Arts and Crafts last year. She took your deposit and left town, telling Georgina to take photos and find something to fill the space temporarily."

They nodded.

"Georgina borrowed the seascape but a buyer came along and Fran needed it. So, she picked it up and sent another replica, the Vermeer, in its place."

"And Twinkle painted the replicas," Michael said.

This was the tricky part, and I was still working out the details. "I thought that at first, based on her skill and history, but now I believe Twinkle learned about them for the first time Thursday. Georgina says Twinkle laughed at the reference photos and came here immediately. I think she was coming to see the seascape in person, but it was gone. She got a good, long look at the Vermeer instead. Then she went back and told Georgina she'd decided to attend the dinner."

"Um-hum," Jim nodded.

"After that," I thought out loud, "there's an hour or so when her movements aren't accounted for. She was in town, and she knew there were at least two replicas. She went to her storage locker at Royale Court, but I don't know why. I think she visited Fran, too. They were partners, after all, with an exhibition planned for the next day, so they had things to talk about. I think she suspected Fran had painted the copies, and perhaps Fran admitted it. Then, at dinner, Twinkle was on a tear. She began listing all the ways an artist could trip up in painting a forgery." I looked at Michael, who was nodding his head. "You suspected she was needling Fran, but Fran knew she was about to be exposed in front of her friends and colleagues." I paused and looked around again. "It must've been excruciating."

"Was this replica business lucrative?" Jim asked.

"Sure," Michael said. "Definitely."

I agreed. "People love fantasy, and replicas of stolen paintings come with ready-made mystique. Buyers can spin their own stories about collusion and robbery, or smuggling, or mobsters, or the big rewards they could collect if they chose."

I looked at Michael. "Twinkle was ridiculing Fran's work without naming her, right in front of her teacher and colleagues. Fran knew she had to act quickly. She'd seen tung nut decorations in the courtyard. She used Stewart's pliers to crack the shells, then chopped the nuts and added them to Twinkle's salad."

"Ohmygod," Michael breathed, eyes wide. "That gives me chills."

"You know her. Tell us. Would Fran do such a thing?"

His eyes bugged momentarily and he swallowed hard. "I was just imagining her developing a phony provenance—without ever guaranteeing it was true, of course. It's so vivid in my mind, I think I might've actually heard it."

Had he been involved? Too late to consider that now. I looked around the room. "What do you think? Who poisoned Twinkle?"

Michael stiffened, closed his eyes, and leaned back for a few seconds. Then he sighed and gave a shivery shake of the head. "That's just so... so *definite*. You know? It's one thing to say she could've, but to say she actually *did*...you know what I mean?"

Jim changed positions in the recliner and stalled. "I don't know Fran, not well, but the elements are there. And who else? Emily's father? I don't think so."

Nita nodded. "I don't like to say, not before the police make it official. But I know it wasn't Stewart. Or you, Michael."

"Or maybe it *was* you," Dolly said, "and you're trying to throw us off the track now."

Michael stared at her then whooped. "Maybe I did!" He swiveled and grabbed her in a hug. "Dolly, you're *precious*."

She laughed with pleasure. "First time I ever accused anyone of murder. Maybe I'll do it more often."

I looked at Riley, who smiled and shook his head. "I don't see a flaw yet, but I'll keep trying."

"I wondered about cracking the nuts," Jim said. "It was on my list of questions."

Nita was unfazed. "We know if Stewart was there, his tools were, too. And it makes sense, finally."

Riley looked at his watch and then at me. If we were going to the pier, we needed to leave. Nita saw it, too, and offered more wine or coffee. I started to get up.

"What've you got there, Cleo?" Jim pointed to the stack of photos.

"One final topic. I believe you got the seascape on your fiftieth anniversary, the day Georgina made the reference photos."

Jim nodded. "Right."

I walked across the room and handed the photographs to Nita. She was surprised, then delighted, and finally verged on tears.

"Oh, Jim. Have you seen these? Look at us!" She perched on the arm of his recliner and bent toward the light, looking at the photos one by one.

"Fifty years." He took the photos as she passed them over.

"Dolly, come see," Nita said.

Michael got up to look, too.

"Where'd you get them?" Riley asked me quietly. "Montgomery? Twinkle's things?"

"I'll tell you later."

He glanced toward the door and raised his brows, and I got my bag.

"Can we keep these?" Nita asked of the photos.

"Yes. Would you give me one?"

"I want one, too," Dolly said.

Nita gathered all the photos, stacked them, and handed me the stack. "Take whatever you want."

I shuffled through and selected one that showed a big portion of the painting in the background, still only a swath of black with some foamy waves. I returned the rest to Nita.

Before she could pass the stack to Dolly, I said, "Look. Is this what I think?" I walked to the recliner and held the photo under the gooseneck lamp, where both Jim and Nita could see it. "What's that in the background?"

"The seascape!" Nita snatched the photo from me.

Jim grabbed it from her. "Let me see that." He nodded immediately. "The seascape. Awfully dark there. I remembered it as green, but that's it. *Storm on the Sea of Galilee.*"

He handed the photo back to me but began to reexamine the others.

"Do you want a different one, dear?" Nita asked me. "One with a plain background?"

"I like this one." I stuck it in my bag to pass to Montgomery, along with my suspicions.

Jim was examining each photo, sorting them according to the presence or absence of the background painting. "Dolly, you want the seascape in back, or not?"

"Cleo, you've made me so happy." Nita walked to the door with us and stretched to give me a hug and a kiss on the cheek. "Take care of my girl," she told Riley and gave him a hug and kiss, too.

"Who took the seascape away, Nita?" I was casting out one last effort to connect Fran directly to the replicas and, grudgingly, admiring the fact she'd made it so difficult. "You said it was too big to fit in a car."

She hesitated then nodded and tapped my hand with a finger. "We were right earlier. Drew got it down and used a dolly to walk it over to Georgina's apartment. Fran picked it up later, or had someone do it, I suppose. I wonder where it is now." Her voice dropped to a whisper and she grabbed my wrist. "But I don't want it back."

Riley and I went to the pier, avoiding the festival by taking a zigzag route through the Fruits and Nuts, a local name for the old residential neighborhood where streets had names like Fig and Pecan and Orange.

We reached the bay and turned north, then zipped through an opening in the line of traffic departing the festival, descended the hill, and parked at the rose garden. The big American flag billowed and snapped in the breeze, the fountain splashed and sparkled, and the roses were pretty again, back in bloom after their January pruning.

Just as Riley cut off the engine, my phone rang. I dug it out of my bag. "Stephanie," I told him, and answered.

"Mackie," Barry said.

I hadn't expected him and was slow to answer.

He screamed. "Mackie!"

"Hello, Barry. How are you?"

Shrieks and giggles. I heard Stephanie reasoning with him, followed by the sound of the phone crashing against something, and then her voice. "Mom? Are you there?"

"Hi, honey. I'm at the pier with Riley."

"This connection's terrible! Barry just wanted to speak to you."

"Do I have a name now?"

"I can't hear you. He came up with Mackie all by himself and practiced it all the way home, and I love it. We'll talk tonight. Enjoy the pier. Love to Riley. I'm hanging up now."

"Love to Riley," I repeated to him as I got out of the car.

He took off his jacket and held it for me. It was too breezy to protest. "Do you have another one for you?"

He got a hoodie from the back of the car and shrugged into it while I explained the call. "I hated Grandma, and Stephanie doesn't want him calling adults by their first names, so we've been at a standoff. The poor kid had to solve it himself. I'm Mackie."

"That works." He nodded approval and the corners of his eyes crinkled. "Wonder what he'll call me."

That gave me a warm feeling. He expected to be around while Barry grew up. I hoped I wasn't about to upset that.

The bay was gorgeous, pale blue and hazy, with seagulls squawking and diving. A pelican family sailed by without flapping, and some little skimmers mined the water just south of us. We joined a train of pedestrians snaking down the pier, dodging running children and men with cast nets or carts.

"Did you learn anything from the murder board?"

"I like that. The murder board. They'll like it, too."

We ambled to the rail and watched twenty little sailboats approaching the yacht club.

"Tell me," Riley said, "what's funny about a big dark painting? Why did Twinkle laugh at the photos?"

I shrugged. "I think it was a poor imitation, by her standards. Jim remembers her using the word *amateur* when she was looking at the

Vermeer. He thought she was referring to Vermeer, but I think she was referring to Fran. Twinkle had her own experience with fraud, you know."

"Let's walk, before we freeze."

We rejoined the stream of pedestrians moving westward, toward the end of the pier and the setting sun.

"Michael said she used words like *patina* and *thread count*. Fran must've botched a few things, and Twinkle was pointing them out."

"Did you talk with Fran?"

I shook my head. "We know she was in the courtyard with the tung nuts. You heard what Michael said—all Georgina's students knew they were poison. She helped Georgina with the food, which gave her a chance to crack the nuts, chop them, and add them to one serving of the salad. She either delivered the plates herself or told Stewart which one should go to Twinkle. It was a small serving. He might've assumed it was for her."

Riley nodded slightly, pursed his lips, and stopped while a Japanese family asked, in perfect English, if he'd take their photograph. He did, and they thanked him profusely.

We reached the end of the pier just minutes before sunset. The platform was crowded with kids watching a pelican beg for fish. When the big orange ball sank below the horizon, we joined in the applause. Some people headed for shore immediately, but I slid into a space against the rail and checked to be sure there were no fish guts.

Riley joined me.

I wiped my hair out of my eyes and took his arm. "Families are tricky, you know, and I've decided not to move into the house right now. I think I need to meet your sons first, and be sure they aren't going to resent me and make us miserable."

He stared then tipped his head back and laughed. I thought he was relieved and amused.

He put an arm around my shoulders and pulled me close. "My sons have strong opinions on every topic, but they'll adore you, I promise. Shall I arrange this meeting? A quick trip to DC next week? I want us together."

"Not so fast. Thing two. Would you like to visit Tuscaloosa for a day or two, this week or next? I'm thinking academe still has a big hold on my heart, and I need to find out more about this job."

His eyes narrowed and his grip on me loosened. "Okay. That's reasonable, I guess. When do you want to go?"

"Whenever they say. If you go along, I'll have to refer to you in some way. Shall I say *partner*? I don't like the word *fiancé*. It's as bad as grandma."

That amused him, too, but there was caginess in the manner of his reply. "We've got a few days. We'll figure it out."

"Okay. If this should work out, I thought we might keep a place here. Apartment or house, your choice. But a foothold in Fairhope for the future."

The smile was gone. "This is sounding damn serious. You're imagining I'll tag along?"

"I was hoping…"

He raised one eyebrow then looked away and gave a little shake of the head. "What if I need to go to DC?"

"Tuscaloosa has an airport, I'm sure."

I'd half expected to see the ring box again, since the pier was such a romantic spot, but there was no sign of it. I was a tiny bit disappointed but told myself it was best, with so many things up in the air.

The park was still busy when we got back to the car. Many people were walking dogs in the twilight, and I petted a pair of Scottish terriers wearing red plaid coats. My phone rang again as we drove up the hill. According to caller ID, it was the Royale Knit Shop.

"Cleo! I was just about to give up," Ann Slump said when I answered. "I've been calling for thirty minutes."

"We were on the pier," I said.

Everyone knew phone service was unpredictable there.

"This is a terrible connection. Did you say you're in town?"

"Almost."

"Would you mind coming by here? I'm at Royale Court and there's something I want you to see."

I agreed, ended the call, and told Riley. "You don't mind, do you? I couldn't hear her well enough to discuss anything."

There were two messages from Patti. On the first one, her voice bubbled with excitement. "You won't believe this. Guess who has offered me a job as a decorator. Michael Bonderant! A decorator! Ha!"

Riley and I laughed.

The phone beeped and Patti's voice resumed. "That wasn't a resignation. In case you wondered."

Tents were still up on the main streets and tree lights twinkled around fluttering new leaves. Artists were packing unsold merchandise and loading boxes and crates into cars and trucks wedged in beside the tents. The intersection was almost blocked. We turned right and then made a series of quick turns before parking behind Royale Court.

I told Riley about Skinny Alley as we went between the old fence and the building and emerged in the retail courtyard. Dixieland music played from speakers mounted in trees and under eaves. The fountain gurgled and splashed, and twinkling lights reflected in its water.

Ann was waiting in front of the knit shop. She motioned for us to follow and headed at an angle across the courtyard. "I'm trying to decide if we should do anything about this. Hi, Riley. I love the new house. Come right this way."

She opened a glass door and stopped in a small, brightly lit anteroom. A second glass door to our left displayed the name and logo of the T-shirt shop. On my right, a flight of stairs went up to a landing, made a right-angle turn, then went up again and out of sight. Windows in random sizes and spots gave us glimpses into the illuminated courtyard.

The space beneath the stairs, on two sides of the little foyer, was enclosed with bead board, painted ivory, and interrupted by doors of increasing height. Big steel padlocks hung from hasps, but one short door was ajar.

"Twinkle's storage locker?" I guessed.

Ann nodded. "Somebody emptied it today. Came in from the T-shirt shop, we think."

There was a clamor up above, a door closing, followed by footsteps and a man's voice. "Ann? Is that you?"

Usher's feet were visible through the balusters, followed by his legs and torso, and finally his round, blond Charlie Brown head. He noticed Riley first then saw me and shouted a greeting.

"Cleo! Haven't seen you in ages." He crossed the foyer to give me a bear hug, then he and Riley shook hands.

"What's in there?" I gestured to the little door.

Ann grabbed the hasp and pulled the door open. The enclosed space was three feet deep, three feet high, and completely empty.

"Sister wants to call the cops." Usher rolled his eyes like it was an absurd idea. "I say they're probably the ones who emptied it. And even if somebody else did, it's not like Twinkle's going to sue me, is she?" He giggled.

"What do you think?" Ann asked.

"When did it happen?"

"Today. After lunch," Usher said.

"Well, we know Twinkle didn't do it." I looked at him. "Who else has a key?"

"Not *who else*." He shook his head. "Twinkle didn't have one, but her name's on the contract. That's why I opened it Thursday when she asked me to."

"How'd she get in otherwise?"

He shrugged. "I don't know that she did. That's what I'm saying. Twinkle was always gone. It's Georgina who takes care of things. I guess she came through the T-shirt shop and cleaned the locker out today. That may seem odd, with her grieving and all, but she's Twinkle's sister. She can do what she likes." He looked at Ann. "No sense making a federal case of it."

Ann was frowning. "You told me it was Twinkle's locker."

He nodded. "It's her name on the lease. But Georgina's the one who uses it. Pays the rent. Comes by every month or so. Takes care of business."

"What do we do?" Ann looked at me and waited, hands on her hips.

I didn't like the situation. "Do you remember when we were with Georgina yesterday and you mentioned the storage locker—"

"And Georgina acted so odd? I certainly do."

"She seemed surprised Twinkle had been here."

"There I was, wondering what Twinkle had in a locker, when Georgina could've told us."

I reached a decision. "I think you should call Montgomery. She'll tell you if she thinks it's a waste of time."

Ann let out a big breath and caved into a tired posture. "That's what I thought. Usher talked me out of it." She gave him a hostile look, and I took out my phone.

Lieutenant Montgomery answered on the first ring and listened while I said that Twinkle Thaw's storage locker at Royale Court had been cleaned out. "I don't suppose the police did it?"

"I'll come," she said when I stopped talking. "Give me five minutes."

I passed the message along and looked at Riley. "We don't need to wait, I guess." I was curious and would've stayed if I'd been alone, but I was giving him the option.

He walked to the locker and bent over to peer inside. "It's easier to stay than to come back." He stuck his head through the opening, craned his neck to look around, then felt along the doorframe. He got up brushing his hands together.

I asked Usher, "What did she keep in there?"

"Paintings, fancy frames. A cash box." He laughed and dropped his voice. "Everybody has one. Just part of business."

Montgomery showed up with a couple of uniformed cops and waggled her thumb from me to the door. "Wait outside. There's a bench by the fountain."

I knew that perfectly well, since I'd been attacked in that exact spot six months before.

Riley was banished with me. He paced around the courtyard, but I plopped down on the concrete bench and immediately felt the cold seeping through my pants. I hopped up and pulled my knit pants away from my rear. Too late. The bench was wet with spray from the fountain and now I was soaked and my panties were stuck to my bottom.

"Let's sit over here." Riley seemed oblivious to my dilemma. He selected one of the tables outside the Gumbo Shop. It was closed on Sundays, but the smell of onions and spices was still there. "We won't have to talk over the fountain noise."

Without Riley's jacket, I would've been freezing. I pulled it snug around me and stuck my hands into fleece-lined pockets. At least we were sheltered from the wind.

"You were going to tell me about getting the reference photos," he reminded me. "Nice of Georgina to pass them along."

My annoyance had a new target. "Well, it would've been, but she didn't. She gave them to Twinkle, and Twinkle threw them away. I found them in the garbage this morning." I told him about retrieving them. "That's what I was reluctant to say in front of Nita. Jim wouldn't care, but Nita might. I cleaned them up the best I could."

He just looked at me, not saying anything. It was a deafening silence, so quiet I could hear the details of the story clicking through the logic centers of my brain.

My mental dung detector went off. "That doesn't make sense, does it?"

"Why?"

"Twinkle wouldn't have discarded those photos. She expected to use them. After she was dead they served no purpose, but Twinkle wasn't here to toss them. And obviously they weren't among the things the police took. Georgina threw them away. Why didn't she just give them to Nita? You saw them. They were excellent photographs." I paused. "Twinkle looked at the seascape and laughed hysterically. And Georgina threw the photos away."

I paused again, and the chill I felt came from within. "You know, I think I've been making a mistake. I think I've been blaming the wrong person."

Chapter 20

It took several minutes to tell Montgomery the story, with all its curves and convolutions. I began with the replicas. "I thought Fran had created them to sell, possibly for a lot of money. I pictured her dangling the possibility that they were the real thing, right down to the slashed edges, and telling some story about smuggling and concealment, or that she'd found them at some estate auction."

"Right." Montgomery nodded, jotting notes.

"Twinkle recognized the seascape when she saw it in the background of Jim and Nita's reference photos, knew it was missing, and went to see it in person. But she found the Vermeer instead, which told her there were at least two replicas. Maybe more.

"I think she saw something in the Vermeer that told her who painted it. I assumed at first that was Fran, even though she was more manager than painter. But today, I saw Georgina with a paint box." I looked at Ann.

She nodded. "She's a painter, too. Never got enough credit."

That's what I had guessed. "Here's my theory. She drew on her photography connections to get good photos of the stolen masterpieces, photos she could project at the right size on a blank canvas. Then, like paint-by-numbers, she painted a detailed replica."

Montgomery filled in the conclusion. "And poisoned her own sister when Twinkle found out."

I nodded. "Georgina could paint. She could handle the technicalities of photographs and projectors. She knew enough about marketing."

"And she'd had a lifetime of sibling rivalry," Ann said.

I nodded. "She told us about Twinkle's self-centered, abrasive behavior Thursday. Twinkle discovered the replicas, then came here and looked in the storage locker. We don't know what she found. Cash? More replicas? And we don't know what she said to Georgina while they dressed for the party. But we know the bullying—needling, to use Michael's term—continued after the other guests arrived. Michael thought it was aimed at Fran, and Fran may have thought so, too, especially if she knew nothing about the replicas. But Georgina knew she was the real target and knew Twinkle was building up to expose her to her former students and to the art community at large. She knew tung nuts were poison. She knew they were right there in the building..." I looked around the table and shivered.

Riley summed up. "Means, motive, and opportunity, Jim would say."

"It may have been spur-of-the-moment, but she didn't regret it immediately. She kept Twinkle away from medical attention for hours, until it was too late to save her. And even when she took her to the ER, she left it to the doctors to figure out what the poison was."

Montgomery was still asking questions when the officers she'd sent to Harbor Village reported Georgina wasn't at home. "Does she frequently go out at night?" she asked.

I didn't know but Ann, sitting in the fourth chair at our table, said no. "She doesn't like to drive at night."

"She looked terrible this afternoon. Maybe she's realizing..." I left the sentence unfinished but had another thought. "She told me recently about an old family place on Oberg Road."

"That's right." Ann told Montgomery exactly where it was.

"There's an outbuilding where Twinkle liked to paint," I recalled Georgina saying.

Montgomery got on the radio and passed along information about Oberg Road. Then she glanced over her notes. "Solly Roka...Did he have anything to do with it?"

I shook my head. "Not that I see."

"And Fran Beck? You were awfully sure about her."

I thought about her cat, sleeping in the window at the gallery, and felt a little foolish. "If Fran was involved, she did a good job of concealing the fact. You'll know more when you talk with Georgina. Or get a look at any records she kept in the storage locker. See if she shared the proceeds with Fran. And I just remembered something else. Georgina was in the courtyard Thursday night, right before they left for the hospital. That's when she put the nut shells in the chiminea. I watched her when I got up to feed Tinkerbelle. When I turned the kitchen light on, she came to tell me they were going to the ER, and she'd checked to be sure the fire was out."

Montgomery sat quietly for a long minute before she signaled a uniformed cop to the table. She gestured to him and told me, "Tell him where the photographs were. In case you missed some."

I began from Harbor Boulevard, directed him to my garage, and tried to pinpoint the correct garbage container. "A translucent bag with a hole in the side. One of the middle containers. The third one if you're coming from—"

"You'll have to find it." She snapped her notebook closed and pushed her chair back. "Where's your car?"

"Out back. There were a couple more prints, I know, but they were torn. Probably goopy by now."

She glared and I stood up. Riley already had his keys out.

She instructed him. "Go directly to the garage. I'll be right behind you."

She could sound ferocious. But she didn't say I couldn't make a phone call on the way. Debra Hollen answered immediately, listened to my message, and said she'd see us at Harbor Village.

* * * *

Before I found the correct garbage bag Jim Bergen showed up, drawn, no doubt, by crackling radios and flashing blue lights. Chief Boozer was there, too, standing with his arms crossed, watching and nodding while Montgomery briefed him. I gave him a wave.

Hunter was the lucky technician who got to dig through the mess after I identified the bag with a hole torn in the side. He found three photos that had been ripped in half and another one with a goopy smear. It was still possible to see large portions of the seascape. Eventually, he pulled out a Walgreen's photo wrapper containing more photos of the seascape, with no people blocking it. Photographs that had been used to find a buyer, perhaps.

Jim came to look over Hunter's shoulder. "That's the seascape." He pointed to a photo. "Where it is now, Mary? Do we know?"

Debra Hollen showed up, too. Jim brought out his little tactical light and the two of them examined photographs over Hunter's shoulder as he cleaned off the worst of the slop. An officer tried to back them off, but Hollen flashed press credentials and they were allowed to stay. They were watching when Hunter pulled out two more photos from the depths of the bag, both gooey with yogurt puddles. At least I told myself it was yogurt. Hollen raised her phone and Hunter obligingly held the photos while she snapped away. She got a photo of me, too, without the slightest warning.

"We need to talk with you and Nita," Montgomery told Jim.

He turned immediately toward his apartment but, after a couple of steps, he looked back at Debra Hollen. "You want to come? We've got another forgery in the apartment."

The two of them went off together, Jim flashing a bright beam of light across the pavement and quizzing her about *WaPo*'s allowance for technical equipment.

Montgomery was about to follow them, but I saw her hesitate. Radio chatter had intensified and she stood still, apparently listening. What was up? She walked toward me.

"Did you hear that? EMTs called to Oberg Road. Apparent poisoning."

I closed my eyes and pictured Georgina's gray face.

As soon as Montgomery departed, the flashing blue lights were turned off. Cop cars crunched across gravel washes, circled, and exited the parking lot. Silence descended. I could no longer ignore my damp clothing.

Riley went to the kitchen and heated soup while I took a quick shower and put on dry clothes. He was putting two bowls on the table when I returned, warm and cozy. I wrapped my arms around him and he hugged back but seemed miles away.

"A penny for your thoughts."

He sighed. "Just thinking. We'll miss all the excitement if we leave here. Remember what a dean's office is like? A mortuary."

I smiled at his choice of pronouns...if *we* leave here. "Did you say mortuary? Maybe you haven't heard about party schools."

* * * *

Monday dawned gray and cool. I stopped at Winn-Dixie for a bud vase, three red roses, and a sprig of baby's breath, and got to the hospital before the parking lot filled up. Georgina might be in trouble but she was still my neighbor and a Harbor Village resident.

"No visitors," the woman at the information desk said. She wrote the room number on a slip of paper and looked around before she leaned across the counter. "Give the flowers to the nurses up there. They'll deliver them. Georgina needs cheering up."

Upstairs, the nurses' desk was empty but I recognized the cop standing in the hallway. He was young and cute and had worked evenings last fall, hanging around the pier to keep the high school kids on good behavior.

"Can I see her?" I pointed to the closed door.

He shook his head. "But I'll give her the flowers."

I scribbled on the card, stuck it into the tangle of little branches, and went back to Harbor Village.

Mondays were always hectic, even without murder and suicide and festivals. Certainly without job offers and the prospect of moving. Today I was seeking comfort from routine. Patti was already at her desk, wearing a denim outfit, red glasses, and red plaid nail polish.

I smiled at the three little turtles on her desk. "Nice weekend?"

She giggled and fluffed her curls and handed me a stack of mail. The phone rang. "People are not liking this Georgina business," she said, reaching for the phone. "I hope you've got some ideas."

I didn't like the Georgina business myself, but the problem was out of my hands now. I walked down the hall to my office and Patti was buzzing me before I got the door unlocked.

I had a nice long conversation with the provost at the University of Alabama. We ended by planning a visit one week away. "I'm looking forward to meeting you," she said, and I told her the same. Like so many things, growing reality made it a little less interesting, but I had a week to think about it.

Earl Wallace's daughter had requested a wellness check. I went up to the second floor to chat with him. He'd recently moved down from Birmingham and didn't know many people yet, but his living area was chock full of books, so we had things to talk about. After a few minutes he agreed to take on the task of organizing Harbor Village's library. I called Dolly to ask if she'd help.

"I guess. When does he want to start?"

"Can you come over now?" I asked. "We'll be there in five minutes."

"I'm coming but I don't want to miss anything important," she said, and disconnected.

I didn't know what she thought she might miss, but Earl and I took the elevator down. I showed him the little library and he dove right in, tidying up.

I was back at my desk a few minutes later when Jim Bergen looked in at the doorway. He was there and then he was gone, and then he was back again, waving Nita and Dolly into the office. I hadn't been notified, and Michael Bonderant wasn't there, but it appeared that the murder board was convening again.

"Riley's getting more chairs," Jim told me with a sheepish smile, "and Carla's sending coffee down. Where's Mary?"

"Mary Montgomery? She's coming?" That was a change in routine.

Nita kicked things off immediately. "Georgina Burch does not belong in jail."

Dolly agreed.

"At least she's going to recover," I said. "Has she been arrested? I ask because there's a cop standing guard at her door."

"At the hospital, you mean," Jim verified. "Not here."

"I should hope so." Dolly was scowling. "Somebody did try to kill her, you know."

"I think she tried to kill herself," I pointed out.

"Well, now…" Jim held up a hand. "Let's don't jump to conclusions. She's entitled to a defense."

Riley came in pushing one desk chair and pulling a second one. I caught his glance and thought he looked a little guilty. He sat in one of the chairs and rolled forward, into the group.

"There seems to be some sentiment that Georgina is a victim," I said.

He smiled faintly and raised his eyebrows. "What kind of person would harm Georgina?"

I saw which way the wind was blowing. One of their own was in peril and the law-and-order crowd had morphed into colluding defenders. Was it confined to Harbor Village, or happening all over town?

"It's difficult to imagine," Nita said, picking at the cording on the arm of her chair. "But someone poisoned her sister. Don't you suppose one person is responsible for both?" She looked up and watched my reaction.

I nodded. "Yes. I think that's likely."

"I've spoken with Georgina," Jim said. "She knows she can't come back here, not right away. But there's a niece in Memphis and I've got a call in to her."

"Can't come back here?" Dolly echoed, turning her scowl on Jim.

"If she's not guilty of anything?" Nita sounded indignant. "Of course she can."

"Who's not guilty?" Lieutenant Montgomery barged in and took the vacant chair. "What's the emergency? I've got about two minutes."

"We need to know one thing," Jim said. "Did Georgina leave any kind of a note?"

"A suicide note, you mean? She didn't die. She's recovering."

"What we want to know is, will she be charged with anything?" he pressed.

She hesitated, then shook her head. "You're asking the wrong person, Jim. The police investigate. The District Attorney prosecutes." She looked at each of us, tightened her lips, and asked Jim, "You're asking for a prediction?"

"Yes," Nita said. "What do you expect will happen?"

She took her time, sighed, and summarized, "The sister was a jerk. She didn't live here. And there's no family or friends clamoring for an arrest. Ms. Burch, on the other hand, has the reputation of a saint. I wonder if they can even seat an impartial jury."

"The prosecutor's budget is tight," Jim suggested. "Might not want to waste money on a lost cause."

She crossed her legs at the ankle, leaned forward, and smiled at the floor. "It all comes down to evidence, people. So far, there's not much. I can't say what the lab might turn up."

"Nothing iron-clad, you're saying." Jim was pushing her toward his own position. "Nothing like a note. So if Georgina moved away..."

She shrugged. "Whether she's here or not, if there's no evidence, they can't prosecute."

"What if she confesses?" I asked.

Everyone looked at me.

"It's a possibility," I said. "I predict it, in fact."

"There's no guarantee even then," Montgomery said. "Some defense attorneys—they might let her plead to a lesser charge. But without evidence..." She waved empty hands. "You want me to say it could fall through the cracks? Yes, things like that happen. This time? Who knows?"

Carla came in with coffee on a cart. Mary filled a cup and came to lean against the wall beside my desk while the others crowded around the cart.

"You're down with this?" she asked.

I shrugged. "I have theories and you know them. I don't have any evidence."

She swilled the coffee down and stood up straight. "The wheels of justice turn slowly. What is she, eighty?"

I nodded. "Not quite. Why is there a cop at the hospital? Is she in custody?"

She laughed shortly. "He's supposed to be keeping her friends away. The third floor was gridlocked before eight this morning."

Nita joined us and said, with a note of apology in her voice, "We just thought, with two of them poisoned..."

"I know what you thought," Montgomery said. "She's got a good lawyer?"

"Jim's working on it."

Montgomery straightened. "I've got to go. There's crime to fight." She took a step toward the door but looked back at me.

"Look at it like this. If she gets away with murder, it's because we didn't find the evidence."

"I think she'll confess."

The murder board adjourned. It was lunchtime but I wasn't in the mood for the dining room. All the talk would be about Georgina.

Riley lagged behind the others. "I'm going to the house. I think Carla left some food in the kitchen Saturday."

"You want company?"

He smiled and reached out an arm for me. "That's the idea, you know. Something to do and someone to do it with."